"You're afraid, aren't you?" Marie demanded

"You're scared to death. What do you think I can do to you? Oh, you're so tough," she said sarcastically. "You can handle anything. Disgrace. Trial. Even prison. But you're afraid of me. Well, let me tell you, Craig Saybolt. You need me. You're just too much of a coward to admit it!"

Craig couldn't stop himself. He stood and strode across the room —a puppet pulled by invisible strings—toward a fate he couldn't avoid. He put a hand out and touched her cheek and she closed her eyes, turning her face sideways into his touch. He wanted to press her into his arms. The need was overwhelming.

Terrifying.

He pulled against the invisible strings, fought them. "You're not really interested in clearing my name, are you?" he asked, the old bitterness back in his voice. "You just want your promotion and that bonus, right?"

Marie's eyes opened wide. "No," she whispered, her eyes dark and shining. "No." But she knew he wouldn't believe her.

ABOUT THE AUTHOR

"You wouldn't believe how wild Alaska is!"
says Carla Peltonen, who writes as Lynn
Erickson with longtime friend Molly Swanton.
"Molly and I had been dying to go to Alaska
practically forever, and doing research for *The
Northern Light* was just the excuse we'd been
waiting for. Boy did we have fun. We hired a
bush pilot to fly us to Valdez from
Anchorage—along the same route Marie
takes in the book. Up and over the glaciers
we flew with our hearts in our throats."
Carla and Molly make their homes in Aspen,
Colorado. They've been writing together for
fourteen years.

Books by Lynn Erickson

HARLEQUIN SUPERROMANCE

276–A PERFECT GEM
298–FOOL'S GOLD
320–FIRECLOUD
347–SHADOW ON THE SUN
370–IN FROM THE COLD
404–WEST OF THE SUN

HARLEQUIN INTRIGUE

42–ARENA OF FEAR

Don't miss any of our special offers. Write to us at the
following address for information on our newest releases.

Harlequin Reader Service
P.O. Box 1397, Buffalo, NY 14240
Canadian address: P.O. Box 603,
Fort Erie, Ont. L2A 5X3

The Northern Light

LYNN ERICKSON

Harlequin Books

TORONTO • NEW YORK • LONDON
AMSTERDAM • PARIS • SYDNEY • HAMBURG
STOCKHOLM • ATHENS • TOKYO • MILAN

Published February 1991

ISBN 0-373-70439-9

THE NORTHERN LIGHT

PROLOGUE

June 20, 1987

CAPTAIN CRAIG SAYBOLT of the super tanker *Northern Light* checked his watch. Thirteen forty-three hours. Noting the time was a routine act for the captain, a habit.

He lifted a hand to salute the state of Alaska's harbor pilot at Rocky Point, where the pilot had left them, then noted the time in the ship's log.

Captain Saybolt's tanker was on its own now, leaving the Valdez Arm, sailing out into the immensity of Prince William Sound. From the lofty bridge, Saybolt scanned the horizon, alert for small fishing boats, automatically sensing the monotonous throbbing of the ship's engines. The huge inlet spread in front of him, a flat pewter surface with black humps of islands that diminished on the horizon. The sky was partly cloudy. The sun was still high at that hour in the late afternoon, but then it didn't set at this latitude until almost midnight and rose again only three hours later.

Far off, where the coast curved around the sound, there was a touch of mist rising from the flat silver water, more black humps and a jagged line of white-topped mountains behind it.

Alaska.

Ahead of him was Glacier Island; he'd passed the land mass routinely dozens of times. He checked his watch, checked his heading. Dead center in the channel. Right on course. Despite the pristine beauty of the sound, its unruffled surface to port and starboard hid dangers for his ship—shallow reefs that could rip out a tanker's bottom.

As the Coast Guard came over the radio, static filled the bridge. "On course Wesco *Northern Light*. Over."

"Roger, Valdez. On course. Pilot departed 1343 hours. See you next trip. Over," Saybolt replied.

The first mate spoke up, rattling the computer printout schedule. "The *Arco Sun* is heading in. We should pass her in about an hour."

"Fifty-two minutes," Saybolt corrected him, glancing at his watch again.

"Yes, sir."

The first mate folded the paper and set it down. It was the latest tanker schedule, updated by fax machine three or four times daily for the benefit of the tanker captains and the pipeline terminal itself.

Everything was computerized now. Pretty soon, Saybolt thought, they'd replace his crew with a computer. They were already doing it to some extent, and his tanker, which should have had a complement of sixteen, was running with eleven men. It was barely workable that way, especially when something went wrong—bad weather, an injury or sickness, a problem with any of the complicated machinery on board.

Fourteen zero one hours. Busbey Island was right where it should be, three miles north of Bligh Reef. Saybolt noted that fact in his log.

"Nice day," the second mate said. "It sure has been a beautiful summer."

"Yes."

"Hot for Alaska. Goddam heat wave."

Not that it mattered in the air-conditioned bridge and crew's quarters, thought Saybolt. "It's clear. I like it that way," he replied. "Visibility must be twenty miles."

"And it never gets dark," the first mate said. "Easy sailing up here in the summer."

"Not always," Saybolt reminded him. The second mate murmured something he didn't hear.

He saw them then, a family of sleek-backed seals sunning on an ice floe two hundred yards to the port side. He reached for the binoculars that lay on the console and raised them to his eyes. He smiled. He'd remember those seals. He'd also remember adjusting the speed to fifteen knots, checking his heading and entering the information in the log. Automatic, routine.

"Hardly a cloud," the second mate said. "What a day."

"Um. Nice weather." These two wanted to make conversation, obviously. It was hard to keep shipboard discipline with men like them, good sailors but too chummy.

He looked out over the water again, the flat silver expanse, the islands sliding silently by, the incredible turquoise hue deep in the heart of the ice floe that drifted away to the south, probably fallen off the immense Columbia Glacier just up the Valdez Arm. A diamond in the rough, a frozen bit of the north that would float on the current until it melted somewhere down the Alaskan coast.

He looked at the compass again, but he trusted his instincts as much as his instruments. He'd navigated this channel in and out many times over the past ten years and knew every inch of Prince William Sound. He trusted himself. He trusted his ship. He trusted his crew—he'd trained them himself. But he never trusted the sea, although it was his home. The sea was like a woman—fickle and deceptive.

The *Northern Light* was owned by Wesco, the Western Oil Company, a Canadian conglomerate, and was headed to San Diego, where it would unload its Alaskan crude oil at an American-owned refinery. It was his normal route, so familiar that he could damn near run it with his eyes closed. When this cycle was over, he was due his sixty days off. Maybe he'd fly down to Seattle and see his kids. Yes, he should do that.

"Increasing speed to seventeen knots," he told the first mate. "Fourteen thirteen hours. Enter it in the log."

"Yes, sir."

"Why don't you two go on to the galley and eat? You can spell me later. We're in the open now. Only Bligh Reef to watch for."

"Yes, sir," they chorused.

He knew they were anxious to leave. He wanted to be alone, and they knew it. He'd eat later in his cabin. That was his usual habit, anyway. Too much fraternizing with the crew was bad for shipboard discipline. He knew that his crew thought he was tough and humorless—and he was. But he was fair, and he'd trained them well. They could be proud of themselves.

The two seamen left the bridge, closing the steel bulkhead door behind them with a clang. Saybolt was alone then, steering the behemoth by himself, like a flea on an elephant, but totally in control. He liked the feeling of power, the comfort he got in his own skill and knowledge. His wife, when she'd been alive, had teased him about his ego. His giant ego, as she'd called it. But it was only that he knew his own worth. He was a natural sailor, a good captain.

Storey Island lay to the starboard, Bligh Island was just beyond it. He noted the time and the sighting. Fourteen fifteen hours.

Two hours out to sea, approaching Johnstone Point, he crossed the path of a salmon fishing boat heading home to Valdez with its catch, the squatty ship cutting an arrow-shaped wake through the smooth water. He waved, not sure if the man could see him, but yes, the captain of the fishing boat raised a hand, too. A brotherhood. Men of the sea. An Alaskan, as well. There was a special bond in being an Alaskan. It was different from being from North Dakota or New Jersey. There was a mystique, an understanding shared by native Alaskans, who lived through the endless cold, dark winters and the frenetic sunlit summer days.

Alaska, the last frontier, the captain thought. It was his final thought before the nightmare began.

CHAPTER ONE

June, 1990

MARIE VICENZA heard the familiar heavy footfalls on the old wooden staircase and sighed.

The routine began. "Oh, my back. Oh, my poor back. Al, what am I going to do? How am I going to work like this?" It was Marie's mother, Sophia Vicenza, beginning the evening litany of complaints to her long-suffering husband as she descended the stairs, getting ready to go to work.

"Papa," Marie's mother called over her shoulder, "are you coming? Am I supposed to stand here on my poor aching feet all night while you hunt for your apron? Sweet Lord," Sophia moaned, entering the living room. "If I had the money, I'd see a *real* doctor for these feet."

Marie looked up from the stack of papers in her lap. "Now, don't get mad, Mama," she said, "but your doctor said that if you'd lose a few pounds, your feet wouldn't—"

"There you go! My own mother weighed more than me, and she never had a minute of pain in her life. It's not my weight. I'm on my feet twenty-four hours a day. after day after day."

Diet was not a word in Sophia's vocabulary, Marie knew. But then, her folks owned a little Italian restaurant in the Mission district in the heart of San Francisco's small Italian community, and one did not lose weight cooking with pasta, olive oil and cheese all day long.

"You'll be in to help out tonight?" Sophia asked. Then, before Marie could reply, "*Papa,* what are you doing up there?"

"I'll try," Marie said, "but I'm not even halfway through this transcript and—"

"Waste of time." Sophia eased herself into Papa's big leather chair. "Give it up."

"You must be kidding. No way."

"Oh, and now you say no to your mother?"

"Mama," Marie tried, "we've been over this a dozen times. If I can save my company that hundred and eighteen million, I'll get a bonus of—"

"Ha! Dreams. And where did all this fantasy come from? You think you're better than the rest of your family? You think you're going to get rich with this bonus? You think you don't have to *work* for a living?"

Marie rolled her big brown eyes, tapped a pencil against her teeth and silently turned a page of the trial transcript. She was thirty-one years old, still living at home, working at the Pacific Group Insurance Company down on Market Street, and putting in two or three nights at the family restaurant. She didn't need her mother's nagging.

"*Papa!*"

"I'm coming, Mama, I'm coming," a tired voice echoed from upstairs.

If Marie could find something, *anything,* that would clear Captain Saybolt of liability, it was worth staying up half the night, night after night, pouring over these two-year-old transcripts from Saybolt's trial. If she could get a bonus from Pacific, she could pay off the mortgage on her folks' house. Then they could sell the restaurant and retire. Her mother could see a "real" doctor for her

myriad aches and pains, and Marie could put funds aside
for Tony's education. All it took was enough money.

"The man's guilty," Sophia said, studying her daughter. "The whole world knows it. Three years ago the
whole world knew it, but not my Marie. Oh, no. *She*
knows what everyone else doesn't. *She's* the hotshot at
that cheapskate insurance company. *She's* the big world
traveler who's flying off to Alaska and leaving her family."

"*Mama.*"

"Don't you Mama me. You tell that company of yours
to pay up. So cheap. All those animals killed up there. It's
a disgrace. And that captain. A no-good deserter."

"He wasn't a *deserter,* Mama...."

But Sophia went on, undeterred. "You belong here,
Marie. You belong with your family and your son."

"Tony's thirteen years old. He'll be fine for a couple
of days. He can eat at the restaurant."

"He hangs out with a lousy bunch of bums," Sophia
said. "*Papa!* And you're too busy to see what goes on. I
never raised you to be a bad mother."

Marie mumbled under her breath.

"Leave the girl be," Al Vicenza said quietly as he entered the living room. "She works hard. She's a good
girl." He came over and patted Marie's dark head.

"Of course she's a good girl," Sophia said, rising with
a groan. "I would raise anything *but* a good girl? She just
needs reminding. That's all. Now come on, Papa, we're
late." Sophia opened the front door, then called, "You
try to come on over and help out tonight. You hear, Marie?"

"I'll try," Marie said, already lost in the pages of the
transcript.

Marie tapped her pencil against her teeth to the ticking of the grandfather clock in the corner. Nestled comfortably in the corner of the deep couch that had been her great-aunt's, resting her arm on a lace doily crocheted by her great-great-grandmother, Marie read on into the June evening, turning pages, nervously jiggling a slim foot, occasionally nibbling on her stubby fingernails. Two hours passed and she'd barely shifted her position. She glanced up at the clock. Seven-thirty. There was something...

Oh, no! Tony's Little League baseball game! She'd promised. What time had the game started? Six, six-thirty? *Oh, no.*

Guilt coiled inside Marie. Maybe Sophia was right. Maybe she *was* a bad mother. But, darn, she'd tried so hard all these years to raise Tony properly. When he'd been a baby, she'd stuffed envelopes at home for a mail order house just so she wouldn't have to leave him. Then, at night, while he'd slept, she'd worked at a fast food joint *and* gone to night college clear across the city so they wouldn't always have to live at her folks' like beggars.

She'd tried. Hard. She was still trying hard, desperately looking for that break, a promotion, a way out of the hole she'd dug for herself when she'd gotten pregnant in her senior year of high school.

Poor Tony. Fatherless, and with a mother who had to work day and night to help pay the bills.

Was he hanging out with a bad crowd? She knew his friends: Pete, Joel, little Mario. They were okay kids. Boys. Thirteen-year-old boys weren't supposed to be angels, for Lord's sake. She wished Tony hadn't stolen that radio from Mr. Linetti's store, but getting caught had surely cured him. After all, he wasn't the first boy to shoplift. He'd outgrow it. It was just all those hormones whirling around in him, changing him, confusing him. When he got home tonight, she'd have a heart-to-heart talk with him. It had been a while.

Marie fixed herself a cup of tea and telephoned the restaurant. Part of her hoped her mother and father were swamped in the kitchen; that would mean money in the bank. Another part of her hoped the place was dead so she wouldn't have to rush the two blocks over to the restaurant and tie on an apron.

"Hello, Mama? It's me. Are you busy?"

A moment of silence. "It's fair. Not so busy. You coming over?"

"Well..."

"I thought so. It's that transcript. You think you'll find something. You won't."

"I might."

"When do you leave?"

"I've told you a hundred times, Mama. Tomorrow, at two in the afternoon."

"You know why that boss of yours is letting you go to Alaska, don't you? He should be arrested."

"Mama..."

"He thinks he can get you into his bed, that's what he thinks. The slob. The *bum*."

"Mama, he doesn't."

"You stay at home. Do your work. Fly to the ends of the earth tomorrow. We'll be all right, your Papa and Tony and me."

"Stop laying this guilt trip on me, Mama."

"I gotta go back to work," she said. "You read your papers. Make us all a hundred thousand dollars." Sophia hung up.

Marie sat down, fingered the stack of papers, and thought: a hundred thousand dollars. Pacific Group could *afford* to pay her a hundred thousand if she could somehow save them that fortune.

She sat there, staring into the middle distance, twisting a long lock of her shoulder-length, ebony hair around a finger, jiggling that foot. One hundred thousand dollars. No more cutting her own hair; she'd stop biting her nails and get a manicure once a week. Buy a car that ran once in a while. She could enroll Tony in that boys' school just outside the city, put aside money for his college education. She could buy a cute little house of her very own, right here in San Francisco. Maybe her folks would come and live with her—sponge off *her* for a change—and get rid of this old, three-story monstrosity that still had cracks in the walls from that big earthquake last year. How many times had they mortgaged it over the years just to pay the bills? Three, four times?

A hundred thousand dollars.

Her delicate hand rested reverently on top of the transcript. What if she *did* find something in this mountain of testimony that everyone else had missed? If she could clear Wesco and this Captain Craig Saybolt of any liability...

Last week Marie had read through the stacks of depositions the court up in Anchorage had on file from three years before. Thick bundles of typed pages in question-and-answer form. The lawyers from both sides had obtained depositions from everyone they could get their hands on: the crew of the *Northern Light,* the pipeline terminal workers who'd loaded Saybolt's tanker, friends and neighbors of the captain, the Coast Guard radar operators on duty that night, anyone with any relation at all to the accident. Anyone who might have any idea what had happened on board the *Northern Light* that fateful afternoon.

She'd read statements from the agent in Valdez who'd serviced the tanker with food, linens, books, and tapes for the VCR on board and who had seen to it that the crew's laundry was done, because she figured if anyone had spent time with Saybolt the day of the oil spill, it had been the agent. Diligently, slowly, Marie had read every word in dozens of depositions—to no avail.

She started in on the actual testimonies given at the trial. Everyone even remotely connected to the Canadian-owned supertanker had been subpoenaed by either the prosecution—the state of Alaska in this case—or the defense, the dozens of lawyers defending Western Oil Company and Captain Craig Saybolt.

They'd even called to the stand a navy captain who had been on board a mine sweeper off the Vietnam coast with Saybolt in 1969, when then Junior Lieutenant Saybolt had deliberately disobeyed orders and gotten his general discharge from the navy.

Prosecution: State your name, age and present address.

Witness: Captain Lindsay Swanson, 43, 210 Front Street, Los Angeles, California.

Prosecution: Spell your name for the clerk, please, Captain Swanson.

Witness: L-I-N-D-S-A-Y S-W-A-N-S-O-N.

Prosecution: Can you tell us, Captain Swanson, how you were acquainted with Craig Saybolt?

Witness: Yes. It was March 1969. I was a radar operator on a mine sweeper. Craig, that is, Captain Saybolt, was an LJG at the time, a lieutenant junior grade. We were on duty patrolling the coast. We saw two fliers eject from their plane. Our orders were to pick up the fliers but not when it might endanger the ship. Well, those two guys were real close to shore, but Craig went in after them, anyway. He got 'em, all right, but the ship took a hit and two men were wounded.

Prosecution: So Craig Saybolt disobeyed orders?

Witness: Yes, but you have to understand—

Prosecution: A yes or no answer will suffice, Captain Swanson. Did Craig Saybolt, lieutenant junior grade, deliberately disobey orders and sail too close to shore?

Witness: Yes, but he saved two American fliers.

Prosecution: What happened to Craig Saybolt after that event?

Witness: He . . . uh . . . well, I understand he was discharged from the navy.

Prosecution: That is correct. For the record, let it be noted that he got what is called a general discharge, a less desirable discharge than an honorable one. Is that not so?

Witness: Yes.

Prosecution: Tell me, Captain Swanson, what is your personal assessment of Craig Saybolt's judgment?

Witness: Well, I . . .

Defense: Objection, your Honor, this is opinion and uncalled for.

Judge: Objection sustained.

But the point had been made. Saybolt's judgment had been questioned. And the circumstances of his less-than-perfect discharge from the Navy had been brought into the open. If he'd made a bad judgment call once, the prosecution had insinuated, he could have done it again. And it had also been pointed out that he'd been hired by a Canadian oil company after he'd been turned down by several U.S. shipping companies, because of his discharge from the military.

His own lawyer called to the jury's attention Saybolt's unblemished record since he'd left the navy, questioned men who'd worked with him and under him, and men who'd supervised him. But the fact of his military record stood.

Marie read on, through more of the same kind of testimony. Saybolt had had a few friends in Valdez, though very few. He must have been a loner, and no one had been willing to stick his neck out for him, not with the whole world watching and waiting. He'd been on his own those two months of the trial, very much on his own.

She leafed through photocopies of some of the physical evidence presented to the courts, items such as computer printouts of vessel loading schedules on the day of the oil spill. And along with the loading schedule was detailed information concerning the estimated time of arrival at the pipeline terminal by a tanker, who was piloting the tugboats and the estimated loading time and departure time.

Marie eyed an aerial photo of Valdez that was included in the Pacific Group file. The Alaskan port was surrounded by tall, snow-capped mountains. There was only a narrow channel from Prince William Sound to the port, an inlet called the Valdez Arm. But then, the spill hadn't occurred in the inlet; it had happened out in open waters when the *Northern Light* had drifted, or been steered, right onto the jagged rocks off Johnstone Point on Hinchinbrook Island. It seemed impossible, Marie thought once again, to have been so far off course.

Stiff, she stretched out her trim legs, rotated her toes and wrinkled her brow. The word impossible sat itching in her mind. Tirelessly she looked back through testimony on the weather that June afternoon. It had been stated over and over again that the day had been unusually clear, that visibility had been ideal.

Saybolt hadn't been sick or drunk or on drugs; he'd undergone the routine blood and urine tests. He hadn't been asleep. He hadn't left the bridge. *How* had the ship hit those rocks? Marie knew how the captain explained the accident, but he could have been lying. Everyone in the world thought he'd been lying. The jury hadn't believed him, either. The evidence against him was just too overwhelming.

Of course, she'd scanned Captain Saybolt's testimony, but suddenly she was eager to study it word for word. She reached for a stack of papers on the coffee table, but the front door opened, distracting her.

"Oh, my aching feet."

Sophia.

Marie rubbed her eyes and glanced at the grandfather clock. Eleven-thirty. Tony, she thought suddenly, where was he, anyway?

"It got busy," Sophia said, plumping herself down. "I knew it would."

"You should have called me," Marie began.

Sophia waved a hand in dismissal.

"And how was your evening?" her father asked as he headed to the kitchen.

"Fine. I haven't stopped reading. Guess I lost track of the time."

Sophia shifted uncomfortably, a plump hand going to her back. "You read all night?" she asked. "I thought Tony had a baseball game."

Uh-oh. "He did. But Mama, these papers might help me get at the truth. There'll be other games. Lots of them. This is my one shot at—"

"Sure, sure, I've heard it before. But you've got only one boy, Marie, and he needs his mother."

"He's *got* his mother."

Sophia lifted a dark brow. "Oh, he does, does he? And where is Anthony right now?"

"He's..." Where *was* he?

"You see? He's off with those bums. Next thing you know, you'll be down at the police station bailing him out."

"Mama," Marie sighed, "give it a rest. He's probably over at Mario's or something. They're watching TV."

"At midnight?"

"It's not midnight."

"Oh, excuse me, it's a quarter till midnight. He's thirteen, Marie. You don't know where he is, and you don't care, either. How have I raised such a daughter? Where did I go wrong?"

Marie's father stood in the kitchen doorway uncertain whether or not to intervene. A look from Sophia made up his mind for him.

"Mama," Marie said, "let's not fight. You're hot and tired, and I've got to get up early and pack."

"You're always too tired to talk."

"You call this talking?"

"Why?" Sophia asked, shaking her head, "why can't we talk anymore? Sometimes I don't think you love me at all."

"Mama." Here it goes, Marie thought. First there were the accusations, then the "you don't love mes," now the tears.

Sophia sobbed and pulled a hanky out of her dress pocket. "I've tried so hard. For you and Tony, I've tried so hard."

"Mama," Al said, "let's go on upstairs. We're both done in."

"Sure, sure," she said, sniffing, rising and trudging wearily toward the stairs. "You'll get the lights, Marie?"

"Yes, Mama, I'll get all the lights. Good night."

"Good—" sniff "—night."

Great, Marie thought, angry at her mother and angry at herself for not helping in the restaurant that night, for missing Tony's game. If she'd been at that game, maybe Tony would have come home with her afterward. Most likely he was at a buddy's watching TV. But what if he wasn't?

She sighed, decided to wait up for him and have that talk, then organized the scattered pages on the coffee table. For Tony's sake, she wished she wasn't flying out tomorrow. Alaska did seem like the end of the earth when she thought about it. And she was leaving Tony's discipline to her poor folks again.

But she had to fly to Alaska tomorrow, didn't she? It had taken her months to talk her boss, Mike, into the expense account for this trip. She'd had to sweet-talk him, put up with his coy touches when no one was looking. She'd had to be nice to him. But opportunities like this didn't come along often. All she'd been given before, as a junior investigator at Pacific Group, were auto accident claims, a few petty thefts and some arson claims. She knew her boss didn't think she had a chance in a million of discovering anything new about the oil spill, but it was that one long shot that had convinced him in the end. The few hundred dollars she'd spend in Alaska was nothing compared to the one hundred and eighteen million dollars Pacific was soon going to have to fork over to the state of Alaska.

And she had to go tomorrow. Because the day after that, Captain Craig Saybolt was to be released from prison in Anchorage.

"He's not going to talk to you," her boss had said. "Saybolt hasn't spoken to anyone from Pacific since they locked him up twenty months ago."

"I'll *make* him talk to me."

Her boss had smiled lewdly at her. "Maybe you will at that."

Of course, seeing how Pacific Group's main office was in San Francisco, the head insurance investigators—all men—had heard about Marie's upcoming jaunt to Alaska. They'd been snickering behind her back for weeks now, shaking their heads. One of the men had even approached her and said, "Four of us spent eight months in Alaska turning over every stone there was. You aren't going to find a thing. And Saybolt? He hasn't talked to anyone from Pacific since they locked him up. Face it, kiddo, the man's guilty. We'll pay off the state's claim and increase our premiums. Big deal."

Marie chewed on a nail, then stopped herself, remembering how unprofessional her nervous habits appeared. Sure, they all thought she was a pushy female who hadn't a clue as to what she was about to tackle. They all thought they'd explored every avenue, over and over. But the fact remained: right up until the moment they'd slammed the prison door shut and Saybolt had quit talking to anyone, the captain had claimed he was innocent. Against all odds, facing an angry world that would just as soon have seen him lynched, he'd maintained his stand. What if he'd been telling the truth all along? To this day, the facts surrounding the oil spill seemed improbable if not impossible. That super tanker, as if it had had a mind of its own, had gone out of its way to strike the rocks.

Marie sat back, glanced at the clock and wondered about Tony for the umpteenth time, then fingered a magazine photo of Captain Craig Saybolt that was clipped to the inside of a file folder.

What an ordeal the man had been through. His captain's rank had been stripped from him. He'd been fired. He'd been humiliated in front of the entire world. Yet reportedly he'd not lost an ounce of the arrogance that he'd displayed during the trial, the arrogance that the press had enjoyed so much. He was supposedly a proud man, a loner, aloof even with his few friends.

Marie's boss was of the opinion that Saybolt was going to leave prison and disappear, drift off into obscurity. And her boss was most likely correct. A man like Saybolt was too full of pride to let the press, or anyone else connected to his past, get hold of him again. But before he vanished, before he even got a taste of freedom, Marie planned on having that long-awaited interview with Craig Saybolt; she planned on having that one-in-a-thousand shot at clearing his name. For Marie, it was success and a home of her own or failure and a future of mediocrity.

She sat there and stared at the face in the photograph. This man, this stranger, had become a part of her life. He dominated her waking hours even though she'd never set eyes on him. The question of his guilt or innocence was as significant to Marie as it was to Saybolt himself; her entire future depended on it.

She studied the lines in the face, harsh lines, brooding lines. What did he look like when he smiled? None of the photographs showed him smiling. Of course not.

She put Saybolt's photo back in the folder and then smiled abruptly. Two days, she thought. In two short days she was going to meet him face-to-face at last, the infamous sea captain who'd allegedly caused enough damage and destruction to the Alaskan wilderness to outrage the entire country. Public Enemy Number One. How could one man, one simple, lone man, be so important?

It was 12:30 a.m. when the front door creaked open and then closed softly. Marie's back stiffened.

"Come in here, young man," she said in a hard whisper.

Tony appeared from the vestibule, his face half hidden in shadow. His thin shoulders were hunched, his dark mop of hair was disheveled. His big, long-lashed brown eyes, so like his mother's, were bloodshot. A fool could see he had been drinking.

Marie tried to collect herself. Yelling at him wasn't going to accomplish a thing. Still, her heart pounded against her ribs miserably. Her boy, her little boy... "Sit down, Tony."

"Yeah? What for?" His words were slurred.

"Don't you mouth off to me. I want to know where you got that beer. I want to know where you've been half the night."

"What beer?"

"Even from across the room, you smell like a brewery."

"So what?" He shrugged.

"I'll tell you what. You don't come in this house, at this hour, reeking of booze and smarting off to your mother."

"I'm surprised you noticed."

Marie's face became suffused in red. "I won't bother answering that."

"Listen, can I go now? I'm tired."

Marie sighed deeply. "You can go to bed, Tony. But will you do me a favor, just one little favor, while I'm up in Alaska?"

"Maybe."

"I want you to *promise* that you'll behave for Grandma and Grandpa. No drinking, no late hours. Offer to help them at the restaurant. I'll pay you myself when I get back."

"Ah, Mom, I don't wanna do dishes. I just got outta school for the summer. Can't I have a break?"

Marie clenched her jaw. "Judging by your report card, I'd say you've been on break since Christmas."

"You know what, Mom?" Tony said. "I don't *care* about the restaurant, and I don't *care* about you." He left then, spinning clumsily on his heels, his slender shoulder banging into the door frame before he thumped up the steps. His bedroom door banged shut.

She winced. *He doesn't mean it,* Marie told herself. It was puberty. That was all. He was confused and hadn't a clue why.

Marie closed her eyes. No. She couldn't deny the truth to herself any longer. Mama was right. Tony was heading for trouble, hanging out with God knew who and God knew where.

Oh Lord.

She blinked back the tears that threatened to fall. There was no time for tears or self-recrimination. What she needed to do was keep her mind on the job at hand, find that key to unlock the mystery behind the oil spill. She needed to succeed. For herself, but mostly for Tony, she had to find some missed detail, some incongruity in an event that had occurred nearly three years ago in a place that was as foreign to her as the surface of the moon. She wasn't going to let her son grow up without any advantages or hope for a better future. He wasn't going to be a street kid or end up like her, with a child to support while he was still in his teenage years. Tony was going to have a shot at college, at a decent life. For Tony and for herself, she had to succeed.

CHAPTER TWO

THE JAGGED SNOW-CAPPED PEAKS stretched endlessly along Canada's west coast. Marie even saw a glacier, a real glacier, before the evening fog hid the view from the airplane windows. But as she traveled northwest, the sun never quite set. The plane was following it around the curve of the earth.

Now, if that doesn't beat all, she thought, neck craned toward the window. *The land of the midnight sun. North to Alaska.* All those tales, movies and novels about the frozen north. The Yukon—no, that was in Canada, wasn't it? The gold rush. Dogsleds. Eskimos—or Inuit, as they called themselves. Mount McKinley, the tallest peak in North America. Mountains and tundra, seals and whales, grizzly bears and mountain goats.

And oil.

She turned on her overhead light and pulled out her map once again.

"Excuse me," she said to the man on her right. Boy, she wished she was traveling in first class so she could spread out her map without bumping into somebody. But Mike, her boss, wouldn't let her. Cheapskate. He had her on really short rations for this trip: she wondered if there was a McDonald's in Anchorage.

The map. Anchorage, a dot on the south coast of a big bay called Cook Inlet. Discovered by Captain Cook. *Gee,*

Marie mused, *I thought Captain Cook sailed in the South Seas. Tahiti and all. Guess the man got around.*

To the right of Anchorage—east—was the huge, ragged-edged expanse of Prince William Sound. On an arm of water that ran north from the sound was Valdez. Pronounced *Valdeez* by the locals, she'd learned from the young man next to her. It was an all-season port due to some warm current or other and had therefore been chosen to be the southern terminal for the Trans-Alaska pipeline. Tankers filled up with Alaskan crude at the terminal then sailed off to ports all over the United States—for this was U.S. oil—even as far as the U.S. Virgin Islands in the Caribbean.

Valdez was 300-some miles from Anchorage, she could see, but she couldn't tell how good the road was. Could she drive the distance? Would she have to fly? Mike would have a fit if she spent the money to fly.

She'd have liked to have gone to Valdez, though, before meeting the infamous Captain Saybolt, but it was too far. She'd like to case out the place, ask around about the man who'd made Valdez his home. Yes, Valdez was definitely on her list of must-dos. Three of Saybolt's former crew still lived there. She itched to know just what those men had to say after three years.

"Oh, excuse me," she said again, as her map again hit the man's elbow.

"I was getting up, anyway," he said good-naturedly.

As her neighbor left, the man on the aisle had to be awakened and Marie had to sidle out of her seat then back in again, but she was then able to spread her map flat over the empty seat and study it more easily.

The path the *Northern Light* had taken was marked on the map. Marie had sketched it weeks ago, studying coordinates in a report she'd received. It was like geometry in high school, and she'd gotten a kick out of it.

She'd marked an *x* on the map on the western side of Hinchinbrook Island, at a spot called Johnstone Point. That was where the *Northern Light* had hit the rocks.

There were so few answers about the accident. She recalled more of the testimony she'd read, frustrating testimony.

Prosecution: Captain Saybolt, how do you explain your ship hitting the rocks on the afternoon of June 20, 1987?

Saybolt: I can't explain it.

Prosecution: Why not?

Saybolt: I had been rendered unconscious. Someone else steered my ship onto those rocks.

Prosecution: Who do you think that was?

Saybolt: I have no idea.

Prosecution: You say you were unconscious.

Saybolt: Yes, I had a concussion. I believe you've seen the medical report.

Prosecution: Two of your crew members also had bumps on the head, from the impact of hitting the rocks. Don't you think it reasonable that your concussion was caused by the same event?

Saybolt: No, I do not. I was deliberately knocked out.

She wondered if his reply had been calm and dispassionate or furiously angry. Darn, it was so hard to tell. She'd read every word Saybolt had spoken in endless depositions and in the two-month trial but still had only her own imagination by which to go.

She could recall his face as easily as she could recall her boss's by now. She certainly thought about Saybolt more often. Of course, his face was familiar enough to everyone, having been plastered across the newspapers and magazines of the world. But a picture was so useless. His expression had been somber in all the photos she'd seen, though he'd had reason to look like that. She wondered once again if he ever smiled. Probably not much in prison, anyway.

Somehow she imagined him as a very angry person, a Captain Ahab figure, harsh and bitter. No whale had eaten his leg, but the media had devoured his freedom and his reputation.

A hard man, precise, a perfectionist, sure of himself. But also prone to take chances, according to his crew members' testimony.

That didn't quite mesh. A precise taskmaster who took dangerous chances? His lawyer had pointed out this discrepancy over and over, but character traits were so intangible. What jury would weigh that small incongruity against hard evidence?

The man on her right came back.

"Excuse me."

"Excuse *me*."

She had to get up again while the man slid past her. He picked up the map that was still spread open on his seat and handed it to her with a quick smile.

"Sorry," she said.

"First time in Alaska?" he asked.

"Well . . . I'm not there yet, but yes." Then, in case he misunderstood, and not to lead him on, she added, "I'm traveling on business."

"What kind of business are you in?" he asked.

He seemed nice. Young, dressed casually, broad-shouldered. An Alaskan, she guessed. Maybe he could answer some of her questions. "I'm an insurance investigator for the Pacific Group."

"An insurance investigator." He studied her, disbelieving.

Oh, she knew what she looked like, and she was used to the reactions of men when she told them she was an insurance investigator. Usually they eyed her size, her curves, her too-youthful face. She wondered how many times she'd been investigating an auto accident claim and had an angry man glare at her and say, "No way! I want a *real* investigator here. Look at my car! Just look at it!"

She shook herself mentally and smiled at the young man. "Do you live in Anchorage?"

"No, I live on the North Slope, the oil fields."

"Oh, you're an oil worker."

"Just had my vacation in the Lower Forty-eight. Now I'm going back to work."

"The Lower Forty-eight?"

"States," he explained. "The lower forty-eight states."

"Oh, sure, I knew that." Too bad, but this guy wasn't going to be able to help her. Too young. She looked at him again. He had probably been in college when the oil spill had happened.

The pilot announced their imminent arrival at Anchorage International Airport. The Fasten Seat Belt—No Smoking sign blinked on. It was 10:51 p.m. Alaska time, an hour earlier than in San Francisco, and the sun was still out. It looked as if it were maybe seven in the evening, not even dusk yet. Amazing.

Captain Craig Saybolt. Well, not really captain anymore, as his license had been revoked. She wondered if he were sitting in his lonely prison cell right now counting the hours until freedom. She wondered if he were still angry or merely resigned to the hand fate had dealt him. She wondered what he'd do now and where he'd go.

He'd been offered a deal by the Alaska State Attorney General: admit his guilt and get a suspended sentence with loss of his captain's papers. He'd turned it down flat, claiming he wasn't going to admit guilt for something he never did. So he went to jail for twenty months. A hard-nose. But a man would be crazy to go to jail when he could get a suspended sentence, wouldn't he?

Unless he was innocent.

Or unless his rigid stand was a ploy to make him appear innocent. And it was effective; it had Marie wondering. And it had been the driving force behind the argument that had landed her this assignment in the first place.

"So," came the young man's voice, "what are you investigating?"

"A client," she said.

"Oh, confidential, huh?"

"Yes."

"Where are you staying?" he asked.

Marie looked at him. Boy, they sure *were* friendly in Alaska.

"I meant that we could get a taxi into town," he said. "I'm not dangerous, honest."

"I thought you were going back to the North Slope."

"Not tonight. I have a flight out to Fairbanks in the morning."

"Oh."

"It's not far to downtown. Fifteen, twenty minutes. You want to share a cab?"

She thought quickly. Mike would like her to save money. "Sure," she said, "that'd be nice."

THE YOUNG MAN in the window seat was only her first experience with Alaskan males. They were everywhere in the airport—tall, young, rugged-looking. Not at all the three-piece-suit city type. They carried duffel bags and fishing gear, and they all looked at Marie openly, invitingly, appraisingly. Maybe it *was* true that there were ten men to every woman in Alaska.

Men, Marie mused as she got her bag from baggage claim, men were okay if you had time in your life for them, if you hadn't already had one really traumatic experience.

She'd been sixteen when she'd started dating Nicolas Umberto, Nick, a neighborhood boy. They'd planned on getting married—a proper Catholic wedding in St. Vincent's Church—as soon as they'd graduated from high school. Then Nick would have gone to trade school, and Marie would have worked. They'd had it all planned. What she *hadn't* planned was her pregnancy in the spring of her senior year. Nor had she expected Nick to join the navy with a buddy. It had all happened so quickly—Nick off in boot camp, her pregnant. She'd waited to tell him on his first leave, but he hadn't come home, and then the letters had stopped, too. She never told her folks who the father was—though they probably knew, anyway—and she'd suffered her mother's tears and recriminations, her father's deep, wounded silences, and she'd suffered the humiliation of living in a tight neighborhood; the looks, the whispers. Oh, yes, men were okay, but better at arm's length.

"Yo, lady!" the young man from the flight called. "Our cab's here."

"I'm coming." Marie frowned at herself, at all her silly thoughts about the past, and hefted her bag, her heels clicking on the concrete as she followed her companion whose name, she'd learned, was Ken. "I'm coming."

"Where to?" the cab driver asked. He was a young man, too, Marie noticed.

"Hey, aren't you Greg's friend?" Ken asked the driver. "I met you at . . . Samantha's."

"Sure, I remember. Last winter, right."

"Ken Phelps."

"Jim Morrison."

They shook hands across the seat. Marie watched, marveling. This cab driver was actually a human being, not a robot programmed to be rude. "You know each other?" she asked.

"We've met. People are friendly here," Ken said.

"So, where to?" Jim asked again.

"The Captain Cook," Ken said. "And the lady?"

Marie pulled her travel itinerary out. "The Denali Motel," she read off. "On Northern Lights Boulevard."

"I know where it is. It's a small town."

The sun was still out, seeming to slide sideways across the sky above the horizon. It was a little dimmer out, an odd, diffused dusk that held no promise of night.

What was so remarkable to Marie about Anchorage was how American it looked at first glance, how ordinary. But it *was* American, after all. It was just a small city that could have existed anywhere in the States. Well, not quite, Marie decided at second glance.

There was an embryonic, unfinished look to the place, as if it were a frontier city trying to emulate the old established ones back home. A kid dressed up to look like his grandfather but with his beard askew.

The setting was something else. Anchorage stood on a flat plain with Cook Inlet on one side, surrounded on the others by jagged, white peaks, mountains that receded back into the interior, rank upon rank. Mountains whose crags glistened with ice and snow even now, in June, in this crazy summer sun.

Jim drove them to the Captain Cook Hotel. Ken got out and pulled his duffel bag after him.

"Have a nice time in Anchorage," he said to Marie.

"I'll be at the Bush Company later," he said to the driver. Then he added, "It's my last night of vacation. Join me there for a drink."

"I'm off at one. Might drop by at that," Jim replied.

Ken handed him some bills. His share of the ride, Marie figured. Good, maybe she'd be able to have a decent breakfast on what she'd saved.

Ken waved. Marie waved. Jim made a U-turn on the street and waved out the open window.

"What's the Bush Company?" she asked.

"Oh, well, it's a strip joint. The best one in town. Kind of a legend," Jim told her.

"Oh."

"Did you want to go there?" he asked. "It might be kind of..."

"No," Marie said, trying not to laugh. "No, I think the Denali Motel will be fine. It's late."

"Not here it isn't late," he said, and she couldn't help noticing how long he kept his eyes on her in the rearview mirror.

She cleared her throat finally, and said, "Maybe you can help me. I need to get to Valdez." Carefully she pronounced it Val*deez*. "What's the easiest way to get there?"

"Valdez. Let's see. You can drive. It's 300 miles. It takes, oh, about eight or nine hours. You can fly Alaska Air, but it's usually booked for weeks."

"Oh, darn."

"Hire a plane. I've been taking flying lessons at a charter service. I can recommend them. Bernair."

"Wouldn't that be awfully expensive?"

"Not too bad. If you could get one or two people to go along, it'd be cheaper than flying commercial."

"Really?"

"Sure. Give Bernie a call. Tell him Jim sent you."

Then, for the rest of the drive, she tried not to notice those eyes on her in the mirror.

As it turned out, Ken had not only paid for his ride to the Captain Cook, but he'd shelled out for her fare, as well. She insisted that Jim take a tip though, and then suggested he might buy himself and Ken a beer later at the...ah...Bush Company.

"Sure you won't come?" he asked, leaning out the window.

"No, thanks," Marie replied, lifting her bag, "but you boys have fun."

The Denali Motel was quite a step down from the Captain Cook, but then she wasn't an oil worker on hazardous duty pay. She waved as he drove away and noticed the shadow her arm made on the road, a long pale shadow in the midnight sun.

Her room was done in institutional olive green with scenes of Mount McKinley hanging on the walls. Denali, she gathered, was the Indian name for Mount McKinley. It was also the name for the national park that surrounded McKinley. Nice touch. The Denali Motel.

She should be tired, she thought, kicking her shoes off and stretching out on the bed. It was after midnight back home. It occurred to her, though, that she actually *wasn't* tired. She felt full of anticipation, ready to do something, go somewhere. It must be the sun. What did people do here in the summer? Did they stay up all night?

But it wasn't night; it was barely twilight. Time to go for a walk or to a restaurant or a movie. Time to saunter on over to the Bush Company. Time for Sophia and Al to start serving the dinner crowd.

No, at this hour they'd be home and in bed. Marie got up and padded barefoot across the room to pull back the heavy blackout curtain. She smiled. The sun was still out.

Tony would love it here. Just imagine, a vacation in Alaska for her son. God, she wished Tony could be raised in a pure atmosphere like this, with maybe a man around to teach him to fish and hunt and do all those manly things. She pictured Tony in jeans and heavy boots and a plaid shirt hiking up Mount McKinley—Denali, that was.

She'd phone in the morning, she decided. Patch it up with her mom, talk to Tony, tell them all how spectacular Alaska was. She'd call first thing.

MARIE AWAKENED TO SUNLIGHT streaming in through a crack in the curtains. She stretched and noticed the papers she'd pulled out of her briefcase last night, still scattered on the bed. She couldn't remember falling asleep. She sat up and saw Saybolt's photo staring at her, and she grimaced. Now she was sleeping with the man. She was becoming obsessed with him; the anticipation was eerie, nerve-racking.

Today, she thought, swinging her legs over the side of the bed, she'd get it over with today, at last. Automatically she reached out and flipped the magazine clipping over. She was tired of looking at that face, tired of asking herself if he were innocent or guilty, tired of wondering. Four o'clock, she thought, she'd meet him and judge him in person when he was released at four this afternoon. She'd rent a car, drive out to the prison. She'd even get there early, just in case. It would be unthinkable to miss him after all this waiting.

Marie squeezed toothpaste onto her brush and looked at herself in the bathroom mirror. What if he wouldn't talk to her? She hadn't actually considered that possibility before. Why *should* Saybolt talk to her? Maybe she had been nuts to convince Mike into letting her try this. There wasn't a darn thing to be done after three years; the fleet of insurance investigators had left no rock unturned. They were all back in the office now on coffee break, laughing themselves silly over the little Italian chick who thought she was smarter than anyone else. Out of Mike's hearing, of course, because they knew Mike had the hots for Marie.

Oh, was *she* going to be humiliated when she got back to work.

She scrubbed her teeth hard and pushed down the moment of panic. She was doing her job, doing Pacific Group a favor. The Saybolt case left an unscratched itch in Marie's professional curiosity. And the questions hung in her mind like unfinished yawns: Why had Saybolt asserted his innocence all along? Why had he gone to jail instead of grabbing the sweet deal offered him?

In the bathroom mirror Marie could see the photo of the captain, still lying on the bed. The picture was facedown, but his face was imprinted in her mind's eye, every line, every detail. She couldn't shake it. No matter how hard she tried to superimpose something else over that man's implacable visage, it persisted in filling her inner vision.

What was he *really* like? She'd read hundreds of articles on him in magazines and newspapers; she'd studied countless pages of his testimony. Yet, she could not get a handle on him. Short of the bare facts surrounding his life and his trial, he remained an enigma.

She stepped in the shower and decided to think about other things, to clear her head. She wondered about Tony. If she called in a few minutes, would she find him home? She wondered if he were giving her folks a hard time already—probably not. He knew she'd throttle him if he didn't behave for these few days. And she wondered about her boss. Was he regretting his decision to let her come to Alaska? Lots of thoughts flitted through her head as she let the hot water massage her neck and back, as she tried to relax and not worry so much about the meeting that afternoon. But every time a new thought wandered into her brain it was too quickly replaced by yet another notion about Saybolt.

"Darn," she muttered, shampooing her hair. "Darn him." She wasn't going to think about him anymore, not till later, not till they came face-to-face at last. . . .

The trial. How had he borne it? All the notoriety, the whole nation pointing a finger at him. Oh yes, everyone had been quick to charge Saybolt, even his employer, Wesco, had been only too glad to lay the blame at Saybolt's feet. And the prosecution, whose job was to find him guilty. Not to find the truth, but to prove guilt. The nation had demanded a scapegoat and immediate punishment, a kind of collective purge for a society that required fossil fuels to run, but a society that would not take responsibility for the harm its habits caused.

You bet, she must have been crazy to have tackled this case, to have given it one last examination. Pacific Group had been ordered by the Federal District Court in Anchorage to pay up the 118 million dollars to the state of Alaska on behalf of Wesco. Pacific ought to have just paid and not listened to Marie Vicenza.

She called home after her shower. Collect.

"Hi, Mama."

"Is it cold up there, Marie?" Sophia asked. "You got your sweater?"

"No, it's warm. Summer. The sun never sets."

"That's a fine thing!"

"Is Tony there?"

"Your son," Sophia said, "he's off with those other rotten *bambinos*."

"They're okay kids, Mama."

"Sure! Drugs and beer! Do you know what he's done now, Marie? He shaved his head!"

"He what?"

"Like a billiard ball. All his pretty curls."

Oh God. "Mama..."

"He looks like a freak, Marie."

"Okay, I'll take care of it when I get home. It'll grow out."

"I'll be dead by then."

Marie sighed. "Is Papa there?"

"He's down at the place." Sophia always called the restaurant "the place." "*He's* working." There was a full load of accusation packed into Sophia's words.

"I'm working, too, Mama." Marie looked at her toes sticking up on top of the olive-green blanket and wiggled them.

"You should be home. You know what I mean."

"I'm doing a job, Mama. You know why I'm here. Do we have to go over this again?"

"No, especially since I'm paying for this phone call. Just come home soon."

"Give my love to Tony and Papa. And I love you, too, Mama."

"Sure, sure, a daughter who flies off to Alaska!"

"Bye."

Marie had breakfast in the coffee shop then arranged for a rental car to be delivered at two o'clock that afternoon. She got directions and a street map and took the bus into the downtown area.

She walked the path along Cook Inlet, watching the mirror-smooth water for whales. The inlet was too shallow for big ships, but sometimes whales were sighted there, or so she'd read in a brochure.

The mountains almost surrounded Anchorage, steepsided, tall, rising directly from sea level to snow. The sun shone.

Men looked at her appreciatively. She passed the Captain Cook Hotel and thought of Ken. And Jim. She wondered if they'd had a fine old time at the Bush Company last night.

At noon Marie returned to her motel, got her papers again and made three phone calls. One to each of the crewmen who still lived in Valdez. There was no answer at two of the numbers, but a woman answered at the third.

"May I speak to Tim Klutznic?" Marie asked.

"He's not home. Can I give him a message?"

"No, not really. Will he be home shortly?"

"Well, no. He's out on his fishing boat."

"Oh, I see." Darn it!

"Can I tell him who called?"

"Oh, no, it's just about insurance," Marie said. "I'll call again."

"Can I give him your name?"

"He doesn't know me, but thanks."

Well, she'd known it wasn't going to be easy. She'd wanted very much to talk to those three men while she was in Alaska. She'd just keep trying. Maybe she'd get to

Valdez after all; if she had a good enough reason, Mike wouldn't be able to complain.

Her rental car arrived at two. She'd hoped to avoid driving, because she really didn't get much practice at it. There was no place to park in San Francisco, so she used public transportation. Frisco was such a small city, really. Al had an old Dodge Dart, which she used occasionally for longer trips. Sophia didn't drive at all.

She got directions from the motel desk clerk, marking them on her map.

"The Rabbit Creek Correctional Facility?" The clerk gave her one of those looks. "Let's see. You take the New Seward Highway south. Here. Then you turn left about ten miles out of Anchorage. There should be a sign. It'll say Rabbit Creek, anyway."

She dressed carefully, not wanting to intimidate Saybolt, not wanting to appear too frilly-feminine, either. She wore a navy blue skirt and a blue-and-white striped short-sleeved shirt, plain but crisp-looking. White sandals with heels. A little makeup. If Marie used too much she tended to look cheap; her coloring was too high.

Okay, she was ready. She squeezed her eyes shut and offered up a prayer: *Let this man talk to me.*

The car started after the second try, but she held the key on too long and a terrible grinding sound came from the ignition and made her jump. Thank heavens it was an automatic. She spread the map out on the passenger seat. New Seward Highway. Okay. She put the car in gear. She was off.

She nibbled on a nail at stoplights, but she had to watch where she was going pretty carefully. Once she was on the Seward Highway, though, it was a piece of cake. The sun was out, the clouds were like white cotton candy and the mountains crowded on her left, funneling her onto the coast road along Cook Inlet.

Captain Craig Saybolt. Guilty or innocent? Would she be able to judge when she talked to him? *If* she talked to him.

Maybe he'd have other people waiting for him. She recalled that he was a widower, but he had a son and a daughter, grown by now, in their twenties. Would they be there? If they were, her efforts to speak to him would be much more difficult. She had a gut feeling, though, that no one would be there to celebrate the captain's day of freedom. She knew from the reports she'd read, from his depositions and friends' testimony, that his relations with his children were not good. It seemed that his wife had died of asthma. She'd had a severe attack at home alone and passed out. The kids blamed their father because he'd been at sea so much. Never there when they needed him. Typical male.

Cars were stopped along the highway, and then Marie saw why. The cliff to her left was crawling with white mountain goats or sheep, or whatever, on the vertical wall. They browsed and paid no attention at all to the gawking tourists. She drove on.

The sign was easy to find: Rabbit Creek Correctional Facility, State of Alaska. She turned left, driving up a long, narrow valley that lay in the shadows of towering rock.

Prison. What if Saybolt really was innocent? How had he stood it?

A tall cement facade, colorless, featureless. Barbed wire, guard towers. A parking lot. Marie took a deep breath. It was only three-fifteen. She'd have to wait.

She steeled herself, got out of the car and straightened her skirt, arranged her features into a professional expression and strode up to the guard house outside the main gate.

"I'm here to meet a prisoner who is being released today," she said to the guard on duty.

"Name?"

"Marie Vicenza."

"*His* name."

"Oh. Craig Saybolt."

The man checked a list on a clipboard. "Yeah. 4:00 p.m. You're early."

"Where can I wait?"

"You can sit in here. He's got to check out with me."

"Do you know Capt—er, Mr. Saybolt?"

"Nah, never met him. I only see the inmates when they leave." He smiled. "'Course, I usually see them again when they return."

"I think I'll take a walk first. I'll be back. Thanks," Marie said.

Inmate. The word made her think of a zoo or an insane asylum. Saybolt had been an inmate for twenty months. What did he do all day? What did he think about? How should she approach him? Friendly and understanding? Professional? God forbid, would she have to pull out all the stops and turn on the sex-kitten act? She'd do it if she had to. This case was important.

She walked a little, studied the frowning walls, watched an eagle soar high up on a thermal current.

She wished she'd brought something to drink; her mouth was dry.

At three forty-five she sat down in the waiting room of the guard house, stared out the window into the prison yard and chewed on a fingernail. She crossed her legs one way and jiggled her foot, shifted, crossed them the other way. Words, sentences and questions crossed her mind like a stock market ticker tape. Should she address him as Captain, even though he wasn't one any longer? Would he be flattered or insulted? He'd better talk to her; she was here to do him a favor.

No one else showed up. No kids, no family, no friends. A spurt of pity for Saybolt shot through her before she shut it down. It was better that no one was there to meet him, better for her.

At 4:05 a man crossed the prison yard with a guard at his side. He was forty-five years old, she knew. He walked straight and proud. He was built powerfully around the neck and shoulders beneath a generic white shirt with rolled-up sleeves. His face was expressionless, closed. His blue eyes, which looked as if they'd seen too much, stared directly ahead. He carried a single small gym bag. Prison issue.

It was utterly impossible to penetrate the wall of his detachment.

He entered the guard house. Marie stood, waiting, straining to see into the man, to get an idea what he was feeling. She stared hard at him, before he noticed her, trying to link the face she saw now with the one in the photograph. This face was animated with all those small details that made a person alive, and that made all the difference. It was as if a figure had suddenly stepped out of the photograph and appeared before her, in the flesh and breathing. It was a singularly wrenching experience.

She was struck instantly by two things about Craig Saybolt that couldn't be seen in a picture. He had an aura of authority about him—cold, unbending command. And, silly thing to notice, despite the paleness of his face, despite the slightly thinning brown hair, he was one damned attractive man.

He spoke to the guard, signed something, hefted his bag and turned to go.

Marie stepped toward him, barred his path and thrust out her hand. "Hello, Captain, I'm Marie Vicenza from the Pacific Group. Could I talk to you a minute?"

A corner of his wide mouth lifted in derision as he paused for the briefest moment. Then he brushed past her rudely and exited the building.

CHAPTER THREE

I KNEW IT, Marie thought, watching his back recede. Well, he wasn't going to dismiss her so easily. Uh-uh. She made a beeline to her car and started it up. She chewed a nail as she backed out, steering with one hand, and put the gearshift into drive. She'd catch him before he...before he what? Caught a cab? Out here? Hitchhiked into town? He couldn't be planning on walking all the way to Anchorage.

But he *was* walking. A solitary figure moving down the gray ribbon of highway, carrying his gym bag. On both sides of the road, clouds clung to the steep walls of the mountains. The sea captain should have been diminished by the scale of the Alaskan scenery, a minuscule figure surrounded by tons of spiraling rock. Yet he wasn't. His back was too straight, his shoulders too squared, his pace too determined.

Nevertheless, Marie thought, pausing at the turnoff to the highway, he'd have to accept a ride from her because there wasn't another car in sight.

She gunned the motor then slammed on the brakes, slowing to a crawl beside him. Reaching over, she rolled the passenger window down then leaned in his direction, trying to keep her eyes on the road at the same time.

"How about a lift?" she asked cheerfully.

He kept on walking.

"Look," Marie called, "you can't hoof it all the way to the main road. There's not a car in sight. Come on. Hop in."

"No thanks." He walked, eyes straight ahead.

Oh, brother. "It's *ten* miles, Captain ... Mr. Saybolt. Be reasonable."

He gave no sign of acknowledgement.

"This is ridiculous," she said, certain that if she didn't get to talk to him now, he would disappear when he got to the city. "I just want to give you a ride," she said, crossing over the center line then correcting the car back onto her side of the road. "I came all the way up here to see you."

He made a disgruntled sound—that was something—but continued on at a steady pace, a big man, strongly built in the arms and shoulders, his long, well-shaped legs moving tirelessly. He probably *could* walk ten miles, she thought darkly.

Marie let the car roll onto the shoulder and come to a full stop. She had considered the possibility that he might not even give her the time of day—but she still couldn't swallow it. My God, she'd spent months researching this case and talking her boss into this trip. Everyone at Pacific was probably waiting for her to fail. Well, she couldn't. She just *wouldn't* fail. Saybolt wasn't going to get away with this.

His figure was receding down the long stretch of highway. She gripped the steering wheel and stared at him. There had to be some way to convince him she could help him.

Suppose she told him she had some kind of proof that he was innocent. That might get his attention—if, of course, he really was innocent. It was a slightly underhanded thing to do, but in this case, the end justified the means.

She put the car back into gear and caught up with him just as he was rounding a long curve in the road. He gave her a cursory glance then deliberately looked straight ahead again.

"Okay," she called, slowing the car, leaning toward him, "I didn't want to tell you this right away. I mean, it may not pan out, but I've got some news. *Good* news."

Her declaration was met with silence. Marie panicked. He *was* going to walk ten miles. She drove alongside him, but he never gave a sign that he saw her. She chewed furiously on a fingernail. What if a car came along the road and picked him up? She glanced quickly in the rearview mirror. Mercifully the empty road stretched away behind her.

Okay, what to do now? How did you deal with such a stubborn person? With Tony one thing worked—she grounded him. That wouldn't work here. She'd tried friendliness. She'd tried lying, for Lord's sake, but he wasn't buying any of it.

She took a breath, held it for a second, blew it out and tried again. "Look, can't we talk for a minute? I mean, here we are, two intelligent adults. I'd like to help you out."

Oops. That was the wrong thing to have said. He shot her a scathing look.

God, she felt ridiculous driving at three miles an hour next to him. He was being unreasonable and pigheaded, and she was tempted to tell him that. However, that probably wouldn't get him in her car, either.

Okay, plan A and B were flops. So what was Plan C? She chewed on her lower lip. If only she could convince him she was truly on his side, the only human being on earth who had any faith whatsoever in him....

"Mr. Saybolt," she began, leaning toward him once more, "say, is it okay if I call you Craig?" Amazingly that got his attention. He lifted a dark brow. "Well, Craig," she went on, adjusting the steering, leaning over again, "we really do have to talk. I've been working on your case, you know, for months, and I believe you're innocent. Honest I do. I'm working my tail off on the proof." Had he slowed his pace? Her heartbeat quickened. "The trouble is," she said, trying to sound matter-of-fact, "I need to ask you a few questions. Get in," she urged gently, smiling. "Come on. Just a couple of questions."

Finally he stopped. She slowed, misjudged the power brakes and jerked the car. She smiled so broadly she wondered if her face weren't going to crack. *Oh Marie, what a bad actress you are.*

He was shaking his head, a grim look on his face. "You people'll try anything, won't you?"

"You've got me all wrong," Marie said as he leaned down to the open window. "Come on, hop in."

For a long moment he only glared at her with eyes the cool blue of an ice floe. She wanted to shiver but held herself in tight control. "Come on, Craig," she said gently, honey-sweet. "I'm on your side."

Another grudging moment passed. She could see his indecision battle his curiosity. She willed him to give in to her.

"Come on," she whispered, still smiling, and then, when his hand reached toward the door handle, she knew she had him. Relief flooded her. Carefully she looked straight ahead as he got into the front seat and closed the door. The shiver took over finally and coursed through her limbs, then fled. She put the car back in gear and steered onto the road, the warm, friendly smile still plastered to her lips.

"Wow," she said, "I sure hate driving like that. Not paying any attention to the road, that is." Babbling. She was babbling away. She couldn't stop. "In San Francisco—that's where I'm from, by the way—I never drive anywhere. My dad's car is a wreck, too. I can't trust it to go two miles without a breakdown. Heck, it's still got the dent in the roof when some bricks fell on it in the earthquake last year."

She braved a glance at him. He was shaking his head slowly, bemused.

"Well," she said, "this is better than walking, isn't it?"

He swiveled his head toward her, and she could feel the weight of his gaze. "Let's hear about this proof you're working on, Miss . . ."

"Vicenza. But call me Marie, please." She swallowed. What *was* she going to tell him? She glanced at the speedometer. Fifty miles per hour. He wouldn't jump out at this speed, would he? She jiggled her left foot nervously.

"Okay, *Marie,* the proof?"

"It's . . . ah, all in the transcript of the trial," she began, searching her brain frantically for something to tell him, something hopeful. "I really have studied it for months," she said. "There's some testimony that just doesn't jibe."

"Such as?" There was a scowl on his face, and the bulk of him seemed to fill the whole front seat.

"Well," she said, "you kept maintaining that you were innocent, but your crew told a whole different story."

"That's news? You haven't got a damn thing, Miss Vicenza, nothing."

"Marie," she said in a small voice.

"You lied back there."

"I didn't . . . ah, lie. I *did* read things in the transcript that don't ring true."

"Bull."

"It's just hard to put a finger on it, Craig," she said softly. "I promise, there's something missing there, something wrong."

"What's missing," he said, "is the truth."

"That's it," Marie replied brightly.

"Spare me."

She gave him a quick, sidelong glance and saw the tick of his jaw muscle. She drove in silence for a few minutes, collecting herself, regrouping. She had to tell him something more, put a name to her feeling that there really *was* something wrong with the whole affair. She had to convince him somehow of her good intentions. Who else had offered to help him, anyway?

She glanced at him again. He was staring out the window, unbending, imperturbable. His silence had the quality of granite. A tough, hard man, someone who could lead other men without the ordinary mortal's need for approval and friendship. Captain Ahab himself. Was she ever going to get him to open up to her?

"Look," Marie said, pointing to a cliff across the road. "Aren't those mountain sheep?"

Obviously bored, he glanced upward through the windshield. "Goats."

"Oh. They're pretty."

"Um."

Then suddenly she felt her front tire catch the edge of the pavement and she was jerking the car back onto the road. Saybolt had put one hand on the dashboard, the other automatically across her chest.

"Holy..." he swore under his breath. "You really *can't* drive, can you?"

Feeling utterly in control of the vehicle again, Marie said, "It was just because I was looking at the sheep... goats. I've got it covered, Craig."

He only raised his brow.

"I'm not the enemy," Marie said after a moment.

"Aren't you?"

"No. In fact, I'm the only one who seems to give a damn what happens to you. Everyone else is writing you off. My company's ready to pay up. We've been *ordered* to pay up. And you know what will happen?"

"No. But I'm dying to find out."

"We'll raise our rates to the general public and close the file permanently."

"What else is new?"

"It's tragic," Marie said, popping the nail of her little finger into her mouth. "I mean, if you're innocent and—"

"*If?*"

"Well, yes, I meant..."

"Hell, lady," he said, "why're you wasting my time? What did you get, a free trip to Alaska?"

"Come on, that's not fair."

"Not much in life is."

"I mean, I do believe you're innocent. I want to help."

"First, you don't believe it at all. And second," he said, "I don't need your help or anyone else's."

Marie let out a breath. It whistled between her teeth. My God, it was Craig Saybolt versus the world. The press was right: the man was arrogant and proud to a fault. A fatal flaw. He'd end up like Captain Ahab, going down in futility and bitterness. She felt as if she'd failed before even getting under way.

They reached Anchorage by late afternoon. Not that the sun was any lower in the sky. The distant mountains were still bathed in noonday light despite the clouds that clung tenaciously to their sides. She felt disoriented, a bit lightheaded, as if she'd not slept properly in days. The constant strain of his deliberate silence was not helping, either.

"You can take me down to the waterfront," he said, pointing to an exit on the highway.

"Oh," Marie said, "I thought you could get a room or something at my motel."

"I'll find my own room."

"What about friends?" she tried. "Is there someone you could stay with?" At least she'd know where to find him.

But he shook his head. "I'll be just fine, Miss Vicenza."

Reluctantly she drove him to a street near the waterfront that struck her instantly as a blemish on the face of Alaska. The small street of hotels and saloons seemed not quite finished. In this part of town, there were vacant lots in between the buildings, trash clung to broken fences in the breeze, and litter was left in the gutters. Obviously this was not an area of prime concern to the citizens of Anchorage. But then again, since the oil-boom days of the late sixties and early seventies, the modernization of the city had come to a grinding halt.

"Is this *really* where you want to stay?" she asked, pulling up to the curb.

"Compared to where I've just been," he said in an embittered voice, "it'll be like checking into the Ritz."

He opened the car door and reached in the back for his
bag. For a moment he hesitated, then he faced her full
on, and she could feel the force of his anger press her to
the door. "Look," he said, "get out of this neighborhood. Drive back to your nice room and pack up. There's
nothing you can do for me. Go back to where you came
from, Marie, and forget about oil spills and has-been sea
captains." He closed the door. "Thanks for the ride," he
said.

"Craig," she said. "*Craig,* listen, I—"

"Go home, little girl" was his final comment.

Frustrated, Marie watched him walk down the street
and round a corner. "Go home, little girl," he'd said, as
if she were of no account whatsoever, as if she hadn't
spent countless hours trying to help him. Some thanks
that was.

She sat in her car and felt her nerves scratch against
one another like fingernails on a blackboard.

Little girl. If only he knew how angry that made her....

She'd really blown it. She should have known, just
from reading the newspaper reports on him, that Craig
Saybolt wasn't going to give her the time of day.

She pounded the steering wheel with her palm. So what
was she supposed to do now, jump on a plane and fly
back to San Francisco, her tail between her legs? How
humiliating! Failure. She could just hear her boss, not to
mention her own mother and her son. Oh yes, they'd all
be saying: "We told you so, Marie."

She decided right then and there—Saybolt wasn't going
to do this to her. She'd worked too hard and come too
far. She'd find him, find his hotel, camp out on his
doorstep until he got it through his thick head that Marie Vicenza wasn't a quitter.

She pushed open the car door and took a deep breath, *Little girl*. The nerve. Who did he think he was, anyway?

Something occurred to her through the haze of her anger just then, and with that sudden insight the anger fled from her. Craig Saybolt had heard the prison door clang behind him over a year and a half ago. He'd shut the world out, the world that had accused him, tried him and found him guilty. And Marie was a part of that world. He was all bottled up inside, wounded, lashing out at the first person he'd met outside the prison walls.

A spurt of unbidden sympathy for him shot through her. She forgot immediately how mad she'd been only seconds before. Instead, she saw Craig Saybolt as a proud, aloof man who'd been forced to face the world alone. Well, she thought, she was going to change all that. Somehow, she'd convince him he needed her. He wasn't going to go this alone, not anymore, not until she had done everything humanly possible to help him clear his name. She'd have her success, all right—that was still true—but in the process she was going to help this lonely soul face a society that had written him off. Marie Vicenza, rescuer, a white knight on a white horse. Now *that* was novel, she thought as she headed down the street, high heels clicking.

There was a problem however: just exactly where had the captain gone?

When Marie rounded the corner she spotted two hotels. There were a few bars, as well. He'd get rid of his bag first, wouldn't he? Then go for a drink or something? She'd check every place on the waterfront until she found him, every hotel, bar, restaurant and park bench.

She began by climbing the three steps to the lobby of the nearest hotel and then peered inside. It was dim and smelled musty. Behind the desk an old man sat napping.

"Excuse me," she began, waking the man. But Saybolt had not checked into this hotel.

Marie stood outside, put her hands on her hips and pursed her lips. There was another hotel across the street, the Downtowner.

Sure enough, when she checked with the clerk, she was told that a man fitting Saybolt's description had indeed checked in. He'd used the name Smith. Marie guessed that ID wasn't exactly required here.

"Can I, ah, go on up?" she asked.

The man looked at her blankly. "Suit yourself."

He probably thought she was a hooker, Marie decided, shrugging as she mounted the stairs.

Saybolt's room, 301, was two flights up. The stairwells were dirty, the old red-and-black carpet, threadbare. Light fixtures hung in the hallways, but most of the bulbs were burned out. It was dim and depressing and stank faintly of urine.

She found 301 and tried to control the too-familiar shiver that this sort of flophouse elicited in her. It was sad, so sad; too many souls inhabited this shadowy world. She should know, having lived on the edge of it all her life.

Not anymore, she thought, raising her hand to knock. She and Tony were going to escape this. Absolutely. And just inside that door was her ticket out. Boldly Marie knocked. She waited.

The second time she rapped on the door it swung open abruptly, catching her off guard. But it was him, his white shirt hanging unbuttoned out of his pants. She noticed that his hair was wet around the temples; she guessed she'd disturbed him while he'd been washing up.

"Ah, hell," he said, eyeing her, "you've got to be kidding me."

Undaunted, she put on her best smile. "You aren't going to get rid of me, Craig, so you might as well talk to me."

For a long minute he stood there regarding her with annoyance. "You're wasting your time," he said finally.

But Marie stood her ground, still smiling. She was aware of the size of him, his six-foot-one frame filling the doorway; his naked chest was far too intimate in this dismal place. A Marlon Brando in *On the Waterfront*. It struck her, quite out of the context of her mission, that she hadn't seen a half-dressed man in an awfully long time. There was a vitality to Saybolt, a male charisma in the way he leaned a shoulder against the door frame, that made the tiny hairs prickle on her neck.

"Let me buy you dinner, at least," she said, though with a little less confidence. "We can talk about whatever you like. We don't have to talk at all if you want."

But he was shaking his head, and she could see anger boiling under his surface. "Go *home*" was all he told her. Then, without warning, he shut the door in her face.

For a time all she could do was to stand there stunned. God, how she *hated* closed doors! Nothing made her angrier than someone—in the middle of a good fight— shutting a door in her face. Tony was a pro at that, and, boy, did it get her blood up! When Tony did it she flew into his room and *really* gave it to him. Better the screaming and yelling, the confrontation, if you were mad. Shut doors were poison.

For what seemed an eternity, she stood in the dingy hall tasting the bitterness of defeat. Sounds came to her ears:

the slamming of doors, the echo of voices, a shrill burst of laughter from the hallway upstairs.

And then she felt tired suddenly, drained. It was hopeless. She should just give up and go home....

Darn it all! Marie Vicenza didn't give up. She'd never given up, not when she was eighteen and pregnant, not when she had an infant and had to go to school and work. She'd be damned if she was going to give up!

She went back down to the lobby. No one paid the least attention to her. *These* Alaskan men were too concerned with where their next drink was coming from, she guessed. And that was fine with her.

She looked around. A fake, dusty palm stood in a green plastic pot. The black-and-white tile floor was cracked. The desk clerk read a newspaper, oblivious.

Shrugging, she plumped herself down in an old, cracked leather chair and picked up a magazine—*Outdoors in Alaska*—and hoped nobody would notice her.

How embarrassing, she mused, jiggling her foot, scanning a photo of salmon leaping to spawn upriver. She flipped a page. A bear, a *big* brute of a Kodiak bear, standing on his hind legs, baring his teeth, twelve feet tall. Wouldn't want to run into him in a dark alley.

How could Saybolt do this to her?

She glanced at her wristwatch. He had to come out eventually. He'd have to eat sometime, at least. Her own stomach was growling shamefully. She'd kill for a whopping serving of her mom's lasagna. Mmm. Dripping with mozzarella, the tomato sauce sweet with basil, cheese on top bubbling as it came straight out of the oven.

Time seemed to have slowed. She kept glancing at her watch, over and over. A minute would pass, two. Where *was* that man?

She wondered then if Tony were eating properly, hanging out at the restaurant with Sophia and Al, behaving himself. Or was he hanging out with those kids, those beer lovers, getting in trouble?

Her stomach knotted up. What kind of a mom had she been, really, working all the time, blind to her son's needs? She'd tried so hard to provide for him. But a woman alone... Frequently the task seemed insurmountable. If only there were enough money, if only she could succeed with this Saybolt business, get that bonus.

What time was it, anyway? Maybe she ought to march herself back up those steps and lay it on the line to him. "Look, Saybolt, you're my one shot at making it. No matter how slim the chances are of saving my company that money, you've got to help me. *Talk* to me."

Should she? Did she dare?

An image of him popped into her mind. He had a forbidding look to him, stern, unreachable. Yet somehow that steely exterior tugged at her, made her want to scratch the surface to see what lay underneath. Was there a human side to him? He did have two grown children, she knew. Had he ached when they'd been sick or hurt? Had he wept when his wife had died?

Actually, she thought as she glanced at her watch, he was a very attractive man, vital and physically fit. She supposed he'd be described as rugged-looking, like a sea captain, though maybe one from a past century. The man had appeal, she had to give him that, in the same way that lots of men in their middle years possessed a certain air of knowledge and authority. Men of conviction, men of honor. But was Saybolt honorable? She'd told him she believed in his innocence. But *did* she? Was her mother right? Was Marie pursuing a dream?

The sun should have moved lower in the Alaskan sky, but it hadn't. Marie looked at her watch yet again. Two hours. He hadn't shown his face in two whole hours, and the sun was still at its midafternoon zenith despite the time. Seven twenty-eight. How was that possible?

Yet she wasn't in the least bit tired. In fact, she was wide awake, alert, nervously so. And she was still hungry, starved. Maybe she should get a candy bar down the street....

The stairs creaked. Her senses sharpened. And then there he was, clad in a brown leather jacket, coming down into the lobby, his eyes straight ahead. He looked grim.

Marie stood stiffly. "Hello, there," she said, dropping the magazine onto the chair. "I thought you'd never come down."

He stopped short and glared at her incredulously. Then he shook his head, shot her another harsh glance and left.

Oh, brother. Marie grabbed her purse and chased after him. Over two inebriated men on the steps, down the sidewalk, her heels clicking as she hurried to catch him.

"Hold up!" she called.

But he kept right on walking.

Great.

Just around the corner, he entered a diner, one of those real old-fashioned, silver-sided trailers that was shaped like a bullet. She could smell the greasy blue-plate special before she even stepped inside.

Where was he? Ah, over there, in a booth. Alone.

Uninvited, Marie slipped into the seat opposite him. He looked mad enough to kill. "Now don't go telling me to buzz off," she said. "I waited half the evening in that awful lobby, reading about salmon fishing." She screwed up her nose. "And I'm famished."

For an unsettling moment he stared at her. Deep down inside she quivered, but on the surface she kept right on smiling bravely.

"At least let me order something," she tried, reaching for the plastic-coated menu. "Um, a BLT and fries. Maybe a chocolate shake. I'm starved."

But he refused to speak to her. He sat there across from Marie, scowling. She didn't know what to make of him and kept having to remind herself that he'd just gotten out of prison—that very afternoon—and there must be dozens of emotions battling one another inside him.

"What are you going to order?" she asked calmly, matter-of-factly.

He stared at her hard for a long moment. It was impossible to read him, to see behind those cool blue eyes that appraised her. "Listen," he finally said, "you must be crazy to hang out in this neighborhood. Have you looked around you, Miss Vicenza?"

"Marie," she said automatically, and then she glanced over her shoulder. The place was crammed full of men. There wasn't a woman in sight except for the waitress behind the counter. Every set of eyes was on Marie. A few of the men behind her grinned openly, an invitation.

"Tough lady, aren't you," he said. It wasn't a question.

"Yeah, I'm pretty tough," she replied. He was challenging her, testing her mettle, wondering no doubt if she was as brave as she sounded. She gave him a little smile. "You bet," she said, "I was tough enough to get this assignment, and I'm tough enough to handle it. In case you haven't noticed, I happen to be the only person around who seems to care about you at all."

And then suddenly he laughed, a laugh that was utterly devoid of humor. "This must be my lucky day," he said. "I've got a new champion, pretty little Marie Vicenza. And she's going to do what a fleet of lawyers and professional investigators couldn't—she's going to prove my innocence." Again, he laughed. "Give me a break."

Marie's foot was wagging furiously under the table. Okay, she thought, no more pleasantries, no more skirting the issue. There was obviously only one way to handle this angry, intimidating man. Straightforward and with no holds barred.

She lifted a slim, dark brow purposefully. "Tell me something," she said, "just satisfy my curiosity." She took a break. "Tell me the God's honest truth. Did you deliberately run the *Northern Light* onto the rocks?" She looked up and met his ice-cold glare and a granite wall of silence.

CHAPTER FOUR

SO MUCH FOR THAT, Craig thought as he walked away from the Denali Motel, where he had deposited Miss Vicenza over her many and varied protests.

What a day. He'd waited for twenty months, more than 600 days, more than 14,000 hours for this day. He looked around at the cars whizzing by on Northern Lights Boulevard, at the trees and grass. He studied the buildings, the shops, the gas stations and restaurants. There were people out, lots of people, even though it was a week night. But that was summer in Alaska—you grabbed it while you could.

All those people he saw and who saw him were free; they could go where they wanted, do what they wanted, wear and eat what they wanted. And not a one of them had the sense to appreciate all this freedom. He supposed they had worries—financial, romantic, sickness maybe. But how insignificant all those problems seemed to Craig.

The sun cast wan shadows as he walked. God, it felt good to be going somewhere, not to be at the beck and call of anyone, neither guard nor warden nor trusty nor other prisoners.

How had he survived?

What a crazy day. He'd meant to relax in his own room, catch a nap, eat a good meal, take a bath to wash the prison stink off him. Take some time for himself.

Yeah, well, he thought, Murphy's Law: if anything could go wrong, it would. That pushy little insurance investigator, Marie Vicenza, was right out of the Murphy's Law textbook.

Annoyance etched deep lines in his face as he wondered why on earth anyone had sent her to talk to him. They must have known he would have nothing to say to any insurance company. He'd said it all three years ago, then again at the trial two years ago, and no one had listened. Why would they listen now?

He'd been barraged by requests in prison. Requests from lawyers, from Wesco, from the insurance companies involved. Fill out this, make that statement, relinquish the right to something else. He'd even received offers to help a writer do a book about him, a TV miniseries, articles in newspapers, magazines and a goddam offer to appear on the *Today* show. They'd do it right in prison, no problem; the warden had already agreed. They'd done everything humanly possible to strip him of his dignity....

And now they were after him again, only this time they'd sent a cute young girl.

Craig walked and wondered about that. He wondered if her superiors hadn't picked her out simply because she *was* cute. Had they planned for him to fall head over heels for her the minute he'd exited the prison gate, because he hadn't had a woman in years?

He wouldn't put it past them. And he wondered, too, if Marie weren't in on the scheme, although he had to admit she hadn't come on to him that way. Maybe she'd been told not to lay the sex-kitten act on too thickly. Damned if he knew. Damned if he cared, either.

He walked, hands in pockets, and shook his head in disbelief. It was over a mile to his hotel, but he wanted to walk. How long it had been since he'd been able to walk where and when he'd wanted. How long since he'd been able to walk in a straight line for more than fifty yards!

He was tired. It had been a long day. But his blood bubbled with a kind of anticipation. Free at last. He should be celebrating. Champagne, a woman; he should call someone he knew. Something.

A car pulled up next to him. "Hey, need a ride?" a man asked.

Craig shook his head, pulled his mouth into a rusty smile. "No thanks, I like walking."

"Okay." And the car was gone, a shiny red sports car of some sort. He didn't even know the new models anymore. Rip Van Winkle.

God, prison. It had been unbearable, yet he'd borne it. He'd shut down his mind, his emotions, and survived. The other men had respected his silence and left him alone.

He shuddered to think of the long days and weeks and months. The sour taste of prison food, the scratch of rough cotton clothes, the endless dreary boredom, the stultifying atmosphere of hate and derision and violence and hopelessness. But he'd survived it. He'd spent some time working in the library, where it had been quiet, and he'd gotten back into reading. Anything. The classics, the latest spy blockbusters, history books on Alaska—whatever. And when he hadn't been reading, he'd exercised in the gym. The long hours of pumping iron had eased the tension he'd too often felt. Because he'd known he was innocent, prison had been a living hell.

He was out, though.

A kind of warmth spread in him. Revenge. That would make up for the time that had been stolen from him. And his career. And his children's love and respect. He would find out who had waylaid him, run his ship onto the rocks and let him take the blame.

Thank God Polly hadn't been alive to witness this nightmare. She would have stood by him. She would have believed him. It would have killed them both.

His stride faltered for a moment. Or would she have? No one else believed him, not even his own lawyers. Not the jury, not his employer, not the state of Alaska, nor the whole damn country.

Not his kids, either. His daughter, Tanya, was twenty-one now. Graduating from that college near Seattle. Polly's brother had custody of the kids, and that was okay. He was a nice guy, and someone had to take care of them. Especially Craig, Junior, who had only been fifteen when the spill had happened. But Craig, Jr., whom everyone called Sonny, was eighteen now. Tanya had never called or written, but Sonny had written once—to tell his father that he was an environmentalist and that his old man was a criminal.

It still hurt.

Craig walked faster. The night air was soft and cool and fragrant. The long rays of sunlight bathed the city in gold. He could taste freedom in every breath he took, in every smell and sound and traffic noise. Freedom all mixed together with bitterness and regret and the need for vengeance.

A young couple walked by arm in arm. The girl was giggling and the boy was trying to kiss her neck. The innocence of youth.

The girl pulled herself away from her date and laughingly said, "No, Bobby, come on. It's *light* out."

Something frozen inside Craig creaked and shifted. People. Everywhere. And to them he was just another guy, not a criminal, not an ex-con, not prisoner number

54709. He was just a man walking at midnight in the fairy twilight of the Far North.

Odd, but he truly could feel his legs getting tired. He'd kept in shape, all right, but he'd never been able to walk like this for long periods of time. Still, it felt good. He could go anywhere he wanted whenever he wanted. He took a deep breath and tasted freedom once more.

He passed through downtown and kept going toward the waterfront. It was familiar to him; sailors hung out there, in sight of the water, even though Anchorage wasn't a deep-water port. It was a wide-open town, though, crammed with sailors and oil workers looking for a good time. They could find it, too.

The bars beckoned with the sound of music and loud voices punctuated by bursts of laughter. But drinking had never been one of his habits.

He smelled the sea then, the brackish odor of mud-flats. The tide was out. God, the sea. It had been a long time. What he wouldn't give at that instant to stand on the bridge of a ship, any ship, the salt spray in his hair, the wind in his face, the great dark clouds amassing on the horizon, the sea rolling beneath his feet. He could taste it, feel it in his blood like an unforgettable woman.

It hit him like a sudden hammer blow. He'd lost his captain's papers; he'd sail no more. The serenity of the previous moment was gone, ruined.

He ground his teeth. He had to find out who'd done this to him. And why. The questions had tormented him for three years.

It had to have been one of his crew. There'd been ten of them that day. One of them, he knew, had hit him on the head from behind and run his ship onto the rocks. Why? What for?

He thought about the ten men as he walked, conjuring up the face of each one. He'd done this a thousand times before. Who was the guilty one? *Who*?

He wandered past bars and cheap hotels down to the path along the bay. A man stepped out from the shadows. "Hey, bro'. You look like you need a little happiness. I got all kinds. What you interested in?"

Happiness. Cocaine, crack, uppers, downers. "No thanks," he said.

The man shrugged and stepped back into the shadows.

The pale midnight sun shone on Craig as he wandered. He needed this freedom, the fresh Alaskan air, the smell of the sea. He needed to make a plan of action. He would have to search out the truth, vindicate himself. He'd have to make them listen this time.

He kicked a stone. How stupid he'd been. Trusting the legal system, trusting his lawyers, trusting Wesco and the Pacific Group Insurance Company.

"Sure, Craig, don't worry," Gene Rearden had told him. "We've got it all taken care of. Hired you the best set of lawyers around." Gene had been the Wesco legal counsel; Craig wondered if he still was.

He remembered standing in Rearden's office, his head still pounding horribly, his stomach nauseous from the concussion. He'd been shaky, horrified, disbelieving. On Rearden's shiny desk lay the *Anchorage Daily News*. The headlines screamed: Oil Spill Devastates Coast. Was Saybolt Asleep on Duty?

He'd put a hand to his face and rubbed his eyes. "Are you going to investigate this, Gene? Someone deliberately sabotaged my ship."

"Of course. There's an investigating team out there already, working with the Coast Guard. Don't worry, they'll find out what happened."

But they hadn't.

He'd been betrayed at every turn. He could still see Gene Rearden on the witness stand, skinny legs crossed negligently, face stained with broken capillaries. "Captain Saybolt," he'd testified, "was a good employee until this unfortunate accident. Of course, Wesco had been a little hesitant to hire him because of his military record, but his previous employers vouched for him. At Wesco we like to give a man a second chance."

Craig remembered how he'd felt then—burning inside, furious, humiliated, helpless. He'd stared at Rearden, trying to wound him with his look, as Rearden had wounded him, but the man had been excused and walked out of the courtroom, carefully avoiding any eye contact with Craig.

He drew in a deep breath. It was definitely dusk now. The sun had dipped behind the horizon for a couple of hours of rest. He should go back to his room and get some sleep, too. He could sleep as late as he wanted now. No prison routine to follow. No job. Nothing to do, no place to go, no one to talk to. Not a friend, not even an old acquaintance to call. He was a pariah.

He leaned his forearms on a railing overlooking the water. His legs really were tired from walking, a good kind of tired. He stared out across the smooth, dark inlet. A few lights bobbed on the surface of the water, small boats. To the south a jet landed at the international airport, its lights winking red and white.

He'd be getting on a plane soon, he figured. Going somewhere. But where? He needed to locate ten men, get their current addresses, talk to them. One was guilty, and Craig would find him and prove it.

There was the matter of his parole conditions—not to leave Alaska without permission. He wasn't through with their punishment yet. But he'd get permission one way or the other.

A woman approached him. He could smell her perfume before he could make out her features. She was blond, and she wore a lot of makeup.

"Hi," she said.

"Hello."

"You lonesome?"

He turned his head sideways as he leaned on the railing and studied her. She was a prostitute. Young, pretty except for the too-thick paste on her face, built like a centerfold. She must have had goose bumps all over with that skimpy outfit she wore.

"No, not really," he said.

"You look lonesome." Her lips pouted prettily, dark red, almost black. She fancied herself Marilyn Monroe, he guessed.

"I'm just fine," he replied.

She put a hand on her hip. "Sure you are, mister. But don't you want some company, anyway?"

Despite himself, Craig felt a stirring in his groin. A woman. Softness, perfume, a few moments of forgetfulness and release. It had been a long time....

"Well, mister? I ain't got all night."

"Sorry, not in the market right now."

"Broke, huh," she said, eyeing him.

For a moment he was going to tell her that he wasn't. Instead, he said, "Afraid so."

"That's too bad. Well, see ya." Her hair curled in little question marks around her face, blond and fluffy.

"Say," she said, cocking her head, "haven't I seen you around, mister?"

"I doubt it," he replied and wondered if she hadn't recalled his picture in the papers during the trial.

"Oh, well." She turned away and shrugged.

"So long." He watched her go, slender pale legs scissoring beneath a skin-tight leather skirt. Idly he wondered if she'd find a man or two that night. He was sure she could. And he wondered if she'd make those men happy for a few hours. Wouldn't it be nice, he thought, if that was all it took?

He stared back out over the water. Small gurglings from the tide coming back in came to his ears. A light from a boat moved across the water from north to south.

Inadvertently he pictured the prostitute's face in his mind's eye. Maybe he should have gone with her. But another face seeped into his consciousness. A small, delicately formed face, very Italian, with huge, limpid dark eyes framed by black, spiky lashes. A curved mouth, a pointed chin.

Marie Vicenza.

My God, what had made him think of *her?*

Olive skin, smooth, flawless. Tiny hands and feet. A determined manner. Funny little nervous habits.

She hadn't known how dangerous it was to be around Craig. He'd been without a woman for two years. Had she considered that? Had her superiors really considered that when they'd sent her to "talk" to Craig. He still wondered.

She was, he guessed, around thirty, although she looked younger. Too young for him. She hadn't worn a wedding band, he'd noticed. Probably divorced. Ms. Vicenza.

Craig rubbed the back of his neck with his hand and tried to get her image out of his brain. He had too many other, far more urgent, matters to dwell on. He had to form a plan of action to find out which man was the guilty one—a solid, workable plan, foolproof. He sure didn't have time to be thinking about women....

But he couldn't lie to himself, could he? Marie Vicenza was a helluva good-looking young woman. If he were less of a gentlemen, he'd have taken her into his hotel room when she'd shown up like that. He'd have gladly taken her.

He could almost feel the texture of the silky skin on her thighs and belly. His fingers clenched inadvertently.

What a persistent little fox. Ambitious, young, *pushy*. That's what women were becoming these days. Equal rights...well it was about time. But on some women it sometimes turned shrill and ugly. Little Marie Vicenza, a user, desperate to get the inside dope. Only there wasn't any.

Ah, hell, it wasn't Marie Vicenza he wanted. He wanted a woman, all right, but not her. It was just that she seemed so desperate. It made her vulnerable. He wondered what motivated her. What truths and lies. He wondered just how far she'd have gone to get his attention.

Hell, he wasn't a saint, but Marie would have been more trouble than she was worth.

It wasn't a woman he needed—no, it was vindication.

CHAPTER FIVE

MARIE FELT HERSELF swimming up from sleep and realized that she was still curled up in the old chair in the lobby of Craig's hotel. Then she saw that ex-tanker Captain Saybolt was standing over her, his hands on his hips.

Uh-oh.

"What in hell are you doing here?" he demanded.

She unfolded her stiff limbs and worked out a kink in her neck. "I fell asleep," she said groggily.

"I thought you were back at your motel."

"I couldn't sleep. I figured you wouldn't call me, so I..."

"Camped out on my doorstep." He turned away momentarily, rubbing his whiskered chin. "Look," he said, facing her once more, "I'm going to take you back to your motel again. Then you're going to stay there. You got that? Following me around like a puppy isn't going to fly, Marie. You can't help me, and I can't help you. Now, come on. Let's go."

Obediently Marie stood. With the desk clerk looking on in mild interest, Craig took her arm, rather roughly, and began to steer her out of the lobby. She had just enough time to reach down and grab her briefcase.

"Take it easy," she said, "I'm coming, I'm coming."

"Sleeping in the lobby," he grumbled under his breath, "in that dump. How stupid can you get, lady."

"I can take care of myself," she said, panting as he dragged her along.

"So you've told me."

Marie frowned. Her brain was clicking on finally, and she remembered the last idea she'd had before she fell asleep. Maybe she could get him to think about this rationally, to calm down, if she showed him the computer printout sheets she'd brought along. If she could get him to just look through the files for one lousy minute...

"Listen," she said when he stopped at the corner to find a taxi, "I've got some information in here that you *will* be interested in." She held up the briefcase, waving it in his face. "The least you can do is look at the stuff. It won't take a minute."

"Forget it."

"Aren't you at least *curious* about what I've got?"

"No."

He searched up and down the street for a cab. Fortunately for her, there wasn't a single one around. He growled under his breath and kept hold of her arm. He probably thought she'd escape him before he could shove her in a taxi and be rid of her.

"It's about your crew, Craig," she said. "It's got all their current addresses and phone numbers—everything."

"I can get that information myself."

"Oh?" She tugged on his sleeve with her free hand. "I'll bet it would take you months to track down even a few of them."

"So what?"

"Like, ah…Claud…ah, Claud what's his name, you know? He's in South Africa. I have his address *and* phone number."

He merely shrugged.

Marie tapped her toe impatiently. "Why are you so stubborn?"

"Born that way." He craned his neck. "Isn't there a single cab in this town?"

"And you're foolish, too."

He laughed without humor. "Foolish. Because I won't play your game?"

"Because you won't let me *help*. My company's kept up on every last crew member, every last detail about the oil spill and the aftermath. Every scrap of information our investigators collected is in the files. It's *all* right in here." She pressed on. "I could save you months of time, years."

He pinned her with a sharp glance. "What makes you think I'm even interested in pursuing the accident? Why're you pushing this on me, anyway? Maybe I want to forget, get on with my life."

"I don't think so," she said quietly. "I think you spent the last twenty months deciding exactly how you were going to prove your innocence when you got out of prison. You have a plan. That's what I think."

"Oh you do, do you?"

"You bet. I think you didn't take the deal the attorney general offered because . . . well, because you're bent on proving your innocence to the world. You want your name cleared."

He studied her for a moment with implacable blue eyes. "But you're not convinced of my innocence, are you, Marie? You're working this case like a long shot at a race track. You figure there's an outside chance I might have been telling the truth, and you're praying that long shot pays off."

"So? What does it matter *what* I believe, what my motives are? The issue is," she said, "I can provide information. Why not use it? Use *me*."

"And that wouldn't bother you?" He'd stopped looking for a cab, at least.

She shook her head emphatically. "Not one bit. Use me. Use all the resources Pacific Group can offer. We don't even have to like each other."

He smiled grimly. "I wonder," he said, "if you're really as mercenary as you sound."

"Of course I am," she replied staunchly. "I can take anything you dish out, Craig Saybolt. This is my job, and I'm good at it. But I'm wondering," she added, "if *you're* smart enough to take advantage of me."

He dropped his hold on her and let out a tired breath. "Okay," he said, "I'll look at what you've got. But then I want you to give me some space. Am I reaching you?"

"It's a deal." She stuck out her hand and shook his firmly. "Where to? Do you want to go to my motel room? We could . . ."

"Let's get one thing clear," he said, drawing his dark brows together sternly, "I don't go to . . . I'm not in the habit of . . ."

"What?"

"Look, there are not going to be motel rooms."

Marie ducked her head, suppressing a smile.

"Let's walk." He cocked his head toward a path leading along the waterfront.

"Sure. We'll find a bench or something."

"Yeah, sure, anywhere."

Anywhere but in a motel room with me, she thought and realized suddenly that there had been a shift in their relationship, such as it was, a subtle tilt. Previously he'd merely been a client of hers, albeit a reluctant one, and now, well, now he'd brought the sex issue into things. He'd clearly pointed out that he was a man and she a woman, and they needed to remember that. To Marie, he'd driven a wedge—more like a splinter, she supposed—between them, making it just that much harder for her to do her job.

Why did men do that? Clearly Craig was a gentleman, a dyed-in-the-wool, old-fashioned gentleman. But it nagged at her that he'd felt it necessary to point out their difference in sex. Just once, she mused, just one time, she wished she could do her job without the sex thing getting in the way.

She glanced at him with a mixture of annoyance and curiosity as they headed away from the seedy side of Anchorage to where the path—a bicycle path—curved along the coastline. It was nicely planted with bushes and bunches of surprisingly luxuriant flowers. Across the street there were several Victorian houses painted in rainbow colors. A few shops, art galleries, restaurants, all restored recently.

"I hadn't thought Anchorage had this much to offer," Marie said, strolling alongside him, her much shorter legs moving twice as fast as his.

"It's got its good points."

"And Valdez?"

"What about it?"

"Is it, you know, cute? Like a fishing village in Maine or something?"

"I wouldn't have used the word 'cute.'"

"What then?"

He looked at her impatiently. "Rustic, I guess."

"You don't talk a lot, do you?"

He stopped short. "Listen," he said, "I had my psych evaluation three years ago. I don't need another."

"You don't need much at all," she whispered under her breath.

Despite the clouds that nestled against the steep walls of the surrounding mountains, the sun still poured down on Anchorage. But it was cool out, especially along the waterfront where a slight breeze stirred in the trees. Marie had changed back at her motel into lightweight tan slacks and a cherry-red summer sweater, but it wasn't enough to keep her warm. Goose bumps raised on her arms and legs as they sat on a bench several blocks from the downtown core.

"You're freezing," he said. He sounded disapproving, as if she were too dumb to know how to dress in Alaska in the summer.

"I'm okay," she insisted. But he took off his leather jacket anyway and offered it to her. She looked at him questioningly.

"Here."

"Well, all right. Thanks. It is nippy. San Francisco can get this way in the summer, too," she stated, but felt once again that he was doing the male thing, subtly pointing out that she was in need of protection. She wasn't certain whether or not to set him straight.

He'd seated himself away from her on the hard wooden bench. He sat facing her though, one arm resting nonchalantly on the back of the bench, hand dangling behind it. She looked up to catch him studying her intently as she wrapped herself snugly in his jacket, and then she almost felt like handing it right back to him. She thought about telling him how irritated she got when men tried to take control but thought better of the idea. Saybolt was too used to having the upper hand. It was written all over him, the need to be in control. She'd swear that she could almost reach out and touch the aura of self-sufficiency that emanated from the man. There was something that held her back, though, that kept her silent for a moment too long as the warmth from his jacket spread into her bones; it was the way he held himself in rigid control, the manner in which he erased all expression from his face.

He had large features, his eyes deep-set beneath dark, arching brows, like the wings of a bird. He had a diabolical look to him at times, a sexy look. A girl never quite knew what went on behind those coolly appraising eyes or what promises lay behind the wide, mobile mouth.

She began to rummage around in her briefcase, acutely aware of his scrutiny, her pulse just a bit too rapid.

He *was* handsome. She had to admit it to herself, although somehow the fact seemed to drive the invisible wedge between them just a little deeper. She sat there shuffling papers in her lap, terribly aware of his gaze on her, of his impatience. There was a change in the air, a new undercurrent, something she'd conjured up that was vaguely disquieting.

"The computer printouts?" he asked, the edge of annoyance ever-present.

"They're right here," she replied, shaking herself mentally. He was, after all, fifteen years older than she was, a man with a load of troubles, a brooding personality. Atlas, with the world on his broad shoulders. "Right, here are the files on the crew." She handed them to him. He took them cautiously, wary of the hand that was feeding him. Somehow, she just could not see this hard, deliberate man running his ship aground. Tightly controlled men like Saybolt didn't make that kind of mistake.

"Um," he said, scanning the sheets.

Marie edged nearer but caught the slight tension in him as she moved. She glanced down at the page he was on.

"My God," he said. "I'd heard about Joey Brown and that accident in L.A., but I didn't know it was listed as alcohol-related."

She nodded. "He was killed when his car went over an embankment. Right through the guardrail, too."

Craig shook his head slowly. "The kid was our cook," he said. "He never drank. He was a complete teetotaler."

"He did *that* time," she said carefully.

He flipped the stapled pages, studying the autopsy report. "Blood alcohol at .175. It doesn't figure."

"Was he a...a good kid?"

"The best. His dad was a restaurant owner in Seattle. I knew them there when I was...when I lived there."

"You got Joey the job on your tanker?"

"Yes."

"I'm sorry about him," she mused aloud.

His head snapped up. "Why should you be? You didn't know him."

"The death of any young person is sad," she said, and an image of Tony, reeking of beer that night, popped into her head. She turned the picture off. "There was another death," she said. "Go on through the files...yes, that's him. Woods."

Craig read the report in utter disbelief. "Woody," he said, "dead. I hadn't heard a damn thing about this. Nothing."

"It just happened this spring," Marie said. "In the Bahamas. He was diving on a reef, I believe. A problem with his air tank."

"John Woods," Craig said, "dead. Amazing. He was my helmsman. I'd been out with Woody a dozen times."

"A moment ago," she said, "you used the word 'amazing.' It did seem odd to me that two of your ten crewmen were dead. And both in accidents. What do you make of it?''

He looked up at her sharply. "I don't make anything of it."

"But you did say 'amazing.'"

"Figure of speech. I was surprised."

"But *isn't* it odd?"

"Not for seamen. A lot of them live on the edge all the time."

"On the edge?"

"Thrill-seekers. Risk-takers. They can't seem to settle down."

"So you don't think this is worth pursuing?"

"Pursuing?"

"You know, look harder into the accidents?"

"And how would you go about doing that? The police files appear closed to me." He tapped a page with his knuckles.

"I suppose you're right." But she wondered. There was that little itch in her head, without substance but nagging, persistent.

"Claud Savant," he was saying, opening another file. "You were right. He's in South Africa. Durban."

"And he doesn't answer phone calls or letters."

"You tried to contact him?"

She nodded. "Yes. About two months ago. There was something in his testimony at the trial that didn't click to me."

Craig lifted that brow.

"He said that he'd never really trusted you. That he knew about the incident with the navy, you know, in Vietnam, and he had always wondered about your judgment."

"I remember," Craig said under his breath.

"Anyway," Marie said, "I had to ask myself, if this Claud Savant didn't trust his captain, why did he sail with him in the first place? Four trips, too. I mean, couldn't a radio operator like him ship out with whomever he pleased?"

But Craig said nothing, only sat there with a frown on his face and a tight muscle working in his jaw.

"Well?" she urged.

"There are plenty of reasons why he testified that way," he said hostilely.

"Such as?"

"Such as he didn't want to appear associated in any way with a captain that could run a super tanker aground. That's why. He was distancing himself," Craig said bitterly.

"Maybe."

He turned to her abruptly. "Look," he said, "they all did the same thing at the trial. What did you expect? I'm not an easy man to... Just chalk it up to the burden of leadership." There was an ironic twist to his lips.

She wanted to say that she understood, that she was sorry, but words were inappropriate. She kept silent.

After a moment he seemed to gather himself, putting the trial in perspective, reading on through the files. His face was utterly closed now, wiped clean of expression. She wanted to reach out and touch his hand, just briefly, to let him know she was on his side, but she couldn't do that, either. He'd take it all wrong.

He read through Able Seaman Tom Marshall's file. Marshall had disappeared somewhere in the States after the Valdez trial, and Pacific still hadn't discovered his whereabouts. Marshall, like so many of the other *Northern Light* crew members, had been brutal on Craig at the trial.

"Bob Bogner, too," Craig said to himself as he continued to flip through the pages. "Vanished."

"Yes. And like Marshall," she said, "he disappeared as if he had a real good reason to. Like he was running."

"What are you getting at?"

"Maybe Bogner and Marshall knew something. Saw something. I mean, you insisted that you were knocked unconscious that day. *Someone* must have done it."

"And you're saying these men took off because they were scared of what they knew?"

"It's a possibility. We can't rule it out."

"Interesting," was all she got out of him. He read on, coming to a file on First Mate Tim Klutznic who was still living in Valdez, running his own fishing boat now. "So Tim got his wish," Craig said. "He finally got that salmon boat."

Marie glanced at the page. "Looks like it. And a new baby, too."

"His wife's a nice lady" was Craig's only remark, but Marie had a feeling that the captain didn't think much of his former first mate.

"Did you and Klutznic get along?" she inquired after a moment.

He put down the papers and stood then, walking to the other side of the path, turning to her abruptly. He looked angry.

"Did I say something...?" she asked.

"Let's get one thing straight between us," he said in a dangerously bitter voice, "I didn't captain that tanker to make friends. It's not a popularity contest."

"Craig..." she began.

But he put up a hand. "My own kids don't even like me. And frankly, I couldn't care less. I'm the way I am. Period."

"But *everyone* needs—"

"No, they don't," he interrupted harshly. "I'm perfectly content being alone. I never needed all those damn trappings. So don't sit there feeling sorry for me. I don't want your goddamned pity, Marie. You getting my message?"

"Loud and clear," she said, eyeing him. Then, boldly, "So, if all that's true, if you're such a cool customer, why'd you save those pilots off the Vietnam coast? Why'd you throw away your career?"

For a moment he looked ready to explode. Then, with great effort, he collected himself. He said only, "That was a mistake," and came back over to the bench, sat down and picked up the files. She let it drop.

With Marie looking over his shoulder constantly, he read through several more files. Engineer Steve Stratford was currently residing in New Orleans, a card-carrying dockworker now. Evidently he had a girlfriend there, a Cajun woman who sang in a club on Bourbon Street. A corner of Craig's mouth lifted in the semblance of a smile as he read through Stratford's file.

"What's so amusing?" Marie asked.

"Um. Bones, that's what they called Steve, spent half his trips out to sea complaining about his lousy love life."

"Oh. Did you ... get along with, ah, Bones?"

"I got along with all of them." He shot her a glance. "I saw to it that they did their jobs. For a captain, that's getting along."

"I see."

"I doubt it."

Then there was the third mate, Jeff Petersen. Marie pointed out that he lived in San Francisco now and had been recently married. He'd even bought a small marina there. Nothing fancy. "I tried to call him," Marie said, "several times, but he was always out working on the boathouse, and there wasn't a phone there. I talked to his wife, though. She sounded young and didn't much want to discuss the trial. Said she'd met him right afterward, anyway."

"Wild Man."

"What?"

"Jeff was known as Wild Man. Not only with the crew, but all over Valdez."

"A party boy?"

"The best. In between trips he had a continual party going at his house there."

"He had a house?"

"Sure. Most of us rented something or other in Valdez. There're always places available. Seamen come and go."

"So it isn't odd that your former crew is so scattered now?"

He glared at her as if she should already know the answer.

"Okay," she said, "I'm getting it. You seafarers are a bunch of wanderers. Rolling stones and all that stuff."

"The sea is in our blood."

"But there's only one of you who's still on a super tanker," she observed. "He's...ah...here it is, Pete Lund. Address in Valdez. He's still with Wesco, too, but not on the *Northern Light*."

"Pete *would* still be at sea."

"Why?"

"Hates towns, people, even dogs and cats. He rarely spoke to anyone on the trips out. Real unfriendly."

"It says here, though, that he and Tim Klutznic were in the same outfit in Vietnam together. They must have known each other. Isn't Tim the one who has the salmon boat now in Valdez?''

"Yes. I didn't know they were in Nam together. They didn't seem friendly.''

"Um.'' Marie began chewing on the nail of her index finger while she scanned Lund's file. "The report was written by one of our best investigators,'' she said, thinking aloud. "He's usually thorough. I wonder why he said Klutznic and Lund were pals?''

"Maybe just because they were in Vietnam together. Does it matter?''

"Everything *could* matter. I mean, what if they were together a lot during the trial, talking, going to bars afterward. The investigator obviously noted some relationship between them. Maybe they had something important to discuss or . . . or hide.''

"Hide?''

"Well, say one of them, Lund or Klutznic, is the guilty party, and he—''

"The guilty party?''

"You know, the one who knocked you out.''

"You almost sound as if you believe that. You're slipping, Marie.''

"Oh, excuse me,'' she said, shrugging, "I forgot. I'm playing a long shot at the track here.'' She looked down at the papers again, aware of his eyes still on her pensively. "Anyway,'' she went on, "maybe Klutznic saw Lund knock you out, or vice versa, and one is blackmailing the other. It's possible.''

"You've got a hell of an imagination.''

"An investigator has to have one.'' She shifted her position, still conscious of his perusal. "That's why you need me. That's why I can help you.''

"Or botch everything up for me.''

"Well, that's hardly my intention."

He was silent for a moment, facing the downtown area now, staring off into the middle distance. She gave him a quick, sidelong glance. The news that Lund and Klutznic had known each other in Nam had taken Craig by surprise. Oh, he'd probably tell her it wasn't important that they were old acquaintances—but Marie could see he was still digesting the revelation. And it *was* interesting that during their work on the *Northern Light* and during the trial the two men had distanced themselves from each other. Very interesting, indeed, she thought. Glancing again at the solemn look on Craig's face she mused: *he thinks so, too.*

She was getting somewhere! She was finally getting somewhere. She hadn't given up, and she was going to get this job done. One more success—a big one this time—and she could take Tony away from that neighborhood.

At that moment Craig Saybolt was just about her best friend on earth.

Well, except for a few things. He certainly wasn't the friendly type, and that nonsense about not going to a hotel room with her still rankled. My Lord, she thought, half the business meetings in the world were conducted in hotel rooms or suites. What had he thought she was going to do, rape him? Use her body as bait?

It hit Marie like a ton of bricks. That was exactly what he thought! Of course!

And then she wasn't sure whether she was mad or amused. *Men,* she thought, shooting him another look. And especially this prime example of the male species. Oh, he was attractive enough, but that obstinacy...

Still, Marie mused, in spite of his constant annoyance with her, his open disapproval, she was enjoying the challenge this man posed. Every minute he spent with her brought her closer to sweet success.

He started to close the folder then paused. "Howie," he said. "I didn't see the file on Howie Mayer."

"Mayer." She cocked her head. "Oh, yes, I remember him. He's in there. Let me see." She took the folders and leafed through. "Here he is."

"Figures," he said, scanning the papers. "The guy always was ready to crack."

"He's been in and out of rehabilitation for years now," Marie said, remembering.

"But still living in Valdez, it says here."

"And still drinking, probably."

"No doubt."

"How did Mayer ever get a job with Wesco with his record?"

"Oh, he'd dry out for months on end. But something always set him off again."

"Such as?"

"His wife left him one time. And I think he has a kid somewhere who's institutionalized. I don't really recall."

Marie searched her brain. "Didn't he testify favorably for you?"

"In a way."

"What way?"

"Hell, I don't recall."

"Of course you do," she said, pushing. "I think Howie Mayer testified that you were a competent captain. Sure he did. And he even stated that he didn't see how you could have run onto those rocks. That was it."

"Lot of good it did me."

"Well, at least he tried to be a friend."

"He tried to tell the truth. That's hardly friendship."

"I forgot. Sorry. You don't *need* friends."

But he didn't dignify her sarcasm with a reply.

They ate a late breakfast at a small bakery around the corner from the new downtown convention center. The place was warm and cozy and smelled of cinnamon and yeast. The tables were covered by generic red-and-white oilcloth. It reminded her of her folks' place in an obscure way—it was friendly, folksy, inviting.

"My parents have a restaurant," she told him in between mouthfuls of a cheese Danish.

"Don't tell me, a spaghetti house."

She raised her brows. "Why, yes, it is. But how did you know?"

"It wasn't real hard to figure out."

"I guess I still look like a waitress," she said matter-of-factly. "Maybe that's my destiny."

"But you're hoping I'm the key to your salvation."

Marie's eyes snapped up to his defiantly. "That's right."

"Thought so." There was the faintest hint of a smile on his lips. The cold blue in his eyes seemed to have thawed a touch. "Tell me," he said, "how'd you talk your company into giving you this assignment?"

"I *created* this assignment," she said. "They'd all written you off."

"But you hadn't," he said. "Why not, Marie?"

"Well, because I read the testimony. I told you...."

He stared at her as if he knew that was not quite the truth, as if he knew about all those weeks of reading his words and studying his picture, of wondering, puzzling over every line in his face. She looked down, uncomfortably aware of the compelling strength in him, the uncompromising pride, the unexpected vibrant, masculine authority of this man, and she knew that the moment of silence had stretched far too long.

"You know," she finally said, turning the subject to a safer one, "you'd probably hate it if I felt sorry for you. I can tell you're not a man who likes pity. So I want to explain how I feel. Honestly I don't mean to embarrass you, but I think it's important." She raised her eyes and was met with a wintry stare. "I know you've been through hell, but you can overcome that. And I don't feel sorry for you. You're too darn mean."

He glared at her, the lines around his eyes stiff and white.

"I shouldn't have said that. It's none of my business," she found herself admitting.

"It's none of your business at all," he said harshly. "You don't have one inkling in that head of yours *what* I've been through. You're too young, lady. You're a damn kid."

"I am *not* a kid."

He snorted in derision. "My daughter's almost your age."

Marie put down her coffee cup and felt her back stiffen. She narrowed her eyes. "Don't patronize me, Saybolt," she said. "You're dead wrong about me. I may look young to you, but I've been fighting most of my life for every bit of success I've had. I get treated like a dog at work. 'Oh here, let's throw Marie this scrap. Oh, Marie will do it, she's just this dumb female from the poor side of town. She doesn't know what's going on.'" She shot him a furious look. "I'm *sick* of being treated unfairly by a bunch of condescending males. You can't even believe what my boss put me through to get this assignment. I work day and night, sometimes sixteen hours straight, just to keep my head above water, and then I have to beg this idiot just to give me one lousy break!''

He said nothing.

"Look," she said, taking a deep breath, aware that her cheeks were flaming, "I didn't mean to blow a gasket, but I *am* capable of helping you. Let's work together on this."

He was silent for a long moment, assessing her. Finally he shook his head. "I don't think so."

"What?"

"Go on home. I can solve my own problems. I work alone, Marie. Period."

"But you can't just . . ."

"Yes, I can." He stood, reached into his jeans pocket and pulled out a few bills, tossing them on the table. "Thanks," he said, "but I'll see you around." And then he was gone.

CHAPTER SIX

SHE FELT as if he'd punched her in the stomach. No, slammed the door in her face—again. She could taste the bitter poison of defeat mingle with the too-sweet cheese Danish. Her stomach lurched and rose into her throat, and tears blurred the crumpled bills he'd thrown with such deliberate finality on the table.

She blinked and swallowed and clenched her fists. Okay, she thought, at least she knew just how much cooperation she was going to get from Craig Saybolt. Big deal. So she'd work alone; she'd done it before, plenty of times. She'd manage.

Valdez. That was where she'd pick up the pieces; that was where it had happened, where it had been planned and where three of the men still lived.

She was positive that was also where Saybolt was going. She knew he owned a place there; it had been in the files. Where else would he go? He couldn't leave the state, because his parole conditions wouldn't allow him to. And he was surely going to lean on those crew members who lived in Valdez, lean on them hard. If there was one thing she'd learned about the captain, it was that he was determined.

Whether he stirred the embers in Valdez or she did, either way, sparks would fly and she'd learn *something*.

All right, she had to get to Valdez. Mike expected her back the day after tomorrow. She had time to get there.

The trouble was, she had no money. She hadn't been entrusted with the company credit card, not Marie, even though the men who traveled regularly for Pacific had their own cards. She had no credit card of her own. Her checkbook balance was pitiful. And she wasn't even sure Mike would reimburse her for an unscheduled trip if she wrote a bad check.

She *did* have one thing of value. You bet. She took it out of her purse, sat there at the little round table and stared at it: her return ticket—Anchorage to San Francisco. It was worth 435 dollars. It would get her to Valdez and back, all right, but then how would she get home?

She stood abruptly. She *had* to get to Valdez. That was all there was to it. She'd worry about getting home later. If she had to, she could call home and have her parents wire her money. Or, as a last resort, she could call Mike and have him send her money for a ticket. God, she'd hate to do that!

She got a taxi back to her motel, chewing her nails and tapping her foot with impatience the whole way.

The first place she phoned was Alaska Air. "Yes, we have two flights a day," the lady said, "but they're booked for two weeks ahead. Can I reserve a seat for you then, ma'am?"

Marie practically slammed the phone down. She toyed briefly with the idea of driving but discarded it instantly. It would take two days just to get there and back; she didn't have the time.

Okay, there was one other way. What had that taxi driver said? Bernair, that was it. She crossed her legs under her on the bed and flipped through the yellow pages and found it under Air Charters.

She dialed. A whiskey-rough female voice answered.

Marie swallowed. "Could I, that is, do you...I mean, I need to get to Valdez."

"You want to charter a plane to Valdez?"

"Yes. And a pilot. As soon as possible."

"Well, sure, honey. Let's see, I could do it this afternoon if I rearrange..." A hand muffled the mouthpiece, but Marie could hear her yelling. "Bernie, you want the Arrow or the Cherokee this afternoon for Bobby?" She came back on. "Yup, we can do that. One way or round trip?"

"One way," Marie said, "but can you tell me first how much it is?"

"The flight's an hour and a half each way, seventy-five dollars an hour, that's 225 dollars. 'Course, you understand you have to pay both ways."

Marie squeezed her eyes shut and gripped the receiver tighter. "Okay, I'll take it. When should I be there?"

"Get out here around two this afternoon. We're at Merrill Field on Fifth Avenue, first hangar to your left."

There was another problem, however. Bernair would never accept a ticket from a commercial airline. So she telephoned the carrier at the airport. Naturally it was a no-go.

"Sorry, but my computer shows your ticket was purchased by a company credit card, and unless you're authorized to—"

Marie hung up. She flipped through the yellow pages once more. It took her five calls until she found a travel agency that was willing to cash in her ticket. "But we have to charge you a fee."

So it was off to the travel agency, then back to her room to pack, check out, get yet another taxi. By the time she got to Merrill Field, she was limp with exhaustion.

The lady in the office, the one with the voice, knew who she was right away. "Just a minute. They're gassing up. Your pilot's Tom."

Marie waited, looking around the small office. A coffee urn was the centerpiece. Various men wandered in and out, getting coffee. Old photographs of aviators standing proudly in front of flimsy airplanes hung on the walls.

A piece of paper was tacked to the wall also. Idly Marie read it: Notice to All Pilots. When she got to the second item on the list she stood up, went closer and read the notice more carefully.

Emergency equipment:

    1 axe
    1 first aid kit
    1 pistol
    1 gill net and tackle
    1 knife
    2 small boxes of matches
    1 mosquito headnet
    2 small signal devices
    2 weeks' emergency rations

From October 15 to April 1:

    snowshoes
    sleeping bags
    1 wool blanket for each occupant

Marie sank slowly back onto her chair. My God, where was she going? Pistols, knives, signal devices, food for *two weeks*!

"Okay, all ready," said a cheerful male voice. "Are you the lady going to Valdez?"

He carried two sleeping bags. One for him and one for her. Would they end up in those bags, in a snow cave somewhere in the wilderness, using the "two small boxes of matches" to burn bits of the plane in order to keep warm?

"Hi," she said, rising, "I'm Marie."

"I'm Tom. Nice to meet you."

Tom was a middle-aged man, tall and stalwart-looking, with a neat gray mustache. His Bernair shirt, sort of a uniform, inspired confidence. But then it was meant to. His smile was gentle, his handshake firm. "All set?" he asked.

She nodded. On shaky legs she followed him out onto the tarmac, climbed up onto the wing and into the cockpit, her heart knocking against her ribs. Tom stowed her suitcase and briefcase away, along with the sleeping bags. Then he flipped switches and pushed buttons, turned knobs and adjusted dials. The propeller—there was only one—began to turn. Tom handed her the headset. "Put it on," he told her. "You can listen to the tower. And you can talk to me later. It's voice-activated."

She put it on. Her lip quivered, and she bit down on it, hard. A sense of unreality shrouded her. What on earth was she doing?

She heard electronic voices in her ears. Tom was saying, "Six—seven—tango reporting. Ready for takeoff, tower, over."

The little plane shuddered, rolled forward, taxied out to a long runway. Tom talked, the tower replied. He pushed on a control, the plane roared forward, faster and faster, then there was a bump and they were in the air, rising over Anchorage, circling, circling, heading toward an impenetrable line of mountains.

Everything changed once they were airborne; Marie wasn't afraid anymore. The little plane throbbed confidently, soaring. All around her she could see other small planes, seeming to float in the blue sky below her and above her and right next to her. She could hear lots of chatter in the earphones—other pilots, the tower and Tom.

She was invaded by an odd notion: she wished Craig were with her, sharing the adventure. Of course, he'd probably flown this route a hundred times and would have been bored. She supposed she was just lonely up here all by herself, and Craig was the only person she knew for thousands of miles around. That was all it was. Sure.

She stared out the window and forced his face from her mind's eye. They were flying along the coast with dark green mountains rising steeply out of the water and a narrow ribbon of a road following the shore.

"We're flying at fifteen hundred feet," Tom said, and she realized he was talking to her.

She nodded vigorously, afraid to say a word and break the spell. Everywhere was water and irregular shoreline and towering black mountains with white snow on their summits. They flew up a broad valley and over a pass in between jagged peaks. It was spectacular; it was breathtaking; it was Alaska.

Glaciers lay like dirty blankets in the valleys, melting now in the summer, looking as if giant bulldozers had scoured channels down their centers. In places they slid into the water, breaking off so that there were icebergs floating in the water everywhere.

"Look," she heard, and Tom tipped the plane on its wing, whirling in over an ice floe.

Seals. A family of seals, glistening dark brown bodies lying on a chunk of ice. A big one, two big ones, three small ones.

Water everywhere, a pale sun filtering through thin clouds to speckle the surface. Black rising spires with snowy crests all around and the icebergs, like uncut diamonds scattered from a giant's broken necklace.

In the middle of the vast surface of Prince William Sound, miles from shore, Marie saw a sea otter, lying lazily on his back, his paws resting on his belly, looking up at the plane. She expected him to wave.

And there! The wakes of three whales, cutting through the still water in rippling Vs.

The walls of ice where the glaciers broke off into the water were striated spires, with bright turquoise hearts where the sun hit them. Marie took it all in with wonder, enchanted, mesmerized. Over and over again in her mind she kept thinking: this was Saybolt's country; he lived here and saw this all the time.

"We're flying up the Valdez Arm," Tom told her. "Now I'm going to contact Valdez control."

The chatter went on in her ears: "Six—seven—tango cleared for landing, Valdez control, runway, wind speed five knots."

Then there were planes around them—one, two, floating effortlessly, and a helicopter. And then, below on the bruise-gray surface of the water, she saw an oil tanker. A huge tanker, sailing right up the center of the Valdez Arm. And despite her best efforts to forget him, she envisioned Craig on the bridge of a tanker like that, the wind in his hair, his sun-browned face as implacable as the mountains that encircled the town below. The master of all he surveyed, challenging the sea. She could see him in that role. Yes, he was made for it.

And suddenly something in her stirred. It had been building inside her, and she'd fought it with all her will. But it had persisted, and now it took control. It was something fierce and primitive and hungry. She'd never known a man like the captain, never even met one. Men like him existed only in storybooks. Her body felt flushed and feverish, and it was all she could do to listen to Tom while he talked to the Valdez tower. Somewhere in her mind she realized that they were descending, and they seemed to be flying straight into a wall of rock at the head of the valley. Below on one side of the bay was a small town, and on the other was the Trans-Alaska Pipeline Terminal with its tiers of huge round storage tanks and its spreading docks. She was there at last. Valdez. Craig's home...

At the last minute Tom turned the plane in a wide, descending circle to the left and came in for a perfect landing on the single runway.

"Well, here we are. Valdez," Tom said, unlatching the cockpit bubble. "Nice trip?"

"Remarkable," Marie managed to say. "Absolutely remarkable."

She hitched a ride into town with a U.S. Forest Service worker. There didn't seem to be any cabs or buses, and he looked harmless, and it was broad daylight.... Besides, it saved her some money, even though it was only two miles. The trouble was, she kept wishing it were Craig she was riding with. She glanced over once from her place in the front of the pickup truck. The man was attractive, Alaskan-style, big and rugged. But he lacked the air of authority that Craig possessed. Somehow she felt like crying. Craig, Craig, Craig—it was always Craig. She'd been in charge of her emotions ever since she'd been eighteen years old. But now... now she was beginning to feel betrayed by her own mind.

Valdez was tiny, a rustic fishing village, a frontier town, despite the fact that the buildings were all relatively modern. She forced herself to listen to her companion. "That earthquake back in '64 wiped this place out. A tidal wave destroyed the town completely, so everything is pretty new."

It was new, maybe, but pretty funky, too. There was a small fishing port, a couple of cruddy motels, shops set up in tents and trucks and trailers, a snack stand in a red London bus, and a sign for Diamond Lil's Food Wagon and Home Style Cookin'.

The man let her out in front of the Alyeska Motel. "Have a good time in Valdez. See you around," he said in parting.

Everyone she saw was young, dressed in jeans and plaid shirts and work boots. She felt excitement permeating the air; this town was raw and wild and lawless. This was Alaska. This was the land that spawned a man like Saybolt.

She got a room in the Alyeska Motel. God, everyone was so darn friendly here. No big-city posturing or suspicion, just straightforward, down-to-earth friendliness, as if each person in Alaska welcomed you into a fantastic secret brotherhood of the north.

Oh, boy, Mike would have a fit if he knew where she was and what she was doing! So would her mother. Marie could hardly believe it herself, and if all her sleuthing came up with nothing, then she'd *really* be in deep trouble. Still, there was something terribly wrong with the whole Saybolt affair. It *felt* wrong.

Marie sat on her double bed and unfolded the map of Valdez she'd picked up at the desk. She took a pen out of her briefcase and circled three addresses, those of Tim Klutznic, Howie Mayer and Pete Lund. She felt as if she were finally closing in on something, nearing a truth. The trouble was, she didn't yet know what that truth was.

She sat back, sighed and stared at the circles. It was going to be easy to get to these men. Valdez was so small she could walk everywhere. And if the men weren't home, she'd just start asking questions. She'd ask neighbors and everyone she met on the street. She'd comb the bars asking questions. It was a small town. *Somebody* would know something that hadn't come out at the trial. Somebody would gossip.

For a moment she let her mind slip back to the flight she'd just taken—the beauty, the thrill of it. She'd been wishing Craig were with her all the time, but what about Tony? Tony with his shaved head. Guilt smothered her. Craig had seen the world. He probably didn't even notice the Alaskan scenery anymore. But Tony, poor Tony, he'd never been anywhere. She wished, oh, how she wished that she could afford to bring him up to Alaska for a vacation. Maybe she could, though, if she got this bonus. And the bonus depended on her going to work—right now.

She changed to khaki slacks, a red T-shirt and a cardigan, in case it got cool. No sense looking like a city girl here; it would only put people off.

She kept the map handy and started walking. The street names in Valdez were a strange mixture: Oumalik, Fidalgo, Fairbanks. Inuit, Spanish, American.

Men's eyes followed her everywhere. It was flattering. And the men were handsome, burly types, Paul Bunyons. She couldn't help smiling back at some of them—they were so openly, genuinely interested in her.

Unfortunately the one man in Alaska who she had to deal with was totally uninterested. Where was Saybolt right now? Still in Anchorage? Or perhaps here in Valdez? Perhaps she'd run into him around the next corner. And what would she do if she did? Give him a cool "Hello, how are you"?

She couldn't help herself, but she still wished he were there with her. She wished she could have shared that wonderful flight with him, not to mention sharing the cost of it. If only he'd believe she was trying to help him! They could do so much more working together. He was intelligent enough to understand that, wasn't he? Then why was he so darn stubborn?

Tim Klutznic's house was on Robe River Drive, a nicely cared-for little bungalow. In front of the house a brand new Ford Bronco was parked. Marie could hear a baby crying inside. Someone was home. After a few moments the door swung open, and Marie was met by a fair-haired, freckled young woman. Obviously Mrs. Klutznic, first name listed as Alice.

"Hello," Marie said, "I telephoned you the other day about insurance."

"Oh, yes," the woman said.

"I wonder, is Mr. Klutznic at home? I'd like to speak to him if I may."

The woman gave her an apologetic smile. "No, I'm sorry, but Tim's out fishing."

Marie's heart sank. "Do you know when he'll be back this evening?"

"Oh," the woman said, "it could be *days*. It depends on how the salmon are running."

"I see." Marie frowned, thinking.

"Can I help you? I mean, I know what kind of insurance we have. Was Tim going to change companies or something? The insurance for the new car is awfully expensive.''

"No, I don't sell insurance. I'm an investigator."

"Oh." The young woman seemed to pale. "Has Tim had an accident or something?''

"No, no, nothing like that. I just wanted to talk to him. I'll try again." She handed the woman one of her cards. "When he comes home, could you ask him to call me at the office? Collect."

"Sure." But she didn't seem sure. She seemed nervous.

A baby's wail came from inside the house again. Alice was relieved. "I guess I better go. I'll give Tim your card."

Nice new car, pretty wife, new baby. His own fishing boat. She recalled Craig's remark when she'd told him about the fishing boat. Something like: "So he finally got his boat." Well, Tim seemed to have everything he'd ever wanted. Maybe he was a thrifty guy, and, after all, the tanker crewmen were paid well. Klutznic had been first mate, too. Maybe he'd saved his money; maybe he was lucky.

She recalled Klutznic's testimony. He'd been faintly damning, not saying too much or too little, giving the impression that he would have liked to defend his captain but that he was forced to tell the truth.

Prosecution: Did you like serving under Captain Saybolt, Mr. Klutznic?
Defense: Objection, your honor.
Judge: Sustained. Irrelevant. Rephrase your question, Mr. Kennedy.

Prosecution: In your professional opinion, was Captain Saybolt a good captain; that is, safe, punctual, fair and so on?

Klutznic: Craig was a good captain.

Prosecution: Can you elaborate, Mr. Klutznic?

Klutznic: He was punctual and fair.

Prosecution: And safe?

Klutznic: In general, he was.

Prosecution: Then when *wasn't* he safe?

Defense: Objection.

Judge: Overruled. Answer the question, Mr. Klutznic.

Klutznic: He prided himself on being on time. He was a perfectionist. Sometimes he took shortcuts, but he always left a margin of error.

Prosecution: How much of a margin?

Defense: Objection.

Yes, in subtle ways Klutznic had really not helped Craig's case. Marie wondered whether he'd meant to or not. She wished she could talk to him, assess him for herself. Maybe he'd be back before she left.

Pete Lund's address was the nearest circle on her map. His place was a condo on Woodside Drive. No one answered her knock. She peeked in the downstairs window and saw a practically bare room, a wide-screen TV set, a big stereo system. Lund worked for Wesco, the only one of the ten crewmen who still did, so he was probably out on a trip. Darn it all.

Lund and Klutznic had been in the same outfit in Vietnam together and were reported to be buddies. But Craig, who certainly should know, had said they weren't. It struck her as significant that they'd hidden their friendship from their captain, and that they'd hidden it during the trial, as well.

She knocked at the apartment door next to Lund's. An elderly lady answered. She had bright blue eyes and a halo of cottony white hair. "Yes?"

"My name is Marie Vicenza. I'm an old friend of Pete's next door. I'm only here for a day, and I wondered if he was out of town. Do you happen to know?"

"Oh, Mr. Lund. Well, I don't know him very well. He keeps to himself. I know he works on a tanker and is gone a lot."

"Is he on a trip now?"

"He must be. I can tell when he's home, because I hear his stereo playing through the wall. Rock and roll, all that wild stuff."

"Has he been gone long?"

"Oh, a few days, I guess. Are you his girlfriend?"

Marie laughed. "Just a friend."

"Well, from the looks of him, if you don't mind my saying so, he could use a friend. He's a sourpuss."

"A sourpuss."

"That's what I call him," the lady stated definitively.

"I wonder," Marie said, "doesn't Pete have any visitors, ever?"

The woman knitted her brow. "Let's see.... Well, every once in a while that other man, you know, the one who was on that ship that spilled all the oil...?"

"Tim Klutznic?" Marie asked.

"Don't know his name. But I saw his picture in the paper, all right. 'Round the time of the trial. Saw him go into Lund's place a few times, I guess."

"Thank you," Marie blurted out, pumping the woman's hand. "Thank you *very* much."

She left then, the gears in her mind grinding away. So Klutznic had visited Lund. Of course, in and of itself their association was nothing. But why had the two men shown a different face to everyone during the trial?

Marie headed back toward the docks again, toward Howie Mayer's address. Her mind refused to leave Lund, though. Pete Lund, the sourpuss. She smiled to herself. The loner who hated everything. He hadn't liked his captain, either, or so it had seemed from his testimony.

Prosecutor: In your professional opinion, was Craig Saybolt a good Captain?

Lund: He knew his stuff. He was smart. But the man was arrogant and a slave driver. Working on his ship was the pits. And sometimes, when he got in the mood, he'd take chances, just for the hell of it.

Defense: Objection.

Saybolt: You son of a bitch. Liar. You—

Judge: Order in the court. Captain Saybolt, be seated or you will be held in contempt of court. One more outburst and I will not hesitate to jail you for contempt. Objection overruled.

Had Lund been deliberately lying? He'd been the hardest on Craig. Had they been on bad terms before the accident? She'd like to know. She'd like to ask Craig.

Howie Mayer lived on Jago Street above a grocery store.

"He's not home," the man behind the counter told her. "They took him away to the drunk tank again. You any kin of his? He owes me a month's rent, and I'm gettin' ready to throw his stuff out on the street."

"No, I'm no kin. Just a friend," Marie said. "Could you tell me where they've taken him?"

"Sure, to the hospital, over on the end of Hanagil Street."

"Thank you very much."

Poor Howie. Another trip to the alcohol ward. Craig had told her that Howie had problems.

It was getting late. Late, but not dark. Dinnertime. She could call the hospital and arrange to see Howie tomorrow. Then, maybe, she could get something to eat.

It occurred to Marie that in her briefcase was the address of Craig Saybolt's place. She had the map. She could...but no, she wouldn't. He'd made it more than plain what he thought about her and her proffered help. Maybe if—no, maybe *when*—she came up with something, she could contact him then. If, of course, he was even in Valdez.

She walked back toward what she guessed would be called the downtown area of Valdez. It was pleasant out—warm and sunny. She could have been in San Francisco, but instead she was practically on the Arctic Circle.

Men kept looking at her, smiling, winking, assessing. It wasn't scary, though, not as it would be if she were walking alone in Golden Gate Park at seven o'clock at night with men staring at her. Not a bit. These men were just friendly and curious. She could tell she'd like them if she had time to stop and talk.

She phoned the Valdez Hospital from her room.

"Mr. Mayer can't have any visitors. He's in intensive care," the nurse said.

"Is he in danger?" Marie asked, alarmed.

"You'd have to ask his doctor that, Miss. Would you like his doctor's name?"

"No, no, that's all right. I'll call back. Thank you."

Marie hung up thoughtfully. What if Howie Mayer died? People did die of alcoholism. That would be a third witness dead. Three out of ten. Despite what Craig had said, that was not a very good survival rate for the crew of the *Northern Light*.

She ate dinner at an aluminum trailer set up in a parking lot. There was a big sign that read, Chinese Fast Foods. And a smaller one that assured customers, Yes, We're Open. The smell of Chinese food drifted on the air like exotic perfume.

She waited in line behind a young man in a T-shirt and jeans. He kept looking at her, so she launched right in. "Do you live here?" she asked.

"Yes."

"Have you lived here long?"

"Five years. Say, are you new in town?" he asked.

"I certainly am. Is this Chinese food any good?"

"It's great. As good as in Chinatown."

"San Francisco?" she asked.

"No, Boston."

"Were you here during the oil spill three years ago?"

"Yes, I was." He looked at her. "Are you from a newspaper or something?"

"No, just curious. Did you know anyone on that ship?"

"Yeah, I knew Joey Brown. Heard he bought the farm, poor guy."

"Awdah, please," a Chinese man called out of his small window.

"Spareribs and fried rice," the young man said. "And for you?"

"Egg foo yung," she replied promptly. "Shrimp egg foo yung."

They talked while they waited for their orders. People strolled up, a few women, mostly men. The aroma of onions and garlic frying in oil made Marie's mouth water. She watched a man triumphantly carry a loaded plate of something luscious to his car, sit on the hood and dig in. The sun shone down benignly on the parking lot.

"So, what's your name?" the young man asked her.

"Marie."

"I'm Harv. What are you doing here?

"A little business, a little pleasure." Casually she added, "I flew in with Bernair today."

"Quite a flight, isn't it?"

"You bet."

"One spayrib, one egg," the cook called out.

"I'll get them," Harv said.

"Oh, thanks. Here," she rummaged in her purse and pulled out a five dollar bill. "This enough?"

They ate leaning back against an old Buick parked in the lot. God, the food was good! Greasy, garlicky, absolutely fantastic.

"So, what did people here think about the captain of that tanker that went aground?" she asked.

"Saybolt?"

"I guess that's his name," she said innocently.

Harv shrugged. "Some thought he took the blame for no good reason, some thought he was guilty as sin."

"What did *you* think?"

"I didn't know Saybolt. It seems he was a hard man. A lot of people didn't like him. Maybe he took a bum rap."

"I guess nobody'll ever know," she said.

"Somebody will."

"Oh?"

"Whoever really did run that ship onto the rocks."

She tossed the empty plastic plate into the trash and said goodbye to Harv. She felt better now that she'd eaten. It was time to hit the bars, she guessed. Maybe a little early, as tongues wouldn't be loosened by alcohol yet, but she'd give it a try, anyway.

She felt pretty confident about bar hopping alone. She wasn't the least bit afraid of getting in any kind of trouble. After all, she'd been taking care of herself for quite a few years now. Besides, Valdez was such a nice, friendly little town. The sun never set here, so she wouldn't have to worry about walking home alone in the dark, and she'd go back to her motel before the bar crowds got really rowdy.

She had guts, all right. She could handle men and flirt and keep the best of them at bay. What she *was* afraid of, though, was that she wouldn't find out a thing about Saybolt or the oil spill.

She walked along the fishing harbor, admiring the boats, looking around for a likely bar. It was nearly eight-thirty at night, but the sun was still bright. Out across the water at the pipeline terminal a tanker was being nudged delicately into place by tugboats.

The Harborside Bar and Grill looked like a good bet. She straightened her back, got a good hold on the strap of her shoulder bag and marched up to the door.

Inside it was dim and smoky. A few people ate at tables in the dining room, but the action was at the bar. Murky, smelly, a big mirror behind the counter. A tough lady bartender in a man's plaid shirt.

Marie found an empty slot at the bar and wedged herself in. "Coca Cola, please," she said. She could always say it was a rum and Coke, if someone insisted on a drinking partner.

She felt a little nervous standing there, packed tightly into the crowd, a female alone in a strange bar. But— what the heck—it was all for that fat bonus, wasn't it?

"You're new in town. Ain't seen you around," said a voice behind her.

She turned. A tall lanky man with a bristly face looked down at her. "Just got in today," she said.

"Here on vacation?"

"Yes, I am."

"Well, I'm a native of this place, and I'd like you to meet some of my friends. You game?"

"I sure am."

He led her to a table where two men and a blowsy red-cheeked lady were going through piles of lottery tickets, cackling like maniacs. "Can't see the numbers!" one yelled. "Light! More light!"

"I'm gonna win me the lottery tonight or die!" cried the lady, laughing like a demon. "Come on, come on!"

What a crew. Unfortunately they were in no mood to talk, especially about dull subjects like oil spills and super tankers.

Marie tried pressing. "Say," she asked the lady wedged in next to her, "you ever see that captain around?"

"Captain?" The woman's breath was a hundred-and-fifty proof.

"Saybolt."

"Oh, yeah, *him*. Naw. He's locked up tighter than the hull of a tanker."

"I wonder," Marie said casually, "if he really did it."

"'Course he did. They found him guilty." The woman shook her head. "What a waste."

Marie raised her brows.

"You know," the woman said, "a waste of a good man. Hell of a looker, too. I met him a couple of times."

"Um," Marie said. "Do *you* think he really did it?"

"I don't know. But my boyfriend—well, he *was* my boyfriend—he knew a few of the crew."

Marie's pulse quickened. "Oh, really?"

But the woman shrugged. "Just met 'em, you know. My boyfriend had a fight with one of them. Guy named Lund, I think."

"Pete Lund," Marie said.

"Yeah, I guess so. I don't know him. He's still around, I hear. 'Course, so's my ex-boyfriend." And she laughed and finished off her drink.

"Did you know any of the other crew members?" Marie asked, knowing she was pressing too hard.

"Nah. They're mostly gone. Klutznic's still here, though. Doing pretty damn well, too."

"Oh?" Marie's ears perked up.

"New boat, new car." The woman lost interest. "I need another drink, honey," she said to her companion.

Marie left several minutes later. She'd gotten all she could out of those folks, and she wanted to move on, feel out another place. The woman's words stuck in her mind, though. Klutznic was doing really well. Was he using the bounty of a payoff that he'd gotten for running the *Northern Light* onto the rocks? And Lund getting into a fight—it figured.

The bright daylight outside hit her like an explosion of fireworks, and she had to put on her sunglasses. They called this night. Amazing. She walked and peeked into a couple of rowdy saloons but decided to hunt out a quieter place, where she could really talk to someone.

The Pipeline caught her eye. Kind of a rundown place, small and homey-looking. Its front door stood open.

"Okay," she muttered to herself. "Forward, march."

The Pipeline had a jukebox that wasn't playing and a big popcorn machine. The long bar was crowded with people, but the place seemed quieter than the others she'd seen.

She sidled up to the bar, pushing through the crowd and the buzz of conversation and caught the bartender's eye.

"A cola, please," she said, and it was just then that she saw his face reflected in the mirror behind the bartender.

His gaze fixed on hers, glacier-cold, and she felt her stomach drop to her feet.

CHAPTER SEVEN

CRAIG TOOK A LONG DRINK from his mug of beer and kept his eyes trained on hers in the mirror.

Marie. Here. It figured, didn't it?

He set the mug down hard on the polished bar and felt an ache in his jaw where he was clenching his teeth too tightly. And to make matters worse, a group of crewmen just off a tanker suddenly sauntered in—seventy days at sea with barely the sight of a woman and they were all over Marie like flies on sugar. He wondered just how she was planning on getting herself out of here in one piece.

"Say." A pipeline worker sitting on a stool next to Craig nudged his arm. "Aren't you, you know, that captain from the ah...the ah, yeah, the *Northern Light?*"

Craig turned his head slowly and fixed the man with an ice-blue glare. "The name's Saybolt," he said.

"Oh, sorry, buddy, I thought you..."

Of course, Craig had expected to be recognized—not in Anchorage maybe, but definitely here in Valdez on his home turf. That was another reason why he had to clear his name. It wasn't just that people gossiped or pointed. No, it was his almighty pride.

He looked up from his beer and found Marie again in the mirror. There was a big, burly Alaskan with a chest the size of a gorilla's nuzzling up to her now. She looked like a doll standing next to the brute. But she was smiling that beguiling smile, chatting away, as if she were enjoying herself. She accepted a beer from King Kong, said something, laughed—tinkling bells—then let him put his hairy arm around her slender shoulders.

Craig glanced down to where his hands were wrapped around the mug. His knuckles were white. She *was* crazy. What she didn't realize was that when a man bought a woman a drink up here in God's great wilderness, it was tantamount to asking her to go to bed.

Dumb female. He ought to let her get just what she deserved.

Craig lifted his beer, stared into the mirror at Marie, who didn't notice him, and shrugged. Her problem, not his.

It wasn't five minutes later when he heard Marie say, "Hey, no, put me down." He came to his feet, cursing his stupidity under his breath, moving over toward her and the apeman.

"Come on," Marie was saying, "that can't be true. No one can lift eight hundred pounds!" She laughed coyly and touched the man's big arm.

"Oh yeah I can," the guy said.

Why was he getting involved? Didn't he have enough problems without walking up to this dude and begging for a new set of teeth? Maybe he'd just keep right on walking past them....

"Look," Craig said, placing himself between Marie and the man, "the lady here is with me."

"That a fact?" The man turned to Marie, brushing Craig aside as if he were of no account.

Craig let out an exasperated breath, swore, stepped back in. He was out of his mind to be getting into this. When—or *if*—he got her out of here, he was going to throttle cute little Marie. "I *said,* she's with me. Come on, Marie," he began, taking her arm none too gently, when suddenly all the air was slammed out of his lungs and he was sprawled across the top of a table, glasses scattering, crashing to the wooden floor.

"My God!" Marie was crying, her hands flying to her mouth.

"Somebody stop Luke before he kills that guy!" came a shout from behind the bar.

"That *is* Saybolt! Sure it is!" said another. "I knew it!"

All hell broke loose.

People stepped back, forming a circle around Luke, Craig and Marie. Catcalls sounded in the smoky air, whistles, cheers. Romans at the Coliseum—and it was thumbs-down for Craig.

Slowly, the air just beginning to suck back into his lungs, Craig righted himself. My God, that hurt. But he was in it now; there was no backing out.

Half doubled over, holding his stomach, Craig made the most of the situation. He coughed, faking the extent of his injury. He swayed. Out of the corner of his eye he could see someone holding Marie back and hear her protests. He sure hoped she was getting her money's worth.

"Ugh," Craig groaned, trying to stand up straight, swaying precariously. Luke was close now, deciding whether or not to finish the old guy, when abruptly Craig clasped both hands together into a fist and drove it into the ape's gut just above the beltline. When Luke staggered, the air gone from his lungs, Craig finished him off with a right to the jaw. Luke went down like King Kong from the skyscraper.

"No way!" someone yelled.

"Saybolt cold-cocked him!"

"He cheated!"

"Luke asked for it!"

"Jerks!" the bartender said. "Look at this place!"

"Lousy fight. Glad my money wasn't on it."

And finally Marie: "*That* was the most immature thing I ever saw!"

"What?" Craig managed to say as he snatched her hand and led her out. "*What* did you say?" The night sun and fresh air bludgeoned him. He stopped short. "Immature?"

"Well," she began, her chin up, "I've never...I have *never* been so embarrassed in my life."

"Embarrassed?" he asked, incredulous.

"You heard me."

"You're *embarrassed?* I don't believe this! You pull a stunt like that in there, damn near get yourself dragged off by that ape, and you come down on *me?*"

"I had everything under control," she said. "He was ready to tell me all about Howie Mayer, who, by the way, is back in the drunk tank, when *you* step in like a...a sophomore in college and come to my rescue! I didn't *need* rescuing, Craig Saybolt."

"I don't believe this," he said again, then cradled his sore fist against his aching ribs.

"Let me see that." She reached for his hand.

"It's fine."

"No, it is not fine." She took his hand and examined his knuckles. "It looks awful. Is anything broken?"

"It's fine." He pulled away from her.

"You should see a doctor."

He only raised a brow.

"Okay then. Be the big tough guy." She lifted her shoulders and dropped them negligently. "I just wish you hadn't interrupted in there."

"By the way," Craig said, ignoring her ridiculous statement, "what are you doing here, anyway? I thought you were on a plane heading back to San Francisco."

She began walking ahead of him, slowly. "I can't go back home. Not right at the moment. I'm just about broke."

"You're . . . broke? But how?"

"I turned in my return ticket to get to Valdez. I only have a few dollars left over."

"That's . . . that's crazy" was all he could say. Still, when he thought about it, he had to give her credit. Little Marie Vicenza sure had a lot of moxie. He shook his head and followed her down the street and wondered just what the devil he was going to do with her now.

Craig was indeed recognized as he walked along the main street with the cute little Italian girl by his side. Some nodded at him, uncertain, others ignored him, a few shot him unfriendly looks. Only one former acquaintance said "Hi," an Indian woman who owned a curio shop for the summer tourists. But then she rented the cabin just down the road from his, and they'd been friendly for years.

Craig wondered if he should take Marie to his place and feed her or something. But he'd only been to the cabin for a few minutes, just long enough to dump his bag and see if it was still standing after practically two years. The cabin had been a mess, vandalized by kids; although it had appeared that nothing was irreparable— just a jimmied lock and a few broken windows. Dusty. Some mouse droppings in the corners. No, he couldn't take her there. But what then?

"Listen," he said, "have you got a room or something?"

She nodded. "At the Alyeska. It's cheap."

"Then I'll leave you there."

She started to say something.

"No," he said, "I mean it. I suggest you call your office in the morning and get them to wire you some money. Don't be foolish about it, Marie. You're not going to accomplish a thing in Valdez."

"I already have."

"Have what?" He stopped short in the middle of the sidewalk.

"I went over to Tim Klutznic's and also Lund's place."

"You didn't."

"I sure did." She told him about her visits, and all the while he felt his thermostat rising.

"Damn it, Marie," he said, furious. If she'd blown it, messed up his plan, he was going to throttle her! "I forbid you to go traipsing around asking questions. You have to let it rest. Let *me* rest."

"I have a job to do."

"Yeah? And so do I. And it doesn't include you."

"You know," she said, unruffled, "I'm getting so used to your nastiness, Craig Saybolt, that I feel like we've been married for twenty years."

"Oh my God" was all he could get out.

"You were correct," she said, chatting away, ignoring him. "Alice Klutznic is a nice lady. Although she was nervous. I wondered about that."

"Will you *please* let me handle this? What do I have to do, beg you?"

"Wouldn't do the least bit of good."

"No, I don't suppose it would."

"So," she said, cheerful, "what do we do now? I've eaten, but it's still broad daylight."

"*We* do nothing. I already have plans. And *you,* well, I suggest you figure out how you're getting home and

stay clear of the saloons until you're safely out of here."
He could lend her the money, he knew. But that was a last
resort. Let her company worry about it. They'd come
through.

"You say you have plans," Marie said. "Care to share
them with me?"

"Absolutely not."

But in the end he did. It was her persistence, her nagging, her pleading, and those big brown eyes—eyes that
a man could get lost in—that did it.

"I can boat out to the site of the spill with you? Really?
Actually see where it happened? Tonight?"

"I said yes. Stop pestering me or I'll change my mind.
And don't forget," he added, "when we get back, that's
it, young lady. You go home."

He got no answer to that, but then he hadn't expected
one, either. And then, as he led her down to the marina
where he'd arranged to have a boat gassed and ready, he
wondered how on earth she'd convinced him to let her tag
along. He'd wanted to see the spot by himself. He'd
thought he *needed* to be alone. But he couldn't just leave
her in Valdez wandering around on her own, stranded,
with every pair of male eyes in the town savoring her.

Lord, but she was a nuisance. Worse, though, she
should have been running for cover every time he gave
her a good dose of his brusqueness. But she hadn't. Odd
girl. Well, *woman,* he supposed, turning to glance at her.

"Is that the marina?" she asked, smiling up at him.

He nodded. Yes, he guessed she really was a woman,
shaped like one—all soft feminine curves, delicate feet
and hands, rich, shoulder-length ebony hair that curled
around her face prettily and gleamed in the sun. And the
scent of her, fresh, warm, sweet. It was her face, though,
that made her seem no more than twenty to twenty-two

years old. Her skin was smooth as silk, with a creamy
glow in her cheeks, naturally rose-colored lips that curved
into an easy, tempting smile. And those eyes—deep,
dark, bottomless wells.

What *was* he thinking? She was a pest, a pushy little
female investigator who thought she had the world all
figured out, thought she'd come up here, solve his problems and get rich off him. Well, he'd give her the pretti-
ness, but her pushiness downright repelled him. She
ought to get married, stay home and raise a few kids.
That would keep her busy and out of everyone's hair.
Darn, but he wished he hadn't told her she could come
along.

"How'd you rent a boat?" she asked.

"In this neck of the woods, money'll buy you anything."

"Oh. Is it far to the site?"

"Not in this baby." Then, frowning, he asked, "You
don't get seasick, do you?"

She shook her head emphatically.

Of course, as it turned out, as he should have expected,
Marie Vicenza had never even *been* on a boat before.

He steered the sleek blue-and-silver powerboat out of
the harbor and said, disbelievingly, "Not even a row-
boat?"

"Not even a canoe," she admitted and huddled back
into the seat behind him, all small and white faced in her
orange life jacket, not sure of herself for the first time
since she'd stormed into his life. He actually enjoyed her
discomfort.

Standing, he turned back to the wheel, adjusted his
heading and increased the speed to ten knots once he was
past the channel markers and no-wake area in the harbor.

The water beneath him felt good, right. The late sun sparkled on the ruffled surface of the bay, and the wind drew its salty fingers through his hair. Yes, it felt right. How had he borne those long months of confinement?

Craig kept to the right of the buoys, well out of the path of a super tanker, the *Sohio Duchess,* which was heading into the pipeline terminal. From a foot above the water where he stood, the big tanker was mammoth, the size of an aircraft carrier. Yes, Craig would give it a wide berth. He saluted the captain on the bridge, a hundred feet out of the water—a lofty perch. The captain saluted him in return, and Craig felt a knot of pain in his stomach. That was where he belonged—up there, not down here, steering this souped-up toy.

"They're big, huh?" Marie was calling over the noise of the engine.

Craig turned and nodded. The wind was whipping her hair helter-skelter. He searched in the storage compartment beneath the wheel for a bandanna—one that wasn't covered with fish scales or oil. He found a passable blue-and-white one and reached back, handing it to her.

"Thanks," she shouted.

"Um," he mumbled, but it was carried away on the wind.

Now that they were well clear of the town and traveling along the inlet, he gave the powerful twin engines more throttle and the bow of the boat lifted off the choppy surface of the water. The craft shivered and leaped forward at a good clip. Silently Craig pointed to the port and starboard at times, indicating the sights, the ice floes, a few seals lazing in the sun, the shoreline of Storey Island to the starboard.

He whipped by a tanker heading out to Prince William Sound and lifted a hand to that captain, too. Behind him, he could hear Marie shouting, "Oh!" as he increased his speed and the boat fled across the bay, its nose at a forty-five-degree angle to the water. An inadvertent smile creased his lips—Marie had settled down and seemed to be enjoying herself. He recalled once, when Tanya was still a kid, taking her out in Puget Sound in a friend's boat that had been very similar to this baby. Tanya had been gleeful, too. And when they'd gotten back to Seattle his wife had been waiting at the dock with Sonny. They'd all been so young then, young and innocent. And now his wife was dead, his kids barely knew him—or didn't want to know him—and he was an ex-con, a pariah among his peers.

They passed through a summer storm that was fleeing across the sound just past Bligh Island, and the rain pelted them, sharp, stinging pellets of ice-cold water. He turned to see if Marie was okay, then slowed his speed when he saw her huddled up in the corner of the long seat, her knees high, her face buried in them. He should have realized . . .

"Come on up here," he called. "Come on, get behind the windscreen."

She rose cautiously, swaying with the boat. He reached out a hand to steady her, and the boat yawed over a wave. Marie was pitched forward, and he caught her to his chest, righting her.

"Oh," she breathed. "Wow!" She looked up through rain-spiked lashes. He could feel her shivering against him, and simultaneously he could feel the warmth of her flesh beneath her clothes. The boat slowed; he let go of the wheel and pulled a yellow slicker out of the nose compartment, wrapping it around her. Automatically he rubbed her arms.

"Sorry," he said, "I guess I'm used to these sudden storms. Don't mind them at all."

"You like this?" She hugged the slicker to her and looked up at the gray sky, blinking away the rain.

"It's one of the few things in life I do love," he said, then helped her down into the protected seat behind the windshield.

They passed through the storm and the layer of mist that fled before it and made Johnstone Point by twelve-thirty, just at twilight. Even though it was still light enough to see, Craig was glad to head into shore—it was never safe to be out in a small boat when the light wasn't ideal.

"So this is it?" she asked, coming to her feet, still a bit unsteady.

He nodded. "The last time I was here..." He fell silent.

"I know" was all she said.

He went into shore on a straight line. The coast was mostly rocky, but there were a few sandy coves that led into the pine forests. The speed boat drew practically no water whatsoever, so they were perfectly safe making shore. Still, he couldn't just beach the boat—he might put a tear in the bottom—so he instructed Marie to keep the wheel steady while he hopped out and towed the boat in with the rope.

"You're leaving me?" she said, her eyes as big and round as saucers.

"Only to tow you in. It's all right."

"What if... what if the rope breaks?"

He climbed down into the cold, thigh-deep water. The current was strong, tugging at his legs, slamming the side of the boat against his shoulder.

"Craig!"

"It's okay. You're fine. Just hold on." Breathing hard, he made shore and pulled the boat in so that its bow rested on sand. Then he secured the rope to a rock and called to Marie to wade in.

"I'll get wet," she said, looking down at the lapping waves. "Oh, well." She sat on the side, pulled off her shoes, tossed them ashore, then hesitated. "Is it cold?"

"Stay there," he said, shaking his head. *Women.* He waded out the few feet and took her into his arms. She wasn't much more than a hundred pounds. Still, the water dragged at him, and he was glad to deposit her safely on the sandy shore. "There. You okay now."

"I'm fine. Thanks. I mean, I almost never get in the ocean. It kind of... you know, frightens me."

"Women," he growled, "don't belong at sea."

"Aye, aye, captain." She saluted him facetiously.

The landscape was glorious. It was difficult for Craig to imagine how the site must have looked three years previously—the black crude clinging to every surface, scarring the pristine land, the mutilated animals—so much loss. Now the coastline was clean. Grass grew in between the rocks. At the base of the tall pines, wildflowers opened to the midnight sun. Birds chirped, and the waves lapped gently against the fine sand in the gathering dusk.

My God, he thought as he stood there, hands on his hips, and studied the land, how had it happened? Why? Such beauty, one of the few untouched environments left on earth. And *why* had it happened?

"It's so... wild," Marie said, "beautiful. I never knew."

But he didn't dare speak; he was too choked up. So he walked instead. He was aware of Marie just behind him, shoes dangling from one hand, stepping over rocks in the dimming light, trying to keep up. He shouldn't have brought her here. No one should see him like this.

"Craig," she called, "wait up!"

No, he shouldn't have brought her. He needed space. He needed time. He needed to heal. But then she was there, next to him, an albatross around his neck.

"It's so silent," Marie was saying in a soft, careful voice, "peaceful and clean."

"It took years," he managed to say. "Twenty thousand workers cleaning the shorelines, and still it took nature to finish the job."

"Amazing."

"It can never happen again," he whispered harshly. "Never." He began walking, more slowly this time, reaching down every so often to pick up stones and feel their smooth clean surfaces, to reassure himself. Ahead of them a flock of birds scurried up the beach, leaving little forked prints in the sand. Everything was as it should be. The silence was overwhelmingly lovely. *He* hadn't been at fault, so why, then, was he feeling so damn guilty?

"You know" came Marie's voice, "we're all responsible for what happened here."

He turned around and shot her a bemused look.

"What I mean is that we need so much, we consume so much. When is it going to stop? When will we realize and stop *using?*"

"Well, I'll be," he said, studying her, suddenly seeing a facet of Miss Vicenza that was not all greed.

"I'm serious," she said, as if reading his mind. "I'm glad you let me come along. I needed to see this. If everyone on earth could just see how beautiful it can be..." Slowly, hesitantly, she reached out and touched his hand. At first he almost drew back, a tide of unwelcome emotions surging through his blood. But he let her take his hand in hers and felt the warmth of her touch in the peaceful twilight, a human touch, full of compassion and its own curious needs. A dozen thoughts crowded, batted around in his head uncomfortably: she really did care about him and about what had happened here; she wasn't completely self-centered nor blind to his purpose here. He felt inordinately embarrassed; he hadn't held a woman's hand since, well, he couldn't even remember. And he wondered, did Marie have someone back home? Was that someone special, caring, loving? Did he treat her fairly? It seemed suddenly important to know these things about her.

He noticed her smiling up at him. "Let's walk some more," she said quietly, her hand still in his, "this is good...for both of us."

They walked the shoreline in silence, until the Alaskan sun crept back over the watery horizon, blindingly lovely, sparkling on the tips of the gentle waves. Birds and squirrels scolded them from the forest beyond, and a family of sleek-backed seals came ashore to catch the first rays of silver morning sun on the rocks.

Craig was bursting with emotions that he'd always kept buried. But here they would not stay hidden. The beauty of the Alaskan wilderness filled him, moistened his eyes, while he was hammered by a renewed determination to find out who was behind the crime that had been blamed on him.

Eventually they headed back to the boat. He knew Marie must be exhausted regardless of her insistence that she couldn't sleep in this crazy summer light. *He* was exhausted, anyway, drained. And then she eyed the boat and the water and looked up at him helplessly.

"All right," he said, "I'll carry you. You'd make a poor sailor, lady."

"Sorry," she replied, but she didn't look sorry at all.

He lifted her into his arms and kept his expression bland despite the feel of her delicate bones and the soft flesh of her breast where it pressed against him. He strode into the water, too aware of her arms clinging to his neck, too aware of the round firmness of her bottom beneath his hand and her scent—fresh, sweet and young. Carefully, he deposited her on the side of the boat, and she swung her legs in—shapely, feminine legs. He looked away, returned to shore for the rope, then waded back out and hoisted himself up. Without acknowledging her "thanks" he started the engines and backed the boat safely out of the cove, then brought her around, heading out into the gulf across the glistening surface. He was ready to give the engines full throttle when suddenly her hand was on his shoulder. The hairs rose on his neck.

"Craig," she said, "before—before when I told you I thought you were innocent...I wasn't really sure that you were. But now, well, now I know it's true."

He felt his insides turn to mush. And abruptly he felt old, terribly, terribly old.

CHAPTER EIGHT

MARIE PICKED UP THE PHONE and dialed her folks'
number. It was just past noon in San Francisco; they
should be home. And so should Tony.

She rubbed the sleep from her eyes. Craig had not deposited her at the motel until close to 4:30 a.m., and at
the time she'd thought she'd never sleep. So much for
that fear—exhaustion had won out over the perpetual
Alaskan sun.

In San Francisco, Tony picked up the phone. "Oh,
Mom, hi." He sounded as if he, too, had just awakened.

"Gosh, it's good to hear your voice," Marie said,
pulling the covers back up to her chin. "What's new?"

"Nothin'."

"How's baseball? You guys winning them all?"

"Geez, Mom, we only had one game since you left. Big
deal."

"Did you win?"

Silence.

"Did you go, Tony?" she asked.

"Naw. I didn't feel good. And they needed me at the
restaurant."

"Grandma told me you shaved your head."

"So?"

"I bet you're ugly as sin."

"It's cool."

She bit her lip to keep from yelling at him. It wouldn't do any good now, not over the phone. "Well, it'll sure be cool in the winter, Anthony."

"Har-de-har-har, Mom."

When Marie talked to Sophia, it turned out that Tony had not worked at all and had gotten in last night at 1:30 a.m.

"You come on home, Marie," Sophia said tiredly. "Your boy needs you."

Marie didn't have any answer to that. Her boy did need her, but she couldn't go home just yet. They disconnected, and Marie stepped in the shower, feeling guilt enfold her like a shroud. It was all fine and dandy for her to think she was going to take the bull by the horns when she got home, but just how she was going to do that eluded her.

Tony sure was at that awkward age. Voice cracking, wrists bony, feet too big. He was a teenager, not much younger than she'd been when—but boys were different.

Poor Tony. Someday, somehow, she'd make it up to him. He had his grandparents, anyway. He was spoiled, really, living with the three doting adults. Well, Marie didn't *dote;* she was too busy. She'd always been too busy trying to make ends meet.

Tony was a good boy. His grandmother worried too much. Still, it was up to Marie to discipline him, and she never had the time or the heart. She guessed she felt guilty. Even after all these years she felt young and scared and guilty.

Kids. She wondered: if she had a child now would she be a better mother? Would things be different? But there wasn't much chance of that, because Marie had no husband.

It was crazy, but she was only thirty-one and hadn't even ever considered getting married. She supposed she was scared deep down inside, scared to death of making a mistake, of being left again. How could she trust a man to be a good husband and a father to Tony? How would she know? Then she wondered how Craig would get along with Tony.

Now, where on earth had that thought come from?

Craig, she thought. He'd gone to his cabin that morning still insisting that she head on back to San Francisco as soon as she got some sleep. She'd offered to help him tidy up his place. She'd offered to make him a very early breakfast. She'd all but gotten on her hands and knees and begged him to let her be a part of his investigation. But he'd stood his ground. The big, strong sea captain had shaken his head, said so long and left her safely at her room.

Marie sat on the bed with her head hanging between her knees, brushing out her wet hair, wiggling her toes, plotting her next move. She wanted to work with him. She felt there were many things his crew members could tell them; one of them at least knew the truth. God, how she wanted to help Craig Saybolt; he deserved it.

And there was another thing, too. She knew he had a plan. He'd had all those months in prison to think it out. She was dying to know what his moves were going to be, how he was going to get at the truth. Darn. Why wouldn't he confide in her?

She flipped her hair back over her shoulders, fluffed it and felt confusion gnaw at her. Maybe she was just using Craig Saybolt after all and kidding herself so she wouldn't feel like such a self-serving schemer. Maybe that was closer to the truth. On the other hand, if she helped him clear his name, that made everything okay, didn't it?

She put on her last clean pair of slacks and a fresh white blouse. She peeked out the window. Heavy, gunmetal gray clouds clung to the surrounding peaks. It was claustrophobic. She couldn't even see the bay because of the layer of fog. It reminded her of San Francisco. She put on her cherry-red sweater, snatched up her purse and briefcase and headed out into the raw afternoon. She wouldn't think about Tony or her mother or even her motives for wanting to help Craig. She'd keep in the forefront of her mind the job she was here to do. She'd take care of Tony somehow when she got home. And Craig, well, she'd forget what it felt like to be carried in his arms, to feel his stalwart body against her, his whiskers that had brushed her cheek once, his hands under her thighs. She'd put all that from her.

She'd convince him that no matter what he was planning, he was still going to need her help and the information Pacific could provide. He just couldn't say no. She wouldn't let him.

She walked, map in hand, looking for Craig's place. Fog curled around her feet and clung to the tree trunks. Invisible birds chirped, their bright voices deadened by the heavy air. Squirrels chattered at her from mist-wreathed trees.

She found his house easily enough. A real, Alaskan, turn-of-the-century cabin, it sat on the outskirts of Valdez, nestled in a grove of pines near the base of the craggy mountains.

She could see two broken windows in the front of the cabin, though he'd covered them. There was trash that had blown up against the north side, and a hole the size of a crater in the drive. Still, smoke lifted up into the mist from the chimney, scenting the air. A fire, in the summer. Alaska.

Marie scratched at his door uncertainly. She refused to speculate on his reaction, although she suspected he'd be mad as a hornet.

She was right.

"Ah, hell," he said, pinning her with those ice-blue eyes.

"Well," Marie said cheerfully, "good morning. I mean, good afternoon. Is that coffee I smell?"

"Oh, for..."

But he let her in. He was wearing jeans—and just jeans, no shirt or sweater. The top button on his pants was still undone. His chest, broad and well-muscled, was pale, sprinkled with fine, light brown curling hairs. The white elastic band of his underwear lay against a surprisingly flat stomach.

Quickly Craig seemed to realize his state of undress. He turned away, sucked in his waist and did up his pants, then fetched a shirt. All the while, she could hear him grumbling under his breath.

"Um, coffee. Can I?" She nodded toward the kitchen counter.

Marie poured herself a steaming mug and stood in front of the potbelly stove in the living room. She glanced around while he went about his business of tidying up. It was a three-room log cabin. Living room and kitchen in one area, two bedrooms and a bath, at the back. It was small and dusty. The furniture was askew, pictures of the Alaskan wilderness hung crookedly. A stereo and TV both looked ancient, and the bookshelves all along one wall were festooned with cobwebs.

It was a mess. But then, after sitting empty for two years, any house would be. She could see what it *should* look like, though, and it pleased her. She felt safe and secure in the cabin. It was woodsy, quaint, rustic.

"I like it," she announced.

"What?" He placed some books he'd dusted back on the shelf.

"Your cabin. Your home."

"Oh. Ah, thanks. I do, too."

"Can I help you straighten up?"

He shook his head. "I can manage."

"You know," Marie said, musing, "I'd love a place like this. Of my own."

"You don't have a place?" He stopped and stared at her.

Marie shrugged as if it really weren't of much importance. "No," she said. "I live with my folks."

"You've always lived there?"

"Yes." She went and poured herself more coffee. "I've never been able to afford anything in San Francisco." And then she added, "I've never been married, you see, and I had..." But she stopped suddenly, realizing she'd almost said: "Tony to look after," and somehow, she just couldn't admit to this tough, rigidly old-fashioned sea captain that she was an unwed mother.

"For some reason," Craig said, going back to his work, "I got the impression you'd been married."

Marie smiled. "Oh, you know, I'm too ambitious, too much of a career woman. No time."

"Still living at home," he said wonderingly.

Shamefully, yes, she thought and wished she'd taken the opportunity to mention Tony. Her son meant everything to her. She should have told Craig about him, bragged a bit, pulled out a picture. But it was too late. He'd know she was ashamed of her circumstances.

"Well," Marie said airily, "do you suppose Klutznic is back in from fishing? We could—"

"*We?* Not again, Marie. I don't mind you visiting. You can drink my coffee, talk to me while I clean up in here, but let's skip discussion about the crew. All right?"

Marie narrowed her dark eyes, ready to do battle. "No," she said meaningfully, "it is not all right."

He held a book in midair and raised a brow.

She went on, undaunted. "I've been thinking. One of your former crew is guilty of causing that spill, and he had a motive. We can assume that much. I figure he was bribed by someone else, an outside party. The question is, why? Why did someone bribe a crew member? What did he or she or they gain?"

"Marie," he began, exasperated.

"I mean," she said, "what was there to gain by spoiling the environment?"

Craig shook his head. "Come on," he said, "you're looking at it from the wrong angle. Believe me, I've had a long time to think this out."

"So, why are you holding back on me?"

"I'm not going to discuss this with you anymore. Forget it."

"*Craig*. The least you can do is tell me what you've got. Two heads are better than one and—"

"Spare me the clichés."

"Please. My company can find things out. We've got connections you don't have. Craig," she said, moving toward him, pleading, "don't shut me out. People will talk to me. You know no one's going to open up to you. Be honest with yourself. You haven't got a friend left since—I'm sorry," she said suddenly, catching the grim expression on his face, "I didn't mean that. I'm ... *I'm* your friend."

He laughed ruefully. "That's a comfort."

"I hope it is."

He ignored her, moved around her, went to the coffeepot. "You know," he said, "you're like a pit bull. You just get hold of something and won't let go."

"My bite's not quite as bad, though."

He did let her help dust a few books. He said it was to keep her busy, to keep her from driving him nuts, but Marie suspected he was sort of glad for the company. She suspected, too, that maybe he liked her a little more than he was letting on.

And how did she really feel about him?

She just didn't know. She knew she liked him, a lot. She wondered if she weren't falling in love just a little bit. Certainly every time she caught him silently appraising her, a little shock pricked her heart. She wanted to touch him, to hold his hand again, to perhaps run a finger along his lips, to feel the strength of his arms. The top two buttons of his shirt were still undone. She ached to place her hand on his skin, to feel its warm hardness under her fingers. But he'd never let her get that close. Yesterday, at the island, he'd been off guard—he hadn't had the will to push her away. But today was another thing altogether; he was back to being the gruff old sea captain, the man who didn't need anyone.

"So," she said, dusting her hands off on her white pants, "earlier you said I was looking at the spill from the wrong angle. What did you mean?"

Craig sighed and sat down in his armchair and stared at her as if deciding just how threatening she was. "What I was getting at is this. No one was out to despoil the environment. I figure it had to do with the oil companies that use the pipeline."

"Was the price of oil driven up? I can't remember from my notes." She sat on the dusty couch across from him and frowned.

"Some. Temporarily."

"But not enough to affect the oil industry in general. It doesn't make any sense. Was the tanker old? Could it have been an insurance thing? You know, like burning down an old building to get the insurance money?"

But he shook his head. "You're forgetting. The *Northern Light* was repaired and is still sailing. She's perfectly seaworthy."

"What then? Why did you say the oil industry was behind it?"

"I'm not sure yet. It's just an idea. I feel like I'm missing something that's right under my nose."

She began to jiggle her foot. "Craig," she said, "did you have a plan you were going to follow when you got out of prison?"

He glared at her mercilessly.

"You *did*. I knew it. And I came along and messed it up."

"I never said that."

"Oh, but it's true." Her eyes brightened. "You were furious when I told you I'd visited Lund and the Klutznics. You had . . . you *have* a plan."

"Damn, Marie, let it go."

"No."

He sighed. "It doesn't include you."

"Why not?"

"Because it's going to involve risks."

"Risks?"

"Tenacious, aren't you." It was not a question.

"Yes. Tell me. I'm on your side. You know you can trust me."

He studied her for a long moment, then settled back in his chair and steepled his fingers under his chin. She could feel the weight of his judgment on her but met his stare boldly with one of her own. It was like looking into a person's soul, seeing behind the facade. Craig didn't trust her. He didn't trust anyone. He'd been wounded too many times, and she stood for the very system that had hurt him. She wondered if he'd trusted Polly, his wife. Or his kids. He'd been at sea a lot. He'd purchased this cabin, too, to put distance between himself and the world, even before he'd been betrayed. Distrust was in his nature.

Or was it distrust? Maybe a man who had taken to the high seas didn't need other people. Maybe he had an ability to go through life with only himself to depend on. Maybe he didn't need someone like her at all....

"All right," he was saying, still holding her gaze.

"All right what?"

"I'm going to tell you what I have planned."

"You are?"

"Yes. I think you'll see why you can't be involved. Maybe," he said, the corner of his mouth amazingly lifting into the semblance of a smile, "you'll go away and leave me in peace."

Marie returned his smile readily. "Maybe, but I doubt it."

Then he leaned forward in his chair. "I have to assume that no one's going to open up to me or you—or anyone, for that matter. Even if one of my former crew members just *saw* something that day, he isn't going to talk. And sure as hell the guilty party won't spill the beans."

"So, how are you going to find anything out?"

"In poker," Craig said, "they call it a bluff. I'm going to force the guilty party's hand."

"How? You don't know who did it."

"I'll assume each man is guilty, that's how."

"I don't . . ."

"Give me a minute and I'll tell you how. I start by seeing every one of them in person."

"But two are dead and two more missing. Then there's Claud Savant in South Africa."

"I know." Craig rubbed his jaw. "I've given it a lot of thought. Joey and Woody are dead. You got me thinking about that. There *could* be something fishy there. Say they knew something, and the guilty party got to them. This is all hypothetical, of course, but I believe I can safely rule those two out. As for Bogner and Marshall, I'll try to track them down if I have to."

"And the other five?"

"I go see each one in person. I tell them I have proof that he's the guilty party. I tell him I want money to keep from going to the authorities."

"Blackmail?" she asked incredulously.

"Sure. If the guy is innocent, I'll apologize later. But if I hit on the guilty one, I figure he'll offer me money to keep quiet."

Marie let out a breath. Blackmail. But what if. . . what if the guilty party wasn't willing to pay Craig off? "You could get yourself killed," she said in a low voice. "What if you name your price and whoever is guilty doesn't want to pay?"

But Craig only shrugged. "I'll negotiate."

"You might not be given the chance."

"Look," Craig said, "I know all the risks. I'm not about to push someone over the edge if I can help it. And whatever he does, at least I'll know I flushed out the one who did this to me. But I think you can see now why you can't be involved."

"But . . . I'm already involved." She thought quickly. For herself, she could handle the danger. But there was Tony. . . .

"I—I still want to help, Craig," she said at last. This was her one chance, really, to see that Tony would never want for something again. The risk was worth it. And . . . and if something did actually happen to her— Marie swallowed hard—then her policy with Pacific would see to it that Tony was taken care of financially. Her parents would always be there, too. "I'll help you," she said with conviction.

But Craig was shaking his head.

"You know I'm right." Marie gave him no time to protest. "They're all going to find out about my involvement. I didn't hide my tracks. Alice Klutznic knows. She has my business card, Craig. It's too late."

"Marie, I can't let you."

It came to her then, and she smiled. "You have no choice, Craig," she said smugly.

"What in hell do you mean?"

"Your plan is fine, except for one small detail. *You* can't leave Alaska. You're on parole."

"I'll get permission. I'll talk to the parole board."

"That'll take time. Weeks maybe. How're you going to put your plan into effect, Craig? You tell me."

"I'll . . ."

"You need me. You really need me. I can get you that permission to travel."

His mouth was set in a hard line.

"I'll call my boss, Mike. I'll tell him I need permission for you to travel to solve the case. If a big company puts pressure on your parole officer, he'll listen."

"Oh yeah?"

She nodded. "I'll do it, too, Craig, but I'm going to ask something in return."

"Talk about blackmail."

"Yes. Or paying a debt. Whatever you prefer. But if I get you permission to travel, I'm in on your plan."

"Marie, don't you get it? Whoever ran that ship onto the rocks could have killed someone. It was pure luck that no one got hurt. He knew the risks then and was willing to go through with it, anyway."

She could feel his eyes on her, probing her inner strengths and weaknesses. "I'm in on this, Craig. I won't give up."

"Over my dead body you are."

Nevertheless, she got him to let her walk with him over to the hospital to see Mayer. He gave her permission grudgingly, and only because she promised not to go into Mayer's room. She suspected Craig hadn't been challenged by anyone, especially a woman, in a very long time. No doubt he was at a loss just how to handle her. And no doubt it had yet to occur to him that he might not win this one at all.

As they walked—the mist caressing her face gently—he repeated the same command a dozen times: "You're staying in the hall while I talk to Howie. I mean that, Marie. Don't push me."

Mayer was out of intensive care, and Craig deposited Marie like unwanted baggage in a waiting area near Mayer's room. She seated herself dutifully and smiled up at him as he shot her yet another threatening glance, then disappeared down the hall. Of course, she hadn't any intention whatsoever of staying there. She was unafraid of his anger; she barely even considered it. What ran through Marie's head as she walked purposefully toward Mayer's door was that Craig was not a trained investigator. He could very easily miss something Mayer said. He could fail to notice Mayer's body language, the hidden words behind the spoken ones, the changes in facial expressions. She'd enter quietly; Craig wouldn't even know she was there until too late, and she'd worry about his reaction later.

Marie opened the door to Howie Mayer's room, stepped inside quietly and stood there, unobserved. Howie was lying on the far bed, beyond a patient sleeping in the near one. She saw Craig sitting by his side, his back to her, speaking to him. Howie was shaking and mumbling. His skin was faintly yellow and sagged from his bones like laundry from a clothesline.

Craig spoke softly. She couldn't hear what he was saying. He must be trying his story on Mayer, although the man was so ill she wondered if he would even understand. Then she saw that Howie was becoming agitated. He struggled to sit up, and his parchment-colored, seamed face came apart, split, re-formed. His mouth opened, and she could hear him babble incoherently.

"Captain...I swear, I didn't want to... Sorry, I'm sorry," he said, his voice growing louder. "Sorry, I didn't want... He made me say all those... Sorry, Captain."

The man in the first bed woke up with a jerk, mumbled something and pressed his buzzer. Craig turned around, saw Marie, stood abruptly, and Howie Mayer stared at her, too, mouth still open, small sounds working their way up from his throat.

The nurse appeared. "He's startin' that again," the man in the first bed said petulantly, and the nurse walked quickly to Craig, put a hand on his arm and asked him to leave.

When they were out in the hall, the nurse apologized, but Marie could still hear the faint mutterings of Mayer behind the door. "Sorry, Captain...didn't want...sorry."

After the nurse left, the silence was deafening. Craig said nothing, just stood there, his fists clenched, the muscle working in his jaw. Then he took her arm with hard fingers and steered her out to the hospital lobby.

"Craig," she said breathlessly, "did he say anything?"

He stopped and took her other arm and held her facing him. His fingers dug into her flesh, and for a heartbeat of time she flinched beneath his wrath. "You liar," he said harshly. "You'll promise anything to get your way, won't you?"

"Yes," she said staunchly. "What was he sorry about, Craig? When Mayer said *he* made me say all those things, who did he mean?"

"I don't know," Craig said tiredly, letting go of her arm.

"Did he mean he was sorry he'd wrecked your ship or sent you to jail or what?"

"*I don't know.* He's a poor sick guy. But that never stopped you, did it, Marie?"

"It was your plan."

"Well, it isn't going to work on Mayer. You just wasted your time."

"Stop trying to fight me, Craig."

He rubbed his hand over his face and took a deep breath. "You are driving me nuts, you know that, Marie? I'm trying to accomplish something here, and you keep...you keep..."

"What? Standing in your way? Stopping you? No, darn it, I'm trying to *help* you, but you're too stubborn to realize it!"

He glared at her. "Okay, lady, you want in? Fine. You're in. Now you pay up. You hear? You get me leave to travel outside of Alaska. You said you could do it, so do it."

"Okay. A deal's a deal. But if I keep my promise—and this is one I *will* keep—then I'm in on this. I want to know everything you know."

She called Craig's parole officer in Anchorage from the pay phone in the hospital. The man gave her the third degree, and she had to use her business voice, the intimidating one. He agreed, reluctantly, to let Craig go for a few days—*if* he heard from the Pacific Group corroborating her story and *if* Craig would report in by phone every day.

She hung up and turned to Craig. "Okay. I'll have to get Mike to call him, but that shouldn't be any trouble."

"Your boss will go along?"

Marie nodded and sighed. "He'll go along with my request," she said, "because...well, he thinks he's going to...well, to get somewhere with me and—"

"I get it," Craig interrupted and gave her a long look.

Marie's back went up. "I don't think you do," she said, her temper surfacing again.

She turned her back on him and called Mike, collect. He accepted, thank heavens, and Marie explained the situation, giving him the parole officer's name and number.

She hung up slowly. Craig was pacing, looking down at the floor. It struck her that he must hate to be in debt to anyone, especially her, and he must despise her for manipulating him. Sometimes, she didn't like herself too much, either. "Okay, it's done," she told him. "Mike's going to call. You're free to travel. Just report in every day." *He must hate that, too, being treated like a common criminal.* "So, what are you going to do now?"

"I'll try Bones first. New Orleans. Then I'll visit Petersen in San Francisco."

"And you'll let me know what happens?" she said, ignoring the fact that he'd never said thanks. They had a deal, after all.

"I'll let you know."

"Craig, *I* could go see Petersen in San Francisco for you," she said casually.

"If you set one single foot near the man..."

"But what if you get hurt?" she blurted out.

He shot her a curious glance. "Are *you* going to protect me, Marie?"

"Well, I...sure, yes. I can cover your back, at least."

"You've been watching too much TV."

"I'm serious," she said.

"So am I."

It worried her endlessly that once he was out of her sight he might well disappear for good. She couldn't fly back and forth to Valdez and check on him, and he didn't have a telephone, either. What was she going to do?

"Craig," Marie said, "you've got to promise me you'll get in touch the minute you land in San Francisco. You have to swear it to me."

"I could call you, I guess," he said. "But you're not to do a damn thing while I'm in New Orleans. Zilch."

"I won't. Honestly. But you have to call."

"I said I would."

"Good." But she still wondered.

He pulled her out of the path of a lumbering Jeep and up onto the curb. "And by the way," he said, "just how *are* you planning on getting home to San Francisco?"

She remembered abruptly. "Oh—my plane ticket. Well, I'll think about it. I'll manage somehow."

"*That* I already know."

"Don't worry about it," she said stiffly.

He started walking. She hurried to keep up. It seemed she was always scurrying around, following Craig Saybolt like a stray puppy. "Where are you going now?" she asked.

He looked at her, irritated. "Home. For God's sake, I wonder why in hell they bothered to assign me a parole officer," he grumbled.

"We should celebrate," she said.

"Celebrate what?"

"Our deal. Drink a toast, seal the bargain." She looked up at him. "Now that we're friends again."

"Is that what we are, Marie?" he asked with sharp irony, and all she could do was pretend she hadn't heard.

CHAPTER NINE

CRAIG SAYBOLT felt as if he'd just been run over by a steam engine, a petite one, perhaps, but nonetheless powerful. He had no inkling how to handle her. He sat in the worn old armchair in his living room and watched Marie bustle around his kitchen as if she'd lived there for years.

"Ooh, dirty!" she remarked, holding up a pot and making a face.

"No one's been here in a while," he said dryly.

"Oh, I know, I didn't mean it was your fault. Really, Craig, your place is adorable. I love it."

Polly had never seen the cabin. When Polly had been alive they'd lived in Seattle in a nice, comfortable, four-bedroom house in the suburbs. And then, when she'd died, it had seemed easier to stay in Valdez more often, to avoid the constant flying back and forth to see the kids, who hadn't really wanted to see him, anyway. They'd been perfectly happy with Polly's brother. They'd had school and their friends and their own lives, which he'd never known much about because he'd been gone so much. He'd been a hell of a lousy father.

He stirred in the chair, feeling weariness drag at his muscles. Maybe that's why Marie had been able to get to him; he was just tired, all done in.

"Thank heavens you left a few things here. I'm sure not in the mood for grocery shopping," she was saying.

He watched her as she turned back to the stove. She wore white slacks and a red sweater, and he could see her panty line running diagonally up her round derriere, denting the firm, young flesh. He switched his eyes away. What was he thinking? First of all, this girl was as dangerous as a storm at sea. But more important, he had no right. She was too youthful, too damn lovely, and he was old and jaded, well past dreaming of the impossible.

He tried not to watch her as she opened cans and looked through his cupboards. Her dark hair bounced on her shoulders, and her hips were round, pulling the white cloth of her slacks when she stretched to reach for something.

So young and so pretty. And never mind her bulldog tactics; he was using her too—calculatingly, cold-heartedly—because she could provide him with his ticket to travel and the information he needed, to boot.

All right, he told himself. *You tried to get rid of her. You tried everything. But she stuck.* She'd asked for it.

So what now? he wondered. Here she was, bustling around his kitchen, oblivious to his lecherous thoughts. He had to get rid of her, for her sake, because he didn't know how long he could sit there staring at that inviting panty line before he cracked.

"No onions, huh?" she asked. "No, I guess not, after three years."

"Marie," he began.

"Yes?" She turned, a spoon in one hand, a questioning look on her face.

"Nothing."

"Now, come on, what were you going to say?"

"I think you should go home."

She smiled brightly. "You've said that before. I happen to disagree. I have work to do here."

"There's nothing more to find out up here. Everybody you want to see is out of town. Give it up, Marie."

She frowned. The spoon was dripping tomato sauce. Absently she caught a drip with her finger and raised it to her mouth, licking the drop with a pink tongue. "I've already found out a lot here, Craig."

"What?"

"I found out you were innocent. That's something."

He turned away, unable to tolerate the emotion he saw shining from her eyes. There was that emptiness in Craig, a cold, hard ball of pain that hurt to be touched, and Marie kept touching it. He didn't want her to put her small, warm fingers on that sore spot and stroke it again, goading it into the light. It hurt too much. Damn it, he wanted to be left alone.

"You know, you really do need someone to clean this place up a bit. It's still full of dust. Do you have a vacuum cleaner?" she asked.

He shook his head.

"A broom?"

"Sure, somewhere. In that closet, I guess."

"I think I'll sweep a little while the sauce cooks. Do you mind?"

"Come on, Marie, leave it. I can do it tomorrow. Aren't you tired?"

"Tired? No, I slept half the day. Didn't you?"

"Some."

"Oh. Well, do you want to take a nap before dinner? I'll bet I could find some sheets. Did you leave them . . ."

"Marie!"

She stood there looking surprised.

He took a deep breath. "Marie, let it be. I'm a big boy. You don't have to do this stuff. I can take care of myself."

She looked hurt. "I was just . . ."

"Okay, I know." He wiped a hand wearily across his face. "I guess I need some room. I'm not used to being crowded."

"I'm crowding you," she said in an uncertain voice. Carefully she put the spoon down on the stove and turned to face him. "Do you want me to leave?"

She was really just a kid. So small and perfect and warm and vivacious, with that Italian zest for life. She showed everything she felt, every nuance of emotion—disappointment, affection, anger, fear. How had he become such an old, lonely, bitter human being?

He studied her face and searched inside himself, touching that sore, empty spot as if it were a bad tooth.

"If you really think I should go," she was saying, still poised there in his kitchen.

"No," he said abruptly, "stay."

She gave him a brilliant smile. He could have sworn her eyes were bright with moisture.

"Okay," she said. "I won't talk so much. I get that from my mother. She's a chatterbox. My dad, well, I think he just doesn't listen after all these years."

She went to the closet and opened it, pulled out a broom and a dust cloth. "I think some animal made a nest in here," she said.

"Probably."

"Where are your garbage bags? Oh, here they are. Gosh, something chewed holes in the box."

"I'll clean it out tomorrow," he said, aware that his voice was gravelly from emotion.

"No, really, I can't stand it. I'll get it. It's just grass and twigs. What do you think made it?"

He forced a shrug. "A squirrel, a rat."

"A rat! Ooh." Busily she piled debris into a big plastic garbage bag. "Where are your trash cans?"

"Out back. Here, let me take it." He stood, feeling shaky, and took the bag from her. Their hands touched, and Craig stopped short as if he'd been felled by an ax. Their eyes met and held, and he could see her breasts rising and falling under the white blouse, pulling the cloth tight so that it gaped at the buttons.

He tore his gaze away and pulled the trash bag from her hands. "I'll be right back," he muttered under his breath.

When he returned she was sweeping the floor. She didn't look up. He fed some more wood into the fire and closed the stove door, giving the handle a decisive twist.

Marie stopped sweeping and leaned on the broom. She looked at him, her head cocked. "You know, I have this suspicion that you either hate me or you're afraid of me. You don't have to feel either way. Can't we keep this on a professional basis? I'm an insurance investigator, and you're helping me with a case. I do this every day, Craig."

Who was she kidding? he wondered. Couldn't Marie see that somehow, somewhere along the line the scenario had altered?

Carefully he asked, "So what do you do when a client is reluctant to work with you?"

She shrugged. "I investigate anyway. I work for the insurance company. My job is to save them money. If I can."

"What happens when your company's client is guilty, Marie?"

"Then we pay up. But we fight like the devil first. Haven't you ever tried to collect collision insurance?" She laughed. "We don't make it easy."

"This particular case was a mighty big collision," he said.

She sobered. "I know. And it wasn't your fault. We have to prove that, Craig."

He was silent for a moment, thinking. A log crackled and sizzled in the stove. A small wind pushed at the plastic covering the windows. "Maybe," he said slowly, "maybe it *was* my fault."

"But..."

"I mean, indirectly. Maybe I was too hard on the men, expected too much. One of them cracked. One of them must have hated me a lot. I should have seen that."

"Stop blaming yourself. And even if that were true, you've paid, haven't you? You've done your time, Craig."

She was boiling water, tasting the sauce, putting in a little more salt. He simply couldn't get a handle on her. She was hard as nails, stubborn as a mule, soft as silk, innocent as a baby. Pretty and small and cuddly, with neat little feet and hands and those big, dark eyes.

Craig walked to the door and opened it, took a couple of deep breaths of cool, damp air, watched a cloud slide down into the black trees.

"I think it's ready," he heard her say. "Too bad there's no garlic bread and salad. Oh well..."

She served him a big helping and set it on the table. She'd found glasses and napkins and silverware. And a candle, which she'd lit. The room had become warm and intimate, too warm.

"Sorry, there's only water to drink," she said. "Unless you have something I couldn't find. A nice Chianti, for instance."

Glad for something to do, he opened the cupboard under the sink. A six-pack of beer was still there, dusty after three years. "How's this?"

"Wonderful. Beer and spaghetti."

She put her own plate down and sat across from him. "I hope you like it. It's Sophia's recipe. Of course, she puts in a few ingredients you didn't have. If you come— I mean, *when* you come to San Francisco, you'll have to eat at the restaurant. It's called the Trattoria."

He ate, realizing he was hungry. It was good, neither restaurant fare nor bland prison grub. Real food.

Marie ate with an appetite, her small pink tongue flicking an errant drop of sauce from her lip. "I never get sick of pasta. You should try Sophia's clam sauce." She rolled her eyes upward in a very Latin mannerism. "And my mother is always inviting men, *single* men to eat at the restaurant. Naturally *I* have to wait on them. She keeps trying to find me a husband. It's embarrassing."

"You've really never been married?"

She shook her head.

"Why not?" He wished he hadn't asked.

She shrugged, a touch of color coming to her cheeks. "Oh, I don't know. I never found the right guy. They're either too serious or too frivolous or they're wimps."

"Wimps?"

"You know, no character, no guts. Wimps." She stopped and looked at him. "For instance, you are *not* a wimp."

"I'm flattered."

"There are lots of men who aren't wimps. Don't get conceited."

"I'll try not to."

Though a bit warm, the beer went down smoothly. It reminded Craig of the night before in the Pipeline. That gorilla. He couldn't believe he'd gotten into a fight over a girl on his second day out of prison. He wondered if his parole officer would find out. Not unless Marie squealed on him.

He couldn't fit his mind around the reality of his being there, at home, eating dinner by candlelight, with a woman he'd only just met. If someone had told him he'd be here, he'd have called him a liar.

"Tell me what you're thinking," she said. "It makes me nervous when you're all quiet like that."

"Nothing important."

"I hate people who say that. Of course, it's important. Is it about your crew?"

"No." He hesitated then said, "It's about you. And me. Here."

"Oh. So, tell me."

"It's not important."

"Really? Well, you can think about me all you want. I'm your friendly neighborhood insurance investigator."

"You're out of your element here, Marie. You know that, don't you?"

"You mean here in Alaska or here in your cabin?"

"Both," he said meaningfully.

"Nonsense. Now, I'll just clean up. That wasn't too bad, was it? Considering. You really should get some fresh garlic. That garlic powder just doesn't taste the same. And onions. We should have stopped and bought some at the grocery store."

And suddenly he broke. He caught her wrist as she reached down to get her plate. "You just don't want to understand, do you, Marie?"

She stared at him quizzically. "Understand what?"

"You don't belong here. It's all wrong. You can't help."

She straightened, shaking his hand off, balancing the plates expertly. "That's really getting old, Craig."

"I don't need a do-gooder. And I sure as hell don't need pity."

She walked to the sink wordlessly, put the plates down and leaned on her hands on the counter, her head hanging. Then she turned around suddenly, and he could see that she was angry.

"You really are afraid, aren't you? Scared to death. What do you think I can do to you? Oh, you're so tough. You can handle anything, can't you? Disgrace. Trial. Even prison—God knows what it was like in there! But you're afraid of *me*. Well, let me tell you, Craig Saybolt, you *need* me. You need a do-gooder, lots of them. And you need my pity, too. But you're too much of a coward to accept it!"

He couldn't stop himself. He stood and walked across the room—a puppet pulled by strings toward a fate he couldn't avoid. "Marie," he said, standing before her, then fell silent.

She was breathing hard, angry, a pure flame in his drab existence, brilliant in her red sweater, lighting up the room like the candle. Pulled by those invisible strings, he put a hand out and touched her cheek. She closed her eyes and turned her face sideways into his touch.

The fire crackled, and somewhere a wind-tossed branch scraped against the roof. He wanted to press her into his arms. The need was overwhelming.

Terrifying.

He pulled against the strings that directed him, fought them.

But the moment waited for him, impatiently, full of suspense. Then at last, inevitably, it passed.

Marie opened her eyes, smiled, raised a hand and laid it over his. "I have a temper," she said, "but I get over it pretty quickly. We yell a lot in my family."

He let his hand fall from her face, but kept her fingers in his. "Why are you here?" he asked.

"It's my job to investigate."

"You also told me that you created this case, Marie. I want an answer. Why?"

She looked away. "There was something about it. The reports...the trial...I kept reading what you'd said and looking at your picture. I felt there was something wrong." She sighed. "I was right, too."

He raised her hand and studied it, turning it over in his, looking at the palm, at the back. She wore no rings. Her hand was small and muscular, and her nails were short. He felt as if someone else were inside him, invading him. He was a stranger to himself.

She pulled her hand out of his. "I bite my fingernails when I'm nervous," she said. "Bad habit. They're ugly."

He knew she was trying to hold on to her sanity. It wasn't working.

"Craig." She put a hand on his arm and her voice rang with surety. "We're going to find the rat who did this to you. You hear me? We'll find him and clear your name."

He looked down at her, a bitter half smile on his lips. "And you'll get your promotion and that bonus, right? This is all for the betterment of Marie Vicenza, isn't it?"

He could feel her hand tighten on his arm and tremble. Her eyes held his, dark and shining. "No," she whispered. "No."

He believed her because he wanted to. Because the open wound in him refused to close. He could feel her liveliness warm him and melt the cold knot of his heart. He felt a terrible, tearing pang for a moment, and then he was dizzy with the strength of his reaction, whirled in a maelstrom of feeling. He pulled her into his arms, unable to stop himself, felt her solid and warm against him, her breasts pressing into his chest. Her face was upturned, her eyes glowing, her pink mouth open.

He groaned. A woman. It had been so long. *This* woman. Marie. He bent his head and touched his lips to hers. Her breath was sweet and hot and drew him like a moth to a flame. He kissed her. She moved her lips beneath his. She murmured something, and her hands stroked his neck, his back, then pulled his head down.

A gong of desire went off in his belly. There was nothing but the roaring in his ears and the spreading waves inside him and her lips under his and her hands in his hair.

Sanity came back in tiny shards. First he saw the red of her sweater, then the fluttering panel of plastic over the window. Then he felt her heart beat against his chest. He became aware of his breath rasping in and out of his lungs, and his loins ached like those of a sixteen-year-old boy.

He pulled his head up and drew in a shaky breath. She laid her head against his chest, and he stroked her hair and marveled at what had happened to him.

He found himself sitting in the big armchair, Marie on its arm, her hand on his shoulder, a faint smile on her lips.

"Tell me about yourself," she said. "I want to know everything."

"You've read the reports."

She shook her head impatiently. "Before that. Where were you born? Did you get good grades in school? Tell me."

He could barely think. He felt as if his whole world had just been turned inside out and here she was, sitting practically in his lap, relaxed, in control. Didn't Marie realize what had just happened?

"You were born in Seattle in 1945," she prompted.

"Ah, it's not very interesting," he got out.

"Come on, tell me, please."

He began haltingly. "I had a brother who died young of polio." He stopped and ran a hand through his hair. *Get a grip, man. Get control.*

"Craig," she said softly.

He fought desperately for control. Yes, he had had a brother. Yes, he remembered. He'd hold on to that thought.

"Your brother?" she was asking.

"Yeah, Ned. I, ah, my parents had a very bad time of it," he said.

"I can imagine."

"I guess I didn't realize how bad until I had kids of my own. Ned's death must have affected me," he said, clinging to the thought, trying to ignore her sweet, fresh scent. "I guess I took to the sea. I felt safe out there on the water, alone." He shook his head then. "I *loved* the sea. Crewed, went to college, but all I cared about was sailing. So I joined the navy. I did well. Junior lieutenant at twenty-six. They had great hopes for me, but Vietnam saw to that."

She patted his shoulder. "Go on."

"That incident, the one they all harped on. It happened hundreds of times in wartime, bending the rules a little. I was just in the wrong place at the wrong time. I got busted for it.''

"They made an example of you."

"I suppose."

"Go on," she urged gently.

"It wasn't a big deal."

"Sure it was."

"Yeah, well, I was given a general discharge, that's about it. But it dogged me. Without that honorable discharge..." He didn't know why he was telling her all this, baring himself. And yet . . . yet it felt good somehow.

She bent her head and laid it against his. "Tell me about Polly."

Polly. Yes, his wife. He'd found it easy to talk to her, hadn't he? But what had she really felt? he wondered. "She felt sorry for me, I guess," he found himself saying. "I met her in Seattle after the war. We went through hard times together. I had to work for some raunchy outfits until I got enough credentials to apply to Wesco.

"Hell, it wasn't a bad marriage. I was gone so much, and she was busy with the house and the kids. It was nice to come home."

"Did you love your wife?" Marie asked quietly.

"She was a gentle person. She couldn't accept strong emotions, so I guess I didn't push my feelings on her. She wasn't well the last few years.

"Then I got that telegram. I was in the Virgin Islands. They sent someone down to relieve me and I flew home. The kids were broken up. They blamed me. But Polly had been sick for years. They knew that."

"Kids have to blame someone when bad things happen to them. All kids do that. So do a lot of grown-ups," Marie said. "It's normal."

He shook his head. "They hated me. It was pretty bad at the funeral. I offered to get a housekeeper and keep the house, but Polly's brother Doug stepped in. Good old Uncle Doug. Well, I can't complain. He took care of them, got them into good schools."

"Kids," she said.

"Yeah, they can be tough. Tanya's twenty-one now. She graduated from college. I got a notice not too long ago, but I was...well, I couldn't go. But Doug kept me informed."

"Your kids haven't kept in touch?"

"Tanya never said a word or wrote or called. Ashamed of her old man. Hell, I don't blame her...."

"I'd say that's debatable."

"And Sonny, well, he wrote a letter once, told me what a terrible human being I was." Craig twisted his lips cynically. "Fine, upstanding boy. An environmentalist."

"Oh, Craig..."

"The worst was the notoriety. Before the trial I couldn't go anywhere without reporters on my tail. The trial was pretty bad, too. When you see those sketches of yourself on the evening news...

"And then jail. Hell. I put in my time. It's behind me. But I can't ever forgive them for locking me up. Closed in, four walls."

She sat quietly, listening, wisely not speaking. Her small, warm hand still lay on his shoulder. He wanted, abruptly and illogically, to weep. What in the name of God was happening to him?

He felt her fingers curl around his arm. The perfume of her hair and body reached his nostrils, and an ebony lock of hair lay against his temple, light as a butterfly.

"I feel as if I know you better now," she said finally, her voice as soft as a sigh.

"You don't know me," he said.

She didn't answer. Her fingers played with his shirt, folding and straightening the fabric. Her touch became unendurable. Suddenly he turned in the chair and grasped her hand in his. "Stop," he commanded.

She drew back, hurt.

"I can't...take it. Marie, please understand. I can't...." He turned away.

"Come here," she said gently, tugging at his collar.

He was being pulled by those strings again, gossamer threads that were as strong as iron chains, only this time she was pulling them. Her face was shining with emotion, incandescent, glowing. There was nothing else in his vision but the bright red of her sweater and her dark eyes, luring him on, dragging at him. He was a man drowning in an unfamiliar sea.

Then he was pulling her onto his lap and kissing her hungrily. She sighed and wilted against him like a plucked bloom. He heard her whisper his name, then all was rushing blood and murmurs and the pounding of his pulse in his ears.

"Marie," he whispered.

Like a man awakened from a long, dreamless sleep he found himself carrying her into his bedroom. And then her clothes were disappearing. He was not sure whether he was peeling them away or she was. He knew only an insatiable hunger.

Her red sweater lay like a flame on the floor, her blouse was unbuttoned, her delicate neck was arched back as she lay under him. He pressed his lips on her pulse, felt it flutter. She made a small sound in her throat.

She was so young, so perfect. He was using her, he told himself in a brief moment of sanity, but then she pulled him close and buried her head in his shoulder, and he knew he wouldn't, couldn't stop now, no matter what happened.

"Marie?" he whispered. "Are you sure . . . ?"

She stared at him, holding his shirt at the shoulders, holding him poised above her. Then she smiled. "If you say another word I'll scream."

She unbuttoned his shirt. Her small fingers teased, then pulled the shirt out of his jeans, then roamed over his skin, tickling, touching, until his nerve endings cried out in sweet anguish.

Her skin was warm and silky and honey-colored. Her breasts were full, swelling. Her panties had lace on them. He stared and stared, until Marie gave a soft laugh and ran a hand along his flanks, making him quiver.

"It's been too long," he said, feeling his skin glow with sensation, as if there were an electrical charge running through him, making his hairs stand on end.

His clothes were gone. My God, he felt free, released from a burden. The room was still light, and he could watch her face and see the way his hand was rough and brown against her paleness. A fine sheen of sweat covered his body.

She rolled on top of him, a sensual, heavy heat. She bent her head and kissed him, and her hair fell around him, a fragrant veil. He was sinking into her scent, falling, falling . . .

Then he was over her, ready. And she closed her eyes and arched up to meet him. She was all warmth and velvet and murmurs, so fragile-looking but so powerfully female.

He rocked over her, watching her face, breathing harder and harder. She clutched at him and gasped. Her eyes flew open, and he could feel her inside, and then he joined her, moving in her, taking her, giving to her, sinking, sinking.

Maybe, Craig thought later, it was even better afterward, when the frenzy was over, and he could appreciate what he had.

"You're exhausted," she said. "Go to sleep." She smoothed his hair back from his forehead.

"Marie..."

She waited, watching him.

"I don't...ah, I haven't done this very often. I don't want you to think..."

Her eyes were deep and dark and luminous. "I don't do this kind of thing often myself. I'm a nice Catholic girl."

He smiled. She said the funniest things. And she did it in total innocence.

"Is that funny?"

"Yes."

"Why?"

"I don't know."

"Well." She shrugged, her bare shoulders pressing into him. "At least I made you smile. Is that the first time you've smiled in three years?"

"Probably."

"I'm glad then."

He ran a hand down her hip. She was so very precious, so perfect. He wouldn't think of what he'd done or was going to do. Not right now. He was too tired, too at peace. He was going to enjoy the moment. The future was on hold.

She quivered under his touch. "No one's ever, *ever* made me feel like that," she said.

He grunted, disbelieving.

But she propped herself on an elbow and looked at him earnestly. "It's true." The heavy globe of her breast lay against his side. "It's true," she repeated. "Now go to sleep."

He slept and woke to find Marie curled up like a kitten against his back. He smiled and rolled over, put a hand protectively on her hip and fell asleep instantly again.

THE ANCHORAGE INTERNATIONAL AIRPORT was crowded, with long lines at every check-in counter. Craig carried his gym bag and Marie's small suitcase and strode through the throng toward her gate.

She hurried to keep up with him, her head only reaching his shoulder, her heels tapping a nervous staccato on the floor.

He knew she wanted to talk, to ask a thousand questions. They shone from her eyes: *Do you care about me? Will I see you again? Did you just use me?*

But Marie was a trooper. She didn't ask. Maybe she was afraid to.

They found seats at the gate to her San Francisco flight.

"I swear I'll pay you back," she said for the tenth time. "As soon as I get to my office. I'll send you a check."

"Don't worry about it."

"But you had to spend a lot of money to get us here. I feel awful. The flight from Valdez was bad enough, and now this one, too...."

"I trust you, Marie."

"I have your address. I'll send it right away. Or should I save it until you get to San Francisco?"

"It doesn't matter."

"But you'll be in San Francisco in a few days, won't you? To see Wild Man Petersen? Maybe I should just keep the check until then."

"Marie." He turned her to face him and held on to her hand. "It's not important. I wouldn't be going anywhere, much less to New Orleans and San Francisco, without your help. Don't worry about the money."

Her eyes clouded, and she looked down at her hands. "I want to help you, Craig, not take your money."

"You are helping me."

Her flight was called. She stood, clutching her purse with both hands. "I don't want to leave. I love Alaska."

"You better go," he said.

"You'll call when you get in?" she asked, and he knew it had been forced out of her by pure desperation.

"I said I would."

She tried to smile. "Well, goodbye then. For a few days, anyway."

"Marie..."

She clutched at his hand then, and he couldn't bear it; he embraced her and she put her face up to his, and his blood boiled, leaping in his veins. He kissed her, hating himself, shot through with guilt and shame, unable to deny himself the succor of her flesh.

They pulled apart, and he saw tears in her eyes, but she grabbed her bag and ran toward the gate, tilting on her high heels, not looking around.

He took a deep breath. Okay, that was over. He'd needed her—in so many ways—and he'd selfishly used her, and now he'd go to New Orleans to talk to Bones.

Forget pretty little Maria Vicenza, he told himself. *She's not for you, sucker.*

He watched her plane roll away from the terminal, move out to its runway and gather speed. He watched it take off, out over the water, and the sun glared blindingly on its silver wing once as it climbed, banked and disappeared.

He wiped his lips with the back of his hand unconsciously, then picked up his gym bag. His face was expressionless, his eyes flinty with determination. He was going to New Orleans. He had plans to make, important plans. Last night had been an interlude. It had been a mistake. He'd lost control. He knew she had, too. But he wasn't going to beat himself up about it. No. Things happened like that between a man and a woman.

He began walking purposefully down the concourse heading to his own gate. He was putting it behind him, putting it all in perspective. He hoped Marie was mature enough to do the same. Nevertheless he felt a stab of guilt knife through him, and he wondered if he would always feel guilty whenever he remembered that sun-kissed Alaskan night.

CHAPTER TEN

MARIE STOOD at the bus stop in front of the Pacific Group Insurance Company's Market Street building, tapping her foot angrily. What a jerk her boss was, chewing her out just now over her unauthorized flight to Valdez and doing it in front of her whole office.

"I should take it right out of your salary," he said, not more than ten minutes ago. "What did you think you were doing?"

She hadn't dared reply. Not a darn word. She'd known he had the power to can her on the spot—and everyone else knew it, too. How mortifying. It wasn't as if the other investigators there—all men—didn't go over their budgets often enough.

Sure, Marie thought, Mike chewed her out in front of everyone, but in private it was always a different story. Then he'd put his hand on her shoulder, smile at her, tell her how they had to keep up appearances. He actually thought she could hardly wait to climb into the sack with him! The creep was married, too!

"Ooh," she mumbled furiously, as she stepped onto the bus. It was not helping her mood, either, that she had to go home now, probably fight with her mom, deal with Tony's latest problems—whatever they were this time—and agonize over Craig's whereabouts.

She stood on the crowded bus and began chewing her nails in earnest. It had been two whole days since she'd gotten home, and there had not been one single solitary word from Craig Saybolt. She wondered endlessly if he'd even gone to New Orleans. She hadn't actually seen his plane ticket, and he might have told her all that bunk just to ditch her.

Oh damn, damn.

The bus lumbered along Market Street, up the hills, down again. She stared blankly at the people out of the window, hundreds and hundreds of them. Swarming the streets. San Francisco was a melting pot. There were the Orientals, who stayed close to home in Chinatown, the street people living in Haight-Ashbury and Golden Gate Park, the BMW yuppies of North Beach, the megabuck socialites of Nob Hill, the dilettantes, the gays, the neophytes, the work-toughened folks of Fisherman's Wharf, the liberal students, the hipsters of the Mission district. Drug dealers, art dealers, money lenders, the wealthy, the poverty-stricken—they all came together in San Francisco, the city on the bay, its famous Golden Gate Bridge rising out of the mist.

She was sick of it. She'd been born and raised in her little Italian community on the edge of poverty and was fed up. There had to be a way out, and Craig Saybolt's case had seemed perfect. But if that didn't work, she'd think of some other way. She wasn't going to grow old, working herself to death like her mom. And neither was Tony. She wasn't going to ride stinky, crowded buses all her life, buses on which a man would rather die than give up his seat to a lady.

She unlocked the front door of the three-story brick house and stopped cold in the vestibule as a thought struck her like a bludgeon. Craig would give up his seat for a woman. But...but did he really care about her? Was he somewhere far away thinking about her, missing her, or was he whooping it up in a bar, free at last, with a laughing blond bimbo plumped on his lap?

Marie hung her jacket on a peg, kicked off her high heels and set her briefcase on the old oak table. She had a dozen reports to fill out, and she'd have to work on them tonight. But her heart wasn't in it.

She cleared her throat. "Tony! Mama! I'm home!" she called up the steps.

But Sophia had already gone to work with Al—and Tony—Lord only knew where *he* was. Maybe hanging out in the park, maybe at a buddy's, maybe robbing the stereo shop down on the corner.

She sat in the living room and put her face in her hands. Where *was* Tony? And where was Craig? She felt suddenly lost and terribly alone. Coming home to San Francisco should have made her feel secure, safe, in control. Yet in Alaska, with Craig, she'd felt all those things. She'd been young and carefree and alive there. She'd walked the streets of Valdez and seen everything through innocent eyes, marveled at the simplicity of life there, at the towering mountains and sparkling water and endless daylight. Sure it would get dark in winter—real dark for months—but Craig's cabin was cheery and warm and welcoming.

Tony would love it there, she mused, tucking her feet beneath her. He'd fish and hunt and hike and camp and boat and do all those things a boy was supposed to do. He'd go to school, play baseball and come home afterward because Craig would be there, and Craig possessed the authority to discipline a thirteen-year-old. You bet.

And Craig would be there for Marie, too. Those cold, long, black winter nights. Craig next to her in his bed, all cozy and loving, his lips on hers, on her throat, her breasts....

I'm going out of my mind.

He didn't want her. He'd used her, just as she'd used him. It was lust. Of course it was. How could she be so stupid as to confuse love with lust? Why? Why hadn't he called?

But oh, how she was attracted to him. Attracted to his air of competence, his worldliness, his silences. He was tackling his case with absolute determination and an unerring sense of justice. He took risks. He sailed the seas of the world boldly, plunging through the storms, needing only himself and the clean salt spray on his face. He didn't even need her.

And that was what was killing her.

Marie forced herself to work on her reports diligently. She even walked over to the restaurant at eight and offered to help. But Sophia and Al had it all in hand.

"There's no business," Sophia said, wiping her big hands on her apron. "Business is lousy. We're going to go broke. Aren't we going to go broke, Papa? Papa?"

"Yes, Sophia, we're going broke," he replied and winked at Marie.

So she strolled on home through the park, searching the growing dusk for sight of Tony. But he wasn't among the kids running along the paths, hiding in the shadows behind the tall trees. Where was he?

The phone rang as Marie got home. Her heart bounded. Craig! Maybe it was Craig! She threw her purse on a chair and ran to answer it.

"Mrs. Vicenza?" a male voice asked—*not* Craig's.

"Yes?" She answered to Mrs. Vicenza; it was less confusing for people.

"I'm Dave Connaroe, Tony's Little League coach."

Uh-oh. "Oh, hello, Mr. Connaroe."

"I'd like to talk to you for a minute . . . about Tony."

Marie slipped off her shoes and wiggled her toes. "Sure. Is anything wrong?"

"Well...Tony hasn't been at practice for a little while, and I wanted to check on him. I tell the boys they have to attend practice, or they're not being fair to the others on the team."

"He hasn't been at practice?"

"Not for a week. We have a game this weekend, and Tony's a good outfielder. I'd like to use him, but I'll have to give his position to one of the kids who shows up to practice. I have to be fair, Mrs. Vicenza."

"Oh, of course, I understand."

"I thought you should know, in case Tony goes home and tells you what a rotten coach I am."

"Oh, you're absolutely right. He can't get away with irresponsible behavior, Mr. Connaroe."

"You know, Tony's a nice kid. But sometimes... Well, some of his friends who aren't in Little League show up at practices and give him a hard time, and you know, he gets kind of an attitude problem."

"Oh." What the coach was referring to was Tony's smart mouth. "I'm really sorry."

"Oh, hey, no big deal. I can handle teenagers. I just wondered if Tony was having problems at home or anything."

Marie flushed. "He's going through a hard time right now. I'll talk to him about practices, though."

"Okay, I'd appreciate that. Thanks, Mrs. Vicenza."

Marie hung up slowly. She closed her eyes tightly and grimaced. How embarrassing. Tony hadn't been going to practice. She thought he'd gone while she'd been in Alaska. Hadn't he told her he had?

Oh, that kid!

At eleven he showed up. "Come in here, young man," Marie commanded, the way Craig might have done, "this very minute."

"Whaddaya want?" He appeared from the vestibule, his jacket askew, his smooth-skinned face shiny and red, his scalp hideously bare.

Had he been drinking again? "Where have you been? I've been home for two whole days, and I've seen you a total of ten minutes. What's happening here, Tony?"

"Nothing's happening."

"Where are you hanging out?"

"With the guys."

"You go to baseball practice? Ever?"

"What's it to you?"

Marie leaped to her feet. Her hands were balled into fists at her sides, but he was too big for spanking. "Do you know that your coach called me tonight?"

"Yeah, so?"

"He says you haven't been to practice in a week, and he's going to give your position to one of the other kids."

"Big deal."

"It *is* a big deal. If you make a commitment, Tony, you see it through. I taught you that!"

"Connaroe's a jerk."

"No, you got it wrong. *You're* the jerk. You let your team down."

"Lay off, Mom."

"Don't you smart off to me, Anthony! I want to know where you go and with whom. If you don't tell me, you're grounded. Period. You can rot in this house for all I care."

He shrugged negligently. "Who's to know if I'm home or not? No one's ever here."

"You think I *like* working?" She waited. No answer. "You think I wouldn't rather be living up in one of those fancy houses in the hills getting manicures all day and sipping wine at night before I go to the opera? Give me a break!"

"I didn't say..."

"I've worked my tail off all my life, kiddo. You don't remember when I had two jobs and was going to night college clear across the city. You were a baby. But I've tried. God knows I've tried." Then suddenly her mouth clamped shut and her hand flew to her heart. "I don't believe it," she breathed. "I sound just like Sophia! I've finally done it. I swore I'd never say the things to you that she said to me. Oh my God."

Tony was looking at her warily. "Well," he said after a moment, "am I?"

"Are you what?" She just couldn't believe it—Sophia. She was turning into her poor, put-upon mother. Next thing, she'd be hunched over, complaining about her feet....

"Grounded?"

"We'll...ah, talk about it. You go on upstairs now and think about where your life's headed. We'll talk at breakfast."

"Sure, Mom."

That did it, Marie thought. She knew with more certainty than she'd ever felt before that she was getting out of the city and changing their lives. Whatever it took. She'd go to Alaska with Tony. She'd go to the ends of the earth—anywhere. But this vicious circle of working and never keeping her head above water had to stop. She was drowning here and pulling her boy down with her.

Al and Sophia trudged in shortly after Tony had quieted down upstairs. Wearily Sophia plumped into her chair. "My back," she sighed. "Al, Papa, what are we going to do about that plugged sink? Papa?"

He sat next to Marie and patted her knee. "Busy night?"

"Yes, Papa. Lots of reports to fill out."

"Reports," Sophia said, scoffing.

"That's the insurance business," Marie replied, hoping Sophia wasn't going to start.

"You heard from that man?" Sophia asked.

"What man?" Marie's back went up.

"That captain. The one who murdered all those bald eagles. As if we had any to spare."

Marie bit her tongue. "I haven't heard from him."

"And you won't."

Al rubbed his jaw. "Maybe she will, Mama. Marie said he was a good man."

"Good man. Ha! Biggest bum on earth."

Abruptly Marie stood, gathered up her papers and shot her mother a wicked look. "I'm going to bed. I'm not listening to this another minute. Craig Saybolt is the finest man I've ever met. Except you, Papa. Good night."

"A bum," Sophia mumbled. Then when Marie was almost out of earshot, "I wonder what really went on up there in Alaska? How have I raised such a naive girl?"

Craig called at 3:30 the next afternoon. Marie clung to the receiver in her little cubbyhole at work, not trusting her voice.

"Marie, you there?"

"Yes, yes, I'm here. Where are you?"

"At the airport."

"New Orleans? *Here?*"

"Here. I'm going to get a cab into—"

"No. I'll come get you."

"You don't—"

"It'll take me...ah...well, I'll hurry. Wait for me out front...."

She grabbed the bus. Raced up the hill to her parents' house, snatched the car keys off the peg in the kitchen then fired up the old Dodge. It coughed and sputtered and blew black smoke down the alley. "Come on," Marie said, pumping the pedal.

Finally she got under way. The old car protested up every hill. The brakes squealed going down the other side. It stalled out twice at traffic lights. She kept glancing at her watch, trying to dart in and out of traffic as if she were in a Porsche. People honked at her. A taxi driver poked his head out the window and yelled, "Where'd you get your license, lady? Sears?"

But Marie was impervious. Craig had called. In a few minutes she was going to see him again, touch him, look into those cool blue eyes. Lord, how she loved that man. How could she have thought it was lust? Silly, so silly of her...

He was there as promised. Tall and confident, proud, handsome. As Marie pulled up to a jerky halt she saw a smartly dressed woman eyeing Craig appreciatively, as she hailed a cab. Marie's heart swelled in pride—he was hers.

"Hi," she said, smiling brightly, clutching the steering wheel with deliciously shaky hands.

He climbed in, filling the front seat with the aura of his self-assurance. She greeted him, expecting the same degree of warmth and pleasure from him, but there was something not quite right. It was as if her world had suddenly tipped off its axis.

Cool. He was cool toward her, reserved. She told herself that he'd been traveling, dealing with airports and crowds, all that inconvenient stuff. He was an Alaskan, used to his space, even his freedom now. Sure, that was all it was.

She put the car in gear. It took too long for the transmission to move into drive. The car rocked unhappily.

Why *was* Craig being so standoffish? She wanted him to lean over and brush her cheek with his lips, as the man in the car in front of her had just done. She felt deflated; the wind had gone out of her sails.

Marie forced cheer into her voice. "Well, I thought you'd never call," she said lightly. "Thought you'd ditched me."

"We made a deal."

She pulled out into the moving traffic, got a honk from a black limo and drove out of the terminal complex. He sat there, too silent, studiously withdrawn.

Words, sentences came out of her mouth. "It was nice out yesterday, but the fog came back in today. The weather's so changeable.

"Um."

"I guess it seems funny here when the sun goes down."

No answer. She dared a look at his profile, snatched her eyes away. A car's rear lights were coming at her rapidly, and she braked too quickly.

"Well," she tried, forcing heartiness into her voice, "how was New Orleans?"

"Okay."

"Hot and humid, I bet. 'Course, I've never been there, but I've heard...."

"It was okay."

"Did you have time to get to Bourbon Street and hear some good jazz?"

"No."

Was he angry at her? He sounded angry, but she hadn't seen him or talked to him since...since that morning at the airport in Anchorage. He'd kissed her then and held her as if he'd felt something, as if he'd cared. What was wrong now?

But nothing stopped her chatter. "Did you see Stratford? You know, Bones. Was he there?"

"Yes."

"Well?"

"Well what?"

"Did you try your story on him?"

Craig glanced over at her. "Yes."

"And?"

"He got mad."

"And?"

"And nothing. He got mad, that's all."

"You told him you knew he was guilty of running the tanker aground. You asked him for money to keep silent, and all he did was get angry?"

"Yes," Craig replied impatiently. "Did you expect him to pull a gun on me?"

"If he *is* the guilty one, wouldn't he have...?"

"Think, Marie. I took him by surprise. If he's the one, he'll have to mull it over, make plans."

"Oh. You didn't push him too hard, did you?"

"No."

"I mean, you let him know you were willing to negotiate?"

"I'm not stupid."

"But do you think...?"

"I *think* Bones is a good guy, if you must know. I think I just wasted my time. Can we drop it, please?"

It was clear Craig was on edge and preoccupied, but Marie didn't know whether it was her fault or not. She'd been weak with relief to see him standing there at the airport, safe and sound—her man. And now, well, now she just didn't know what to think or do or say. She felt swamped by confusion, a little afraid, thrust from one emotion to the next with no control. To top it all off, it had begun to rain and the wiper blades needed replacement.

"Watch out!" Craig said when she pulled out into a passing lane and nearly hit another car coming up on her left.

"Oops" was all she could say.

He wanted to be dropped at a hotel near Fisherman's Wharf, a place he knew, but she was reluctant, afraid he'd disappear, afraid he didn't want to be with her. She thought of telling him her recently discovered view on success—how unimportant it seemed suddenly—and how she'd learned that there were other, far more urgent things in her life now, such as her love for him and her need to get Tony out of the city at any cost. But Craig was in no mood. It was as if he had no patience with her, as if she bored him to distraction, as if he thoroughly disliked her.

"Isn't Fisherman's Wharf that way?" Craig asked, pointing.

"Oh, yes, it is. But I'm starved, and I thought you'd like some home cooking. I mean, my folks' restaurant is practically home. Aren't you hungry after airplane food?"

He said nothing for a long moment, and that, in itself, told her he wasn't sure he wanted to be with her at all. Her heart thumped against her ribs frantically. Finally he said, "I'll go to your folks'. Sure, why not?"

They sat at an intimate table for two by the front window. The place really was charming, a true ma-and-pa operation in the heart of San Francisco's Mission District. The tables were covered in red-and-white checked oilcloth. The candle was stuck in a Chianti bottle. The lighting was low, the heat too high. The air smelled of garlic and oregano and olive oil. Marie saw her mother peer through the kitchen door into the dining room, say something. Then Al's face appeared, too. If they came out right now and embarrassed her.... And, oh my God, what if Sophia came over and started in on Craig?

"Nice place," Craig was saying, "cozy."

"Oh, thanks." How awkward. Maybe this had been the biggest mistake of her life.

The waitress sidled over. "Hi, Marie, wanna cocktail?" She pulled the ticket book out of the pocket of her stained red apron and stared at Craig appreciatively.

"I'll have a red wine, please. Craig?"

"Same." He looked up at the waitress. "Thanks."

It struck Marie that he was being nicer to a total stranger than he was being to her. Why? What had she done? He couldn't have forgotten that night, the intimacy.... It had to have meant something. Under the table, she wiggled her foot nervously.

"What's good?" he asked her.

"Oh, ah, the lasagna. Or maybe the chicken cacciatore. It's Sophia's specialty. Of course, there's the veal parmesan, or you might like the spaghetti. My father, Al, makes a wicked meatball. There's the Italian sausage sandwich, too. We get the sausage from—" She glanced up from her menu abruptly, realizing she was babbling. He was staring at her, utterly expressionless. She felt her cheeks flush and wondered why it was always so darn hot in this place.

He took his eyes from hers and looked at the waitress. "Lasagna, please."

"I'll have a salad," Marie said, "the usual, you know. And garlic bread. Fresh, not yesterday's heels. Thanks."

The girl left them, came back with two red wines, left again. Craig was silent, obviously uncomfortable, gazing around the dining room as if he were on another planet. He never looked at Marie.

But she studied him, all right, a frown creasing the bridge of her small nose, the stubby nail of her little finger in her teeth.

What had happened? She desperately wanted to ask him but didn't have the nerve. And there he sat, a man who three days ago had seemed like a savior to her, someone who could rescue her from the drudgery of her existence and hand the world to her on a silver platter. He was strong and handsome and silent. He commanded not just her respect but the respect of everyone who met him. He was a leader of men, a hardened sea captain, a man who could live alone in a cabin in the woods with no insecurities. A rugged individualist.

She loved him. She eyed him and felt her heart swell and loved him so much it had become a physical pain. Why didn't he love her? Couldn't he see that he needed her?

"So," she said, "I have your check here." She reached into her bag and pulled out the envelope. "And, let me tell you, it wasn't easy."

"I told you it didn't matter."

"Of course it matters. You spent nearly eight hundred dollars of your own money." She thrust the envelope at him. "Here, take it."

He took it, laid it down negligently on the tablecloth. He never even looked at the amount.

"You're going to forget it. Don't you think—?"

His glance silenced her. "My boss had a fit," she finally said, chattering nervously. "He had a tantrum right in front of the whole office. Sometimes I feel like quitting, he's such a jerk.''

"Then why don't you?"

She looked at him in surprise. "I need a job. I mean, I have to work. And I like that job. It's the best one I ever had. I worked my way up from receptionist, and now I have a chance to really get somewhere. I can't quit."

"You can do anything you want, Marie."

"Oh sure." She dug at the wax dripping on the Chianti bottle with her finger. "That's what you think. It isn't so easy, not for us ordinary mortals."

The salad came. The garlic bread. The lasagna. They barely spoke and tension seemed to crackle from every nerve ending in his body. It was catchy. Marie felt her nerves scrape and go raw and could hardly get a bite of food past the lump in her throat. She tried talking about his case, about Wild Man Petersen, whom he'd see tomorrow, about the restaurant, her job, the weather, the Giants baseball team. But when she mentioned baseball she thought about Tony and his coach and Little League, and she remembered that opportunity she'd missed in Valdez to tell Craig about her son. Now, while Craig was in this mood, was sure not the time.

"Well," Marie said, sighing, "I'm stuffed. As usual."

"The food's good. Really." He gave her a half smile, but he was there in body only, his mind elsewhere, his gaze shifting away to a spot over her shoulder.

"Would you like some dessert?" she asked. "The spumoni's good."

"No. Thank you."

"Coffee?"

"Fine."

"Black? In Valdez, you drank it black, didn't you?"

"Yes, sure."

"Craig," she began but caught the movement out of the corner of her eye: the approach of Sophia and Al. Oh, sweet Lord.

"No, no, sit," Sophia was saying, waddling toward them, indicating for Craig to stay seated, "we aren't formal here."

"Mama . . . Sophia," Marie said, "this is Craig Saybolt. Craig, my mother. And this is Al, well, we call him Papa here." *How could they?*

"Nice to meet you, Sophia, Al." Craig half rose and shook both of their hands. If he hadn't been bent over, he would have towered over the two of them, Marie noted.

"So you're the captain," Sophia said, placing her hands on her hips. "Marie's told us a lot about you, Mr. Saybolt."

Craig merely nodded.

"Yes, she has. And what a terrible thing, prison. My, my."

"Mama."

But Sophia raised a hand. "It's no secret, is it, Mr. Saybolt? Whole country knows who you are."

Craig had an ironic twist on his lips. "It's no secret, Mrs. Vicenza."

"Well, well," Al said, shuffling his feet, "I've got work to do. Nice meeting you, Captain." He retreated, but not before Sophia shot him a look.

She turned back to Craig. "And what are your plans now?"

"Mama . . ."

"I'm only asking," Sophia said, shrugging. "You *are* my only child. Isn't that so, Mr. Saybolt?"

Clearly Craig had no idea how to handle Sophia's bluntness. He simply sat there, a grave look on his face, and let her rattle on.

"If I know my Marie, she's got some fancy plans. She says she's going to prove you're innocent."

Oh no. "Mama," Marie said, "you're giving Craig the idea that I've discussed his case with you. That's not fair." She looked at Craig with desperation. "I really never said a thing. Honestly."

He looked as if maybe he believed her.

"I've got cooking to do," Sophia said, as if she were the only person on earth who truly worked. But she had a parting shot for Craig. "I don't want my girl here mixed up with this business of yours. It's bad business, Mr. Saybolt. Bad," she murmured, then did an about-face and waddled back toward the kitchen.

Craig raised his brow and fixed Marie with an icy stare.

"I'm sorry," she said. "Sophia is just like that. She's protective."

"So I gathered."

"And I *am* her only child. And she says whatever she pleases. Always has." What else could she say, that she wanted to kill Sophia, that she had never been so humiliated in her whole life? "I'm sorry," she mumbled, "honestly I am."

"Of course" was all he said, and his eyes held hers for so long she felt as if she couldn't breathe in that place, as if all the air had suddenly been sucked out of the hot room in a big whoosh.

"You should be glad," he finally said, "that you have a mother to worry about you."

He was looking down, swirling the liquid in his coffee cup. She could hardly hear what he said then, because someone at the next table was laughing, braying like a donkey.

"What?" she had to ask.

"I've got to talk to you, seriously."

"Well, sure," she said, abruptly uncertain.

"Your mother was right."

"What does my mother have to do with anything?" she asked.

"It's bad business. She's right. You shouldn't be mixed up in it." He was still swirling the cold black coffee in the cup.

"Do we have to go over that again?" she asked, watching fascinated as the liquid in his cup moved in a glinting sheet.

"Yes." He looked up. His eyes were flat and gray. "There can't be anything between us, Marie. It was a mistake."

She froze inside.

"I don't want to hurt you, God knows, but things got...out of hand. I'd been in jail, well, too long. You're a beautiful woman, Marie, but that doesn't excuse what I did."

She couldn't talk. He was still looking at her, his face glacial in its composure. She wanted to cry. She wanted to scream. She did nothing. She wiped all expression from her face, in case he could read the agony there.

He'd used her. Too long in prison, too long without a woman, without *sex*. He'd used her.

"...Ashamed of what I did," he was saying. "I like you, Marie, I really do. But there can't be anything between us. My life is just too..."

"Oh, Craig," she said, interrupting, plastering a smile on her lips despite their trembling, "don't say another thing. This is so silly. You can't believe how relieved I am!"

He stared at her impassively.

"Seriously," she rushed on, "I was feeling like such a fool myself. And I didn't know how to tell you. I was so embarrassed." She laughed then and shot him a big smile. "How ridiculous. This is so ironic," she said and took a sip of her wine. "Don't you think so?"

He said nothing.

"Well, with me it wasn't prison, of course, but it's this crazy drive I've got. You know, this success thing. I thought, well, I thought if you and I were...intimate," she rolled her big brown eyes playfully, "well, that you'd let me help more. You understand."

"Sure," he said slowly, studying her, "I understand completely."

"Silly," Marie said, unable to stop, fighting the burning behind her eyes, "you doing it for information and me for a big fat bonus from my company. Some adults we are."

"Look, Marie," he began, but she was already rising, waving gaily at their waitress, desperate to feel the cold drops of rain on her burning cheeks, to hide her face in the growing shadows of dusk.

CHAPTER ELEVEN

MARIE THOUGHT ABOUT calling in sick to work. My God, but she felt like something the cat had dragged in. She'd be surprised if she'd gotten more than four hours' sleep all night.

She sat hunched over a cup of coffee at the kitchen table, chewing on a nail, her hair stringy, her old bathrobe on, her bare feet cold on the cracked linoleum floor. She hurt inside as if someone had been punching her in the stomach all night.

Men.

Sophia came bustling into the kitchen. The air of her passage, charged with energy, hit Marie like another fist. She cowered over her coffee cup.

Sophia stopped, put her hands on her hips and opened her mouth.

"Don't, Mama," Marie said quickly. "I have a headache."

"You have a headache! I guess you do! So, that's the man. That's the one, the one that's going to make you rich." Sophia snorted in derision. "Oh, yes, I know that look in a woman's eyes. I'm not dead yet. You're a fool. He's a no-good."

"Don't, Mama."

"So, you finally found one and look. Look! A jail-bird. Twenty years older than you."

"He is not twenty years older than I am," Marie said halfheartedly.

Sophia waved a hand, dismissing the fact as inconsequential. "Not even Catholic."

Wearily Marie said into her coffee cup. "So what, Mama?"

"So, this is what you bring home? All those men out there, and you pick a criminal?"

Her head came up. "He is *not* a criminal. He is not guilty. Someone set him up."

"Sure, sure, I've heard that before."

Marie couldn't bear her mother's ferocious caring another second. "I've got to go get dressed, Mama."

She put some clothes on. She tried to make her face up in the bathroom mirror, but every time she brought the mascara wand up to her eyelashes, her eyes filled with tears.

God, she hurt inside.

She thought she'd found someone, a man she could love and trust and admire, one who needed her as badly as she needed him. Ah, they were all the same, she guessed, eighteen years old or forty-five.

He'd needed a woman, and she'd been handy. More than handy—she'd pushed herself on him in a disgraceful way. It was her fault. She was so dumb sometimes.

Everything was her fault. She looked at her blotched face in the mirror and hated herself. Thirty-one years old, and what did she have to show for it?

She'd done a lousy job raising Tony, too. She'd been self-centered all her life, wallowing in self-pity, using her lack of money as an excuse to stay at home. She was too lazy or too chicken to go out and face the world on her own.

Yes, it was true. She'd always had a million excuses why she couldn't move away. from home, but the real truth was that she had it easy at home, leaning on Mama and Papa. It was absolutely true what Sophia had said: she was a bad mother. She couldn't even deal with her own problems, much less Tony's.

She brushed her hair out roughly, punishing herself. Why wasn't she one of those women who bore up under adversity, who became better because of it?

She went downstairs. Tony was wandering into the kitchen, his eyes puffed with sleep, his bare scalp looking obscene. Anger flashed on inside her as if someone had pushed a button.

"Tony," she said, "you're going to grow your hair out."

"Oh yeah?"

"Yeah. Starting today."

"Who says?"

"*Me*. Me, your mother. *I* say. You got that?"

He looked at her, mouth open.

"I've got to go to work. You behave yourself. Go to baseball practice. Don't be a bum, Tony."

"Why not? It's fun being a bum."

"I'll tell you why not. Because it's in really bad taste, that's why. Think about it. Help your grandmother."

Okay, she was going to start. You had to start somewhere. Tony's hair was a good place. His *lack* of hair.

She could be a good mother. She had to straighten out her priorities. Tony came first. When this case was over, she'd work on being a better mother, a better human being. She'd think about getting her own apartment. Just her and Tony.

She was listless at the office, unable to keep her thoughts on anything. She worked on her report, but every word she wrote brought to her mind a scene from Alaska. Just writing his name, Craig Saybolt, caused pictures to flash in her head. Craig walking out of the prison, the first time she'd seen him. So proud, even in the shadow of those awful walls. His face, now so dear and familiar, with a smile on it. His first real smile.

She could close her eyes and feel his hands on her and how her body had quivered and glowed to his touch.

"Is that report ready yet?"

"Huh? What?" Her eyes snapped open. "Oh, Mike. Soon. It'll be ready soon."

"It better be good. Names, dates, places."

"I'm working on it." She deliberately kept her voice cold; she wanted him to know she was still angry at him.

Her boss sat on the edge of her desk, suddenly chummy. "I want to apologize for the other day, Marie. You were way out of line, but I should have kept it between us."

"You're right." She kept her eyes down on her report, focused on the words she'd written on the report form: "rendered unconscious by unknown person or persons."

"Okay, I lost my temper."

"I noticed."

He leaned forward, his voice edged with ire. "You know, Marie, I can't protect you forever. If you don't come up with something concrete, and soon, you're off the case."

"I'll find something, don't worry."

Then he reached out a hand and laid it on her arm. She wanted to shrug it off, but didn't dare. He was her boss. "You look tired. You're working too hard. Don't you have some time off coming?"

"I have to finish this case first."

Mike smiled and clucked his tongue and shook his head. "You've really taken this case to heart, haven't you?"

"Saybolt is innocent, Mike."

"Okay, good. Prove it. Save us a hundred million and change. You have two weeks to do it. The check will have to be cut soon."

"I'll prove it, Mike."

He patted her arm patronizingly. Mike infuriated Marie, treating her with a combination of condescension and harassment.

She smiled up at him, playing the game. She knew all the other employees in the office were watching and snickering: *There goes married Mike after Marie again.* "Gee, Mike, you know how grateful I am that you're letting me handle this case. I'll do a good job, I swear it. We're really on to something, like I told you."

"That's good, Marie. You know, I sort of feel like you're my protégée. I'd like to see you do well."

"Mike, I'm going to have to go to Alaska again." She held his eyes with hers deliberately. If she were a man, one of his invaluable male investigators, she knew he'd spring for a second trip with little trouble. After all, the chance of proving Saybolt's innocence and saving one-hundred-eighteen million was worth the price of another plane ticket. But Marie wasn't a man.

"Again?" he was asking, raising a brow. "What for?"

"To check those men out, the crewmen who live there. I've put in phone calls, but they're never home. I've got to track them down and talk to them."

"I don't know, Marie," he replied doubtfully. "It's not like running over to Oakland."

"This is a big case, Mike. It'll be a feather in your cap when I find something up there." She put her hand on

Mike's knee. "I can't do it from here. You're the one who taught me to go straight to the scene. There're some real inconsistencies with two of the crew up there. Our own investigators spotted it months ago. I want to follow it up, Mike. It's going somewhere. I can feel it."

His face fell into lines of self-indulgent pleasure. He put his hand over hers and gave it a squeeze. "One more trip up there, that's it. And no more chartered planes to Valdez, for God's sake."

"Okay, Mike, I promise.":

"I'll give Chelsea the okay. She'll reserve a ticket for you. Give her the information she needs." He frowned. "And you better dig up something solid up there, Marie. Or I'll have to answer for your expenses. They're getting tough about costs these days."

"I know, Mike. Honest, you'll never regret this. It's the right thing to do."

"Okay, okay, so I'm a chump. See you when you get back."

Marie smiled and left it at that.

She tried to look busy all afternoon, but in reality her mind went over and over one scenario, around and around like a broken record. Craig was talking to Wild Man Petersen. My God, the name—Wild Man—was scary enough. Craig accused the man of running the ship onto the rocks. Petersen went berserk and tried to kill Craig. Craig was lying wounded somewhere in an alley or in the dirty water of the bay. He needed her.

She got up from her desk and went to the ladies room. To get some quiet she locked herself in a stall, alternately chewing her nails and rubbing her temples to dispel her headache. Nothing worked. Craig was hurt, dying, calling her name through cracked, bloody lips.

Or worse. Wild Man had confessed, and Craig, triumphant, not needing her a bit, was on his way to the police with the signed confession. Then he'd be exonerated, get his job back and leave for Alaska without ever seeing or talking to her again.

She wished he'd call. She'd given him her home phone and her work phone. He'd promised to let her know what happened with Wild Man.

God damn him! He better call! If she didn't get a man out of this case, she'd like her promotion and her bonus!

The day crawled by in curiously jerky time. The minutes dragged and the hours flew. Mike kept smiling at her through the plate glass window of his office. The girls around Marie giggled and whispered. She didn't give a hoot.

She rode home on the bus. It had started raining. Fog drifted in from the bay. It reminded her of that day in Valdez—the fog, the cheery fire in Craig's cabin, the way he'd made love to her. She'd watched him as he slept that night and memorized every line of his face, the wide mouth, the way his hair was receding from his forehead. She loved the way he looked—solid and strong and dependable.

Oh God, why was she thinking about that? It was over. It had been a one-night stand, and he'd even apologized.

So had Mike apologized to her. Wonderful. Two apologies in two days.

"You look like a hag," Sophia remarked when Marie got home. "I'm late. I'm leaving for the place. Don't bother coming by, because it's raining. It won't be busy. Not that you'd bother coming by, anyway."

"Okay, Mama. I probably won't see you if you're late. I'm beat. I'm going to bed early."

"He didn't call, did he?"

"Who, Mama?"

"You know who. That captain. The deserter. The jailbird."

"Oh, for heaven's sake, Mama, stop that!"

Sophia shrugged heavy shoulders, pulled her raincoat on and got out the old black umbrella. "Papa! Come on!"

"Where's Tony?" Marie called after Sophia and Al.

"In his room. For once." Then the door closed and her parents were gone.

Marie hung her jacket up and went into the kitchen. A pot of minestrone simmered on the stove. Sophia had probably brought it from the restaurant. Good, she wouldn't have to cook.

She yelled up the stairs, "Tony, I'm home!"

His voice came down, muffled. "I'm listening to tapes!"

Nice kid. Probably losing his hearing by the second with his headset turned up high.

Why didn't Craig call? She sat at the kitchen table, chewing on a fingernail and listening for the phone. He hadn't wanted to call her at work, that was it. He'd wait until he was sure she was home, then he'd phone. Any minute now.

Should she call his hotel? No, not yet, not until she couldn't bear waiting anymore.

She must have sat there for hours before the phone out in the hall rang. She jumped, her heart flying into her throat. She let it ring once, twice, afraid to go pick it up in case it wasn't Craig. Then she heard Tony thundering down the stairs and his voice, his young, cracking voice. "Hello. The Tone here."

Her heart stopped dead, waiting for Tony to say the words, "Mom, it's for you." But he didn't.

So, it was one of his juvenile-delinquent friends. He'd obviously been expecting the call.

She was going to do something about Tony, something constructive. She'd decided that morning, but she'd do more. Especially when school started. Tony was going to have a curfew and rules about his homework.

He was a good kid. He loved her, despite her failings as a mother, and she loved him. He was just adolescent and confused. All those hormones raging around inside of him. She remembered how it felt. He'd come around, father or no father.

"Man," Tony said, coming into the kitchen, automatically opening the refrigerator door. "Man, that was some kind of weird."

Marie looked up at him. "What was?"

"Some guy on the phone. Said to tell you he knows where we live and where I play baseball. He said to tell you to be careful or something."

"Knows where we live ... where I play baseball ... to tell you to be careful ..." Marie's brain whirled.

"Weird, wasn't it?" Tony was saying, then he put the milk carton to his lips.

"Be careful ..."

"Mom?"

"Oh my God," Marie whispered, her heart freezing. Her temples began to pound furiously. She could barely think. She knew only that someone had threatened her son.

Abruptly she stood and went to him. He was as tall as she was, her baby. She hugged him and felt his bones poke into her, felt him shrink in embarrassment.

"Hey, Mom, what in....?"

"Tony." Tears welled in her eyes. She'd done the unforgivable. She'd put her child in danger.

"Mom!"

He was pulling away. She let him go, but held his arms in hers and stared him right in the eye. "Tony, listen. That phone call..." She swallowed. "I don't know who it is. It has to do with this case I'm on. Tony, are you listening?"

"Yeah, sure."

"Whoever it is is trying to stop this investigation. By threatening you."

"Oh, come on, Mom."

"No, it's true. You'll have to go stay with someone. It's not safe."

He frowned. "Geez," he said at last, impressed. "It wasn't even local."

"What?"

"It was like a long distance call. You know, like muffled."

Marie thought a moment. From Alaska? Or it could be from anywhere. "I don't care, Anthony. We're going to play this safe."

"Cops and robbers, man. Maybe this could be cool."

He was so precious to her. She was flooded with fear and fury and absolute determination. *No one was going to hurt her son.*

She looked at him fiercely, protectively, but there was a glint in his eyes, too. "You know," he was saying, "if my dad were around, he'd beat that creep up. Maybe I should—"

Marie grabbed his arms roughly and shook him. He was so surprised he was speechless. And she knew then that the moment of truth had arrived. She couldn't let him go on believing the lie. Not now. She dropped her hold on him and looked at her hands as if just realizing the violence of her reaction.

"Mom?"

"Your father," she said, whispering, heart aching painfully, "we told you your father was dead."

"Yeah. So?"

Marie closed her eyes and sent up a prayer. "He isn't. At least, I don't think he is...."

Tony jerked upright.

"Tony," she stopped and caught his eye, her heart pounding sickeningly. "We weren't married, Tony—Tony. Your dad and I..."

"You think I'm dumb, Mom? You think I didn't know?" Tony said angrily.

Marie could only stare at him in wonder. He knew. Tony knew all along.

"That's the trouble with you," her son said. "You treat me like a kid."

"Oh, God." Marie swallowed, ashamed. "Why didn't you tell me?"

"You didn't want to hear it."

Of course, he was right. She'd never been able to confront the fact that her son was no longer a baby. Talk about denial, she thought, and bit her lip to hold back her tears.

"Do you...hate me, Tony?"

He shook his head. "Naw."

"Should we talk...now? Do you want to know everything?"

Tony lifted his shoulders and dropped them. He was trying so hard to be cool. She could see two big spots of red rising on his cheeks. "I pretty much know everything, anyway," he said. "Mario told me. His mom told him, I guess."

"How long have you known?" His friends, of course, they all knew. Marie had been born and raised with a lot of their parents. Dumb, she was so dumb.

"Aw, I guess I knew when I was a kid. Ten, maybe."

"I see." She studied his young face. "Tony, did you ever want to go and find your father?"

"Naw." He put his hands in his pockets. "Someday, maybe, I don't know."

"Okay. I suppose if you do, someday, Tony, I'll do everything I can to help."

Tony cocked his head. She could see he was shuffling his feet. "It's not so bad," he said then, "being without a father. I got Grandma and Grandpa."

"You have me, too," she put in carefully. "From this moment on, Tony, we're never going to keep secrets again. Do you want to shake on it?"

"Sure." He shrugged and put out his hand awkwardly. Marie took it and pumped it and then pulled him into her arms until he squirmed.

"You know," he said, freeing himself, "if you wanna get married someday, Mom, I won't stand in your way. If I'm why you don't have a guy around..."

"Oh, Anthony," she said, her heart swelling with love, "you're not why. I promise. It's just that...well, I'm so busy all the time."

"Aw, you'll crack this case. We'll be rich and maybe you can date or something."

Marie smiled. "You think I should date?"

"Sure. Chris's mom does. And she isn't even pretty like you."

THEY WERE STILL in the kitchen talking, making plans about where Tony would stay until the Saybolt case was solved, when Sophia and Al came trudging in.

"You're early," Marie said. "No business?"

"Three tables all night." Sophia sighed, sagging into a chair. "I should stay open and pay the help to sit around?"

They all ate hot garlic bread and minestrone at the kitchen table. Tony, for once, ate with them. He carried around with him an endearing new air of self-importance. It made Marie keep smothering smiles.

Tony even offered to help with the dishes, and Sophia wanted to take his temperature. "He's sick," she said. "He's not acting normal."

It wasn't until later, sitting on the couch in front of the TV set with Tony and her folks, that Marie had time to think.

Someone knew she was investigating the Saybolt case, and that someone didn't want it investigated. All right. That meant that she was in danger, Tony was in danger and Craig was in danger. It also meant that there *was* a guilty man out there, and she or Craig had flushed him out of hiding.

Alice Klutznic knew Marie had been snooping around. So did Howie Mayer, if he were capable of remembering anything. And Craig had been to see Bones in New Orleans and Petersen here in San Francisco just today. Had one of them discovered Craig's connection to her? Was one of them in touch with the others?

What about the Lund-Klutznic connection? Alice Klutznic had said Tim was out fishing. Maybe he was.

But Lund. He'd been gone on a trip. Was he docked in the States? In San Diego? In San Francisco? He could have called Tim's home. Alice could have told him about Marie's visit. *Had Lund been watching her?*

Dear Lord.

She glanced over at Tony. He thought this was all a game. But he wasn't going to talk her out of sending him to a friend's. It was better to be on the safe side. For all she knew, someone might even be watching their house at that very moment.

Craig. He had to know, too. And he wasn't going to like it one bit.

The reflection of the television screen flared on the walls, bilious green, while the laugh track chattered away meaninglessly. Al was dozing in his chair.

"Excuse me," Marie said. "I've got to make a call."

"To the jailbird," Sophia remarked.

Craig wasn't in his hotel room. God, she wanted to talk to him. Where was he? Maybe she should call Petersen. But that would really mess things up if Craig were on to something. She'd better wait.

By the time she got back to the living room, Al was awake, Sophia was looking very angry, and Tony was just finishing his story about the weird dude who'd called and threatened him. "It's about Mom's investigation, see, like in the movies. If she keeps after him, he's going to kidnap me or something," he said proudly. "Cool."

"Marie, is this true?" her father asked.

"Well, actually..." She shot Tony a look.

"Did a man call here and threaten Tony?"

"Well, not really."

"Sure he did, Mom." Tony lowered his voice: "'Tell her I know where you live and where you play baseball. Tell her to be careful.'"

"Oh, God," Marie breathed.

"Stay away from that captain," Sophia said. "It's all his fault. He's made you crazy in the head."

"Oh, for goodness' sakes, Mama, I'm only doing my job."

"It's just a bluff," Tony put in.

"Drop the case, Marie," Al said. "You were always too ambitious for your own good. Now look what's happened."

"I can't believe you'd say that, Papa. An innocent man was put in jail. Don't you want me to help him?"

"God knows that he's innocent," Al said.

"Well, God helps those who help themselves, or someone else in this case. You taught me that, Papa," she said.

"I also taught you that the family is the most important thing. You protect your family."

"I'm going to take Tony to a friend's. He can stay there for a few days. Joel's. His father's a policeman."

"Aw, Mom, I want to stay here and see the action," Tony said.

"You do what your mother says for once," Sophia said. "They probably put a bomb in the car. And you'll go turn it on and boom! That's the end of my daughter and grandson."

"Don't be ridiculous. Whoever it was was only trying to scare me off. He's not really going to do anything," Marie said.

"That man has you crazy. You'd do anything for him, wouldn't you?" Sophia said.

"You go to your boss tomorrow and tell him you're off the case," Al said. "You hear me, Marie?"

"Hey," Tony said, coming to his feet abruptly. "Can I say something?" He looked truly angry. His bare, bony head glistened in the light from the TV. They were all struck silent. "My Mom's gonna break this case wide open. You gotta quit treating her like a kid."

It was a long moment before Sophia caught her wind. "See?" she said, glaring at Marie, "see what you've done? Every day he's sounding more like you."

And Marie couldn't hold back a smile. "Yes, he is, isn't he?" she said and caught Tony's hand in hers.

CHAPTER TWELVE

WILD MAN FINISHED TELLING his joke, laughed loudly and patted his golden retriever on the head affectionately. Craig eyed him carefully and wondered, why was Jeff Petersen so damn glad to see him? His reaction should have been just the opposite, more like Bones's reaction in New Orleans: shocked, uncertain, angry and finally afraid.

But not Jeff. He was behaving as if they were long-lost buddies.

Jeff sat in his living room and nodded toward the kitchen where his wife, Carolyn, was feeding the baby. "Some girl, huh? I can't believe how lucky I am, Craig."

"Sure. She's very nice, Jeff," Craig replied and sipped on his beer.

"Yeah, and we hit it off right away. Met her at a singles' joint down in the city. Love at first sight." Jeff smiled, remembering. "She's smart as a whip, too. Computer sciences. Of course, Carolyn's busy with the baby now, not working, but she helped me with all that paperwork when I bought the old marina. I never could handle that red tape stuff. Yep, love at first sight."

It must have been, Craig thought, because they'd only been married a year, and the baby was six months old. "So," Craig asked, "you moved here right after the spill?"

"After the trial I did," Jeff said.

"The trial," Craig repeated, holding his gaze.

"Pretty bad." Jeff shook his dark handsome head. It was his good looks and his fly-by-night lifestyle that had earned him the nickname. Women loved Wild Man, fawned over him, practically stood in line to get him into bed. It had been said in Valdez that Petersen was responsible for half the fatherless children in town. Hard to believe he was settled down now, that he owned a house in Pacifica, south of the city, and a small but thriving marina.

Craig glanced around the living room. It was what Polly would have called Swedish modern. The rose carpeting was deep pile, cushiony under Craig's feet. The drapes were heavy, custom-made, the wood blond, the glass-top tables chrome-trimmed, the paintings ultra-modern—Craig couldn't interpret them. The lamps were big, bold, handmade ceramics. There was nothing cheap about the appointments. Tanker crewmen made good wages, for sure, but *this* good? Of course, the bucks could have been Carolyn's, making her all the more attractive to Wild Man. And the marina, maybe a wedding present from Carolyn to her new husband.

"I'll tell you," Jeff was saying, "you sure got crucified at that trial."

Craig fixed his stare on his old crew mate.

"And what are you doing now? Traveling, looking for work? How'd you find me, anyway?"

"I found you because I was looking for you, Jeff."

"Well, I'll be."

"Anyone need another beer?" Carolyn walked in with her son propped on her hip. She *was* a beauty; a tall, buxom blonde with green eyes and spiky dark lashes and legs that even Craig couldn't fail to notice.

"No, thank you," Craig replied.

"I'll have one, babe," Jeff said, "but I can get it."

"I'll get it. I have to stir the stew, anyway. Can you stay for dinner?" she asked Craig.

"No, but thanks. I have plans." He looked at her and felt a twinge of guilt for what he was about to pull on Jeff. If Jeff wasn't involved, it seemed a shame to rattle his cage. Still, Jeff *could* have been the one who'd knocked him out that fateful day. He was a man who'd try anything once. The cozy family setting was fine, but Craig remembered a time when Wild Man, drunk on his butt, had slammed a guy over the head with a barstool just for looking at his date. For the umpteenth time, Craig asked himself why one of his crew had done it. It had to have been that an outsider had offered big bucks. But who? And to what end? It certainly must have had something to do with the oil, he was sure, but what? Ridiculous thoughts stormed his head. Maybe a solar energy company had paid a crew member to wreck the tanker in order to discredit the oil companies. Or maybe nuclear power advocates. How about the oil companies themselves? He'd discussed that possibility with Marie. But what in the name of God could an oil company gain by discrediting itself?

Or had it been radical environmentalists who'd wanted to prove to the world how badly man could wound the environment and thus spur stricter safety legislation?

Craig sometimes wondered if this mad charade wasn't going to drive him insane.

"Boy," Jeff was saying, watching his wife leave the room, "she's a catch, all right." He turned back to Craig. "So, you were saying you came to see me. Long haul just for a visit. Should I be flattered?"

"I don't think so," Craig replied in a meaningful voice. "You see, I figure you owe me, Petersen, and I'm here to collect the debt."

Jeff smiled and shook his head in innocence. "Whoa there, you've lost me. *I* owe *you?*"

"That's right. I spent almost two years in prison for you, old buddy, and now I'm here to give you a chance to pay up."

Jeff came to his feet and scratched his head. He was still smiling. "I'm afraid you've lost me, Craig."

"Oh, I don't think so. We both know exactly what I'm talking about."

"What . . . ?"

"The spill. I've finally got the proof that you did it, Petersen. It took a while, but I've got it."

"You've got *what?*"

"Proof you were behind the wheel when the *Northern Light* hit those rocks."

Jeff whistled softly. "You're crazy. You've been locked up too long, friend. I had nothing to do with that spill. I was eating dinner, if you'll recall."

Craig smiled thinly. "It's hard to recall when I was unconscious the whole time."

"That was *your* story." Jeff walked over to the window, pulled aside the drapes and stared out. "Listen," he said, "I'm real sorry for what you've been through, but I can't help you. You've got it all wrong. I don't know who told you what, but it's wrong."

"Oh, I don't think so," Craig said coolly. "I can see you need some time to think about this. It's obvious you figured you'd gotten away with it. Sorry pal, but it's time to pay the piper. I want five hundred thousand. Consider it cheap compared to the twenty months I put in for you in that rat hole."

Jeff had fallen silent. He kept the look of innocence, of disbelief on his face. He was either totally at a loss and unafraid, or he was a hell of a good actor.

He dropped the curtain. "Craig," he said quietly, presumably so that Carolyn couldn't overhear, "I feel real sorry for you. Prison must have been hell. I wish I *could* help, honestly. But all I can do is suggest you see someone . . . you understand, a doctor, someone you can talk to. A professional."

A corner of Craig's mouth lifted, but the smile never reached his cold blue eyes. "Five hundred thousand," he said, "Or I go to the state attorney general in Alaska with what I have." He stood, put down the empty beer can. "Nice seeing you, Petersen. I'll be in touch. You can count on it."

"Hey, Craig . . ."

"Thanks for the beer. Tell your wife goodbye for me, will you?" He left, satisfied with his performance, positive he'd finally seen a glimmer of uncertainty in Petersen's eyes at the end. Or, maybe, Craig thought as he stepped into the awaiting taxi, he was reading Petersen all wrong.

CRAIG FOLDED A SHIRT and tossed it impatiently into his suitcase. He kept seeing Petersen's face when he'd first shown up at his door. It was as if Jeff hadn't been the least bit surprised to see Craig there, as if he'd expected the confrontation, was all prepared for it, right down to his line about Craig seeing a doctor. And if that were true, someone, one of the crew, had warned Petersen.

It could have been Tim Klutznic, who'd reportedly been out on his fishing boat in Prince William Sound. His wife, Alice, had no doubt told Tim all about Craig and Marie's visits when he'd returned.

Or Lund. A neighbor might have told him that Craig or Marie had been snooping around. Either one of the men could have contacted Petersen.

There was, of course, Howie Mayer, still in detox, but very possibly capable of making a simple telephone call.

But most likely, Craig decided as he sat on the edge of his bed, it was Steve Stratford in New Orleans who'd forewarned Wild Man. It didn't mean, though, that either man—or any of the crew whom Craig had been in touch with—was the guilty party. Shipmates were close, kept in touch over the years, and Craig showing up the way he had would have been news. Especially showing up and demanding hush money.

Damn. He wondered if he were accomplishing anything at all or merely wasting his time—free time he'd dreamed about for over twenty long months.

And then, of course, there was Marie. Little Marie Vicenza. If Craig was right in his belief that one of his former crew was guilty, then Marie might be in danger, too.

He rose, paced his room and threw his shaving kit in on top of his shirts. Hell. It wasn't *his* fault Marie might be in danger. She'd put herself square in the middle of this mess. She'd sat in his cabin and insisted she could handle it. It wasn't his doing at all.

He wondered then about the dinner last night at her folks'. That hour had possibly been the worst of his entire life. He'd made the decision on the flight in from New Orleans to get her out of harm's way no matter the cost to either of them. But, my God, it had been hard. He'd hurt her, hurt himself. Yet he'd had to do it. There simply was no other way of getting her off his back and off this case.

What a front she'd put up. Her face had been wiped clean of any emotion. She'd managed that too-big smile and even laughed and come up with that lame tale of how she'd been using him, too.

Sure, Craig knew that at first she *had* used him for her own selfish reasons. But somewhere along the line, when he hadn't been looking, she'd become emotionally involved. Worse, he'd taken advantage of that and made love to her when he'd known all along that there never could be a relationship between them.

He wondered, though, allowing himself a weak moment, just what Marie really did see in him. He knew he was a tough old sea dog, a loner. He'd neglected his own kids because he hadn't a clue how to handle children. He was hard on everyone around him, harder on himself. How she'd found a single redeeming factor in him was beyond comprehension.

He stood at the window and gazed past the wharf and myriad waterfront shops and fine seafood restaurants to the dusk-shrouded bay beyond. The Golden Gate Bridge lifted from the water, its huge steel girders arcing into the evening sun. And there was Alcatraz Island, all but deserted now. He felt his nerves scrape against his skin. Prison. Some of the men had done okay locked up in that isolated Alaskan hole, but not him. He'd been too used to the sea spray, to the wild raw cold, to the solitude. He'd always needed the wind in his face. He'd needed to be in command, to make his own decisions, to be free. Prison had damn near beaten him. He supposed now that the only thing that had kept him going was the anticipation of sweet revenge.

Was that why he couldn't deal with Marie? Was he too preoccupied with getting even, just using the fact of possible danger to her as an excuse? Was that why he hadn't called his kids? Revenge could eat at a man, consume his soul. It could destroy him, as prison hadn't.

He'd promised to call Marie. Well, she'd backed him into a corner and forced him to promise.

The truth was, he really didn't want to call her. He'd have to be polite and answer her questions, and she was full of questions. Like a kid.

"What did Petersen say?" she'd ask. "How did he look? Did you believe him?"

He couldn't face her, nagging, wheedling, begging. She was so damn *committed,* throwing herself into the case one hundred percent, putting herself on the line.

For him.

He should call Marie. She'd worry. That was funny. Nobody in the world was worried about Craig Saybolt, not one person, except for this nobody little insurance investigator.

Was that why he'd slept with her?

He wouldn't phone. Why open barely healed wounds?

So, one more night here in civilization. He'd take that early flight tomorrow morning, check in with his parole officer in Anchorage and get back to Valdez. He'd see Klutznic and Lund in person. Maybe one of them—guilty or not—could give him some leads on the two missing guys, Bogner and Marshall, or maybe one of them even knew how to reach Claud Savant in South Africa.

Maybe one of them knew something about the deaths of Woody and that fine kid Joey. Someone knew something—one of the remaining eight men. And one of those men had cold-cocked him and steered his tanker onto the rocks. Of that he was certain. He just wished he could be more certain who that someone was.

Craig stalked around the small room, smelling the irritating odor of too-strong cleaning agents and room deodorizers. God, he wished he were home. Clean air and the sea and wood smoke. Well, he'd be home soon.

THE NORTHERN LIGHT 211

He wondered if, indeed, someone was going to come after him to try to silence him. It would be ironic if one of the men actually came up with half a million dollars to shut Craig up. Either way, he'd have his man. He only wished Marie hadn't caught that flight to Valdez and poked her nose into his affairs.

Why in God's name he hadn't walked away from her that first day, the day he'd tasted freedom, he'd never know. He should have kept going, hitched a ride later, shut her out from the first moment. But she'd hit him up with that line, "I have proof you're innocent," and he'd fallen for it, hook, line and sinker. What nerve she had. He shook his head, remembering. Little Marie.

Could she be in danger? He couldn't imagine, couldn't bear the thought of anything happening to her.

He rubbed his jaw, sat on the bed. No, he didn't like it, not one bit. He wasn't even sure he could cover his own back much less hers, here in San Francisco. It struck him then that Marie should probably stay at a friend's or take a vacation—whatever—until this was over. He'd call her from the airport, tell her that, insist on it. If she gave him any trouble he could always contact her boss to see if *he* couldn't talk sense into her.

And speaking of her boss... Craig recalled Marie complaining about the man, something about the guy expecting her to put out for him if he let her work on Craig's case. What a jerk. Not that Craig doubted Marie's ability to handle the situation, but the whole thing galled him. She shouldn't have to put up with it. Under different circumstances, Craig would have liked to march into that office and confront the man. But he was hardly in the position to do that. Besides, Marie's relationships were not his affair.

He got up from the bed and paced his room. Maybe he should go out and get something to eat. Some great food in Chinatown. Sure, why not? He remembered a place he and Polly had once gone to when they were young and poor and she'd come down from Seattle to meet him. It was a tiny, crowded two-story restaurant with a dumb-waiter to haul food up from the kitchen. The waiters yelled in Chinese. You pointed at characters on the menu, and it had cost three dollars a meal.

He had to get out of this room.

He grabbed his leather jacket and his room key. The elevator was busy, so he walked downstairs. The stair-well smelled faintly of urine.

He waved down a taxi at the corner. Something kept nagging at him, like a name he couldn't remember. Oh, yeah, he should have called Marie. But he'd already de-cided what to do about that. He'd phone her from the airport tomorrow morning.

"Chinatown," he said to the cabdriver.

The man shifted a wad of gum from one side of his mouth to the other. "Anywhere special? Chinatown's a big place."

"You know a restaurant that has a dumbwaiter, two stories, nobody speaks English?" Craig inquired.

The man turned and stared at him. "What street?"

"I can't remember," Craig said. "Right in the middle of Chinatown."

"Good luck, buddy. I'll drop you off on Grant Street. Ask somebody there."

The taxi pulled up a long hill and stopped at the traffic signal at the top. Craig stared out the window at all the quaint Victorians with their tidy bay windows and painted gingerbread trim and thought about his own place—isolated and crude, but warm and welcoming.

He'd be glad to be out of the city. He'd be glad to get all this behind him, to be reinstated as a captain, to feel the sea rolling beneath his feet once more and to return to his cabin on the edge of the Alaskan wilderness. Maybe his kids could fly up from Seattle from time to time and pay visits. He and Tanya and Sonny could get to know one another again, put the past to rest. There was room in the cabin, and at times it did seem kind of empty.

It hadn't seemed empty when Marie had been there.

Disturbing images flashed through his head: Marie at his stove, Marie sweeping the floor, the line of her panties showing, Marie stretched out beneath him, naked, her lovely soft skin covered in a fine sheen of perspiration, her warm breasts against his chest, her silky smooth legs entwined with his, her back arching, the white column of her neck straining, her cries, his own, and the aftermath, the touching, the quiet intimacy, the soft squeak she made once in her sleep.

What if something *did* happen to her? The possibility was remote, but it was there nonetheless. He'd call her. He owed her that and a whole lot more. He'd call her as soon as he got to the airport . . . in the morning.

Craig leaned forward. "Turn around," he said suddenly to the cabbie.

"Wha'd you say?"

"Turn around and drop me on Dolores Street."

"But that's miles . . ."

"You're getting paid. Just do it."

"Sure, why not?" The cabbie shook his head and muttered something about what kooks people had become since the earthquake.

The Mission District of San Francisco had a personality all its own. It was now essentially Hispanic, but there was also a close-knit community of Italians, like the

Vicenzas, Marie's people. Craig had the driver let him off at Mission Park, where he gazed around, getting his bearings. Over there, around the corner, he believed was the Vicenza's restaurant, so Marie's house must be two blocks away on the far side of the park.

It was dark out. He began to head into the park but hesitated. There were dozens of kids milling around, lounging on benches, roller-skating, smoking home-rolled cigarettes that he doubted contained tobacco. Most of the kids were teens. Some looked older—high school dropouts, he guessed—and most wore leather jackets and either had shaved heads or sported multicolored Mohawks. He took another glance into the dark heart of the park, heard a siren wailing nearby and decided to walk around the perimeter rather than cross it diagonally. He was in good shape for forty-five, but not good enough to take on Saturday night specials and switchblades.

He walked, alert, and wondered about Marie. She'd been born and raised here, had probably played in this park. She was streetwise, or at least she claimed to be. Still, he hated to think of her walking home from a night's work in her folks' place and having to face this. Despite her toughness, she was still a woman and a damned attractive one at that.

It irked Craig, as he checked a street sign, that he felt this protective thing for Marie. The only other female in his life that had touched him so profoundly had been Polly. He'd thought—he'd believed from the depths of his being—that it would never happen to him again. He hadn't felt love for Marie, he thought, not at first. He'd liked her, enjoyed the sense of comradeship with another human being. How funny he'd feel like that with a woman, a young woman. Damnedest thing.

Banks of fog so typical of the changeable San Francisco weather had begun to roll in off the bay and creep along the low-lying streets and alleyways. Streetlights glowed in halos of muted brightness, and wisps of mist curled around Craig's legs as he headed down Marie's street, checking the numbers on the houses. He'd just stop in to tell her she needed to stay at a friend's for a bit, maybe take a vacation until all this was over. Then he'd feel much better about her safety.

He was glad he'd told the cabdriver to drop him off here instead of in Chinatown. Marie would listen to him; she'd know he was right. It was foolish to take needless risks. And it was better to tell her so in person. He'd treated her shabbily.

He pulled up the collar of his leather jacket against the unexpected dampness and headed up the little sidewalk in front of her house. Like every other house on the block, it was built of brick. But then, after the turn-of-the-century earthquake and subsequent fire, the inhabitants of San Francisco had rebuilt the old wooden structures in either brick or stone.

It wasn't much to look at. A few flowers grew in a window box outside, but they were scraggly, uncared for. There was a small lawn on either side of the walk; the grass grew in sad patches. Strangely there was a bicycle chained to the porch, a kid's bike—a niece or nephew of Marie? He was almost sure she'd told him she was an only child, but maybe he'd misunderstood. Maybe she had a younger brother or sister.

As he walked up the two stone steps to the porch, light spilled out from the living room and fell in a patch on an old, broken swing. Somehow, the sight depressed Craig. It was so typical of a poor neighborhood that had seen its heyday before the Great Depression.

He took a breath, mentally preparing what he was going to say to her, and rang the bell that had been painted once but was now chipped. Marie's home, he was thinking. She'd been born and raised here, was maybe—probably—destined to spend the rest of her days here, stuck forever on the edge of poverty. She deserved a whole lot more, a hell of a lot more.

Craig had not finished the thought when the door swung open abruptly, and he was faced with a kid, thirteen, maybe fourteen years old. His head was shaved just like the boys Craig had seen a few minutes ago hanging out in the park.

"Yeah?" the youth asked, as if Craig were soliciting.

He cleared his throat. "Is, ah, your…ah…sister, that is, Marie in?" he asked.

CHAPTER THIRTEEN

MARIE WAS STUFFING clothes into Tony's duffel bag when he called upstairs. "Mom!"

She lifted her head. What now?

"Mom! Some guy's here to see you!"

It didn't sink in right away. And then, when she realized it could only be one very special guy, a quick spurt of adrenaline jolted through her heart. "I'm coming," she breathed. Then, louder, "I'm coming."

Craig. It *had* to be Craig. Oh my Lord. She flashed a frenzied look into Tony's mirror, combed her fingers through her hair and pulled her sweater straight. He was here, downstairs. He hadn't phoned. He'd come in person.

She took a deep breath and set her shoulders. Okay, so he was here. She'd be stupid to read too much into it. Her heart danced with gladness then sagged with dismay. How was she supposed to feel?

It struck her then, like a bolt of lightning sizzling through her body: Tony. If it really were Craig down there waiting for her, then he'd just met her son. "Mom," Tony had yelled up the steps to her. Mom.

Oh dear sweet Lord above. Automatically Marie crossed herself. She'd really done it now. Oh boy, oh boy.

With as much dignity as she could muster, she headed toward the steps. *Oh Lord, oh Lord, give me strength.* Her knees felt watery, and she had to force herself to move down each step. She held on to the rail for dear life. It was as if all those years of Tony's existence, of the circumstances of his birth, had come crashing down on her, and she felt, abruptly, fiercely protective of her son. If Craig said one word, made one derogatory remark to her, no matter how small...!

Then there he was. In her home. In her vestibule. Standing there by the front door. Big, strong, filling the space with that arrogant power of his. And Tony. He was lounging casually against the wall. He had an insolent look on his face, as if he were already instinctively on the defensive. She found her voice when she reached the bottom step. "Why, Craig. What a surprise."

"Hello, Marie," he said.

"I thought you'd call." But she never gave him a chance to answer. "Tony," she said admonishingly, "you should have asked our guest to come in and sit down." And she launched into inanities. "Oh, Tony, have you even introduced yourself? This is Mr. Saybolt. Craig, this is...Tony."

Utter silence pulsed in the small entranceway.

"Well," she began, letting out a breath, "let's go into the—"

But Tony straightened and half barred Craig's path. "Aren't you the dude who was in prison?" he asked.

Marie spun around on her heel. "Tony!" She was frozen, faint with embarrassment.

But Craig needed no help from her. "When you address me, son, it's either Mr. Saybolt or sir. You got that?"

She drew in a sharp breath and looked from one to the other. Tony was going to open his mouth again for sure. He wasn't used to anyone speaking to him like that. He'd probably come out with some smart-ass, foul remark, and she'd die. Poised right there in the vestibule she'd shrivel up and die.

The words hung in the air for too long. The two of them stood face-to-face, neither backing down. Marie held her breath.

"Okay, *sir*. Are you the man who was in prison?" Tony finally asked.

"Yes, I was in prison," Craig answered.

"But you weren't guilty," Tony said. He was eyeing Craig warily.

"No, I wasn't."

For an unsettling moment, Tony seemed to be weighing Craig's statement, deciding. He had never been a child to give his trust easily, and Marie usually had faith in his judgment. She stood there wanting to intervene somehow, but she knew that this confrontation was out of her control. They were like two dogs sniffing each other, circling, assessing. Finally, as if the bristling hairs on Tony's back relaxed, his demeanor altered. Marie sensed that he believed Craig, that in the space of a few short minutes her son was ready to accept this authoritative stranger. She crossed her fingers, awaiting Tony's next move.

"Tell me something," her son began a moment later, "what was it like in prison? I mean," he looked Craig squarely in the eye, "was it, you know, cool? Were there a bunch of righteous dudes in there?"

Craig eyed Tony hard, and Marie marveled at her son's choice of words. She wasn't sure whether to laugh or cry.

But Craig handled it. "No, it wasn't cool. And the dudes were sad criminals, not good enough to make it on the outside like real people."

"Oh." He sounded disappointed.

"Uh, Craig, come into the living room," Marie said, intervening. "Would you like some coffee?"

"Am I disturbing you?" he asked, taking his eyes from Tony. "It's kind of late."

"Oh, no, not at all. My folks have gone to bed, and Tony and I were just getting ready to... Well, I was going to take him to a friend's house."

"I'd like some coffee," he said, "if you're making some."

"Please, come on in. Sit down. Would you prefer a drink?" She bustled ahead, nervous, straightening a doily here, a pile of magazines there, praying the two of them weren't going to start in again.

"No, coffee's fine. Thanks."

Gratefully she disappeared into the kitchen. What a crazy situation. On the one hand, Tony seemed to know instinctively that this man could pose a threat to him, even though Marie was certain her son couldn't possibly suspect what had really happened between her and Craig.

She heard him ask Craig a question—something about being locked up in a prison cell—and while she grimaced, Craig replied, an honest reply, his voice careful and level.

She wondered over and over what Craig was thinking. He knew now that Tony was her son. He must be sitting in there remembering how she'd told him she'd never been married. Oh God. And she wondered why he didn't just stand up and march out of her house. Inside she was cowering, ashamed of her lies, humiliated.

Her fingers were clumsy. She spilled coffee grounds on the counter. Black. He liked his coffee black. She waited for it to brew. Should she go in and talk to him while the water boiled? She couldn't. She needed to compose herself. She kept hearing the high piping of Tony's voice, then the low rumble of Craig's. What on earth were they talking about now?

Eventually she carried the two cups of coffee into the living room, setting one down on the table next to Craig. She sat on the blue overstuffed chair across from him, her knees together like a schoolgirl's, holding her coffee cup in her lap.

She smiled, but no one looked at her.

"So, how do you steer those big things?" Tony was asking.

"There's a rudder and a tiller and a wheel. But it takes a long time to turn. There's a helmsman who helps control the steering, too."

"How big is a tanker?"

"Some run a thousand feet long. Mine was only seven hundred. A small one."

"That's like, wow, longer than a football field," Tony said. "How fast do they go?"

"The *Northern Light* did twenty-three knots, tops."

"That's like twenty-three miles per hour?"

"Close."

The leaded glass lamp shone in spots of color on Tony's shaved head. Her son. Just what did Craig think about him? And what was Craig thinking about her? She was actually grateful to Tony for all his boyish questions. They must be keeping Craig from thinking too much at all.

"How come," Tony was asking, "all that oil spilled out so easy? I mean, like, did the ship crack open or something?"

"Well, oil tankers are really just hollow shells of reinforced steel. Big empty tanks. When they hit something, like rocks, even though they're going slow, they're so heavy with the oil inside, it ruptures the shell."

"If you didn't make that accident happen, then who did, man . . . sir?"

"*Tony.*"

"Gee, Mom, I only asked."

"You're giving our guest the third degree. That's rude. Where are your manners?"

Tony sulked. "Sorry." But he kept right on asking questions, regardless. He was hearing about a world as alien to him as another planet, a world that must have sounded fascinating to a thirteen-year-old boy who'd been stuck in a city his whole life. But the time came to cut it off. The time came when Marie knew she had to face Craig alone. She wondered what he'd say, what he'd ask her about her son. Maybe he'd say nothing at all.

She cleared her throat. "Tony," she said, hoping her voice was even and calm, "I want you to go on upstairs and finish packing. Craig . . . Mr. Saybolt and I have things to discuss."

"Mom . . ."

"Now, Tony." She held her breath and prayed.

"Gee."

"Go on. And don't forget your sleeping bag." She watched as her son rose and slouched out of the room, and her heart felt as if it were going to burst in her chest. She didn't know if she could face Craig alone. What was he going to say? Why hadn't she told him? *Coward,* she thought, and finally, inevitably, she turned back around to face him. She felt, crazily, as if she were on trial for her life.

Craig fixed her with a merciless glare. She knew it must be the same one he gave his crew when they did something wrong. Her coffee cup rattled on its saucer.

"That is your son?" he asked.

Slowly she nodded, her lips pressed together. Her foot jiggled.

"You lied to me. You told me you were single," Craig said after an endless moment.

"I am," she whispered. "I always have been."

It took Craig a minute to digest the revelation. She watched him, her heart pounding heavily in her chest. She should have told him. The moments of silence passed, stretched out like beads of water clinging precariously to a thin thread. Her nerve endings shrieked. Then finally his expression altered. He was figuring it all out.

She held her chin up despite the cringing in her belly. He was disgusted, she knew, absolutely disgusted. This proud, honorable man was repulsed by her. It was a long moment before she realized he was speaking, that his voice was soft and careful.

She fought back tears. "What?" she asked, a whisper of anguish.

"I said, I bet that was no picnic."

She looked at her hands that were clutching the coffee cup in her lap. Her vision was blurred. She raised her shoulders and let them drop.

"I thought he was your kid brother," Craig said quietly, a little uncertain.

"Ha," she said.

"I can't believe you have such a big boy. You're too young."

"I am *not* too young. I told you that before, but you wouldn't believe me. When are you going to stop thinking of me as a kid?" she asked.

"Right about now, I guess." He sipped his coffee. It must have been cold, but he didn't seem to notice. "I'll be damned," he said thoughtfully.

She wanted to confide in him. She wanted to tell him what it felt like to be eighteen and Catholic and unmarried and pregnant. The scorn, the loneliness, the panic, the awful fear that life was over. She'd like to dump it all on his shoulders. She'd like to dump on someone, for once in her life, who'd gone through hell, too. Someone who'd understand. But Craig wasn't interested in her. He didn't deserve her confidences.

He sat there staring at her, bemused, struggling with his new knowledge. Marie, the mother, not Marie the unattached swinging single. He was looking at her differently, but she was exactly the same person she had always been.

She wondered then, fleetingly, if Craig had known about Tony, about her past, would he have been so tender and loving that night in Alaska? She guessed it didn't matter, though, because one way or the other he'd admitted that he'd been using her. What good was it going to do her to mull over the past? She had Tony and herself to think about. Their future. And sitting before her now was the ticket to success. She wasn't going to let it go, either.

She looked up and met his appraising glance. With false bravado she asked, "Did you see Wild Man?"

He nodded slowly.

"Well?"

Craig shrugged. "He was cool. Nothing bothered him. He said he didn't know what I was talking about."

"Oh." She frowned. "So what does that mean?"

"Either he's lying or he's telling the truth."

"Wonderful."

"He showed me his new baby. Introduced me to his wife. He has a nice place. Fine, upstanding citizen."

"Do you think he's lying?" Marie asked, all business now, her tone so cool and impersonal he did not recognize it.

Craig took a long time to answer. "I'm not sure. Something doesn't ring quite true. He acted like he was prepared. You know what I mean?"

"Maybe he's the one."

"Maybe. But I have no proof, nothing to go on."

"What are you going to do now?" she asked.

"Go home. Wait for Lund and Klutznic to get back. Dig around."

Silence fell like a dark curtain between them. Marie could hear Tony thumping around upstairs. Wishing it didn't matter to her, she nevertheless wondered what Craig thought of her son and his shaved head. She'd bet *his* son had never shaved his head, or let his hair grow too long, either. Craig would be a tough father—tough but fair.

"Well," he said.

"Well," Marie said at the same time.

"I'd better be going."

She stared at the brown liquid in her cup. "Why didn't you call me? You said you would. I waited all day."

"I was busy."

"All day? Oh, really?"

He didn't answer.

"I worried about you. About the case, that is. What if Petersen had panicked and pulled something? Gone after you, for instance. Followed you?"

"What could you have done about it, Marie?"

"I don't know. Something. You should have called."

"Sorry."

She eyed him, wanting to bite back her words but unable to stop herself. "Why did you come here? Why did you bother? You could have let me lie awake another night worrying.''

"I wanted to check on you."

"Why?"

"I don't know. Just a feeling I had. You know I didn't want you to get involved in this."

"What do you care?"

"Oh, for God's sake, Marie."

"Sorry." She smiled falsely.

"Marie . . ."

She held a hand up. "No, never mind. You don't owe me a thing. You lent me money to get home. I got your parole officer to let you leave the state. You're right. We're even. You're a big boy, you can do what you want to do."

"Marie . . ."

She stood. "I have to take Tony over to Joel's house now. We better go."

"Isn't it awfully late?"

"Yes, it's late. But I want Tony out of here. He had a threatening phone call earlier," she said, thinking aloud.

"What?"

"Somebody, some man, phoned and told Tony he knew where we lived and where Tony played baseball and I'd better be careful."

Craig bolted from his chair. He looked so furious Marie drew back from him. *"What?"* he asked.

"A man phoned—"

Craig cut the air with his hand. "Who was it?"

"Tony didn't recognize the voice."

"Long distance or local?"

"I don't know for sure. Tony thought it was long distance."

"What did the man say? Tell me again."

She repeated the warning. Craig stared at her with frightening intensity. She'd have almost thought he truly cared. Then he swore and pounded a fist into his hand.

She tried to make him see reason. "Just think, you got to somebody. Your plan worked."

He swore again.

"Now you'll be able to prove your innocence. Aren't you satisfied?"

"I just wonder if the price won't be too high," he said tightly.

"The price?" she repeated. "It was just a bluff, Craig. Surely you don't really think—?"

"Don't I?" he demanded. "And I notice you've got your boy upstairs packing."

"Well . . ."

"Don't tell me you aren't worried."

Marie sighed. "Okay, so I'm taking precautions."

"I can't believe I let you get into this mess. I knew better."

She almost felt sorry for him. "You couldn't have stopped me," she began, but the menacing scowl on his face silenced her.

It was decided—by Craig—that he was going to ride along to Joel's house with them.

"I knew it," he muttered more than once as she drove, "I knew I should have sent you packing. Damn it."

Tony, on the other hand, was enjoying himself thoroughly. He sat in the back seat on the way over to his buddy's house and looked terribly self-important.

"How far to this kid's house?" Craig asked, and he turned and glanced out the back window.

"A couple more blocks," Marie said.

Craig pinned her with a hard glance. "Make a few random turns," he said.

"What?"

"*Turn* down a street."

"Oh, wow, cool, dude. Mom, he wants to shake the tail!" Tony said from the back seat.

"This is ridiculous. Do you really think someone is following me?" Marie said, struggling with the steering wheel; it kept pulling to the right.

"Someone knows who you are, where you live. He knows about Tony and probably a lot more, too. Obviously someone has followed you."

"I'll watch our backs," Tony said, twisting around. "Don't worry. I can spot a tail."

She turned a few times, right and left and left again. Then she got stuck on a one-way street for a few blocks until she could get back to Joel's house.

"Nobody's behind us," Tony said. "There was somebody, but he turned off."

"Oh, for heaven's sake, it was probably somebody going home," Marie said, exasperated.

"Maybe," Craig muttered.

"It's taken fifteen minutes to drive six blocks," she said under her breath.

"That's okay, Mom. It's cool. Wait till I tell Joel."

Marie shook her head. Kids. "Look, Tony, you be careful. Don't come home. Call me at work, okay? Don't even go to the restaurant. Promise? This is serious. I want your promise, kiddo."

"Maybe I'll put on a disguise and come back. Would that be okay?"

"No," Marie said.

And Craig: "You pull a stunt like that, son, and you'll answer to me."

"Stay at Joel's," Marie said firmly, "no matter what."

"Are you going back to Alaska, Mr. Saybolt?" Tony asked suddenly.

"Yes, soon," he replied distractedly.

"Are you going to be a captain again?"

"I hope so."

"Boy, I sure wish I could go on one of them tankers."

"One of *those* tankers," Marie corrected him automatically. The car lurched as she braked too quickly at an intersection.

Craig sighed, ran a hand through his hair and turned to the back seat. "Tell you what, Tony. When I get my captain's papers back and have a new command, I'll show you around my tanker. How's that?" Craig smiled. "Sometimes we sail right into San Francisco harbor."

"Righteous, dude. I'll go for that!"

Sure, Marie thought. That'd be the day.

They dropped Tony at Joel's house. He shook Craig's hand in a gentlemanly fashion and reminded him of his promise.

"I'll call in the morning, Tony." Marie said. "And be good. Say thank you to Joel's mother."

"Sure, Mom. See you."

"Give me a kiss," Marie said, afraid suddenly, feeling as if she were losing her only child.

"Aw, Mom."

"Come here."

He leaned down toward the open car window reluctantly. "Geez, Mom."

She kissed his cheek. "Be careful, Anthony. Be polite. Now scoot on in there."

"Okay, okay."

She sat there, hands on the steering wheel, watching him heft his duffel bag and run up the steps. She had a sinking feeling, as if she'd never see him again. Crazy.

"He'll be fine," Craig said.

"But will I be fine?" she muttered, jamming the gear-shift into first.

Marie drove down the quiet street in silence. She assumed she was going to drop Craig at his hotel, but he'd never actually said as much, so she merely headed that way. All the while he sat there next to her, frowning, deep in thought. She wondered just what he was going to do when she told him about the conversation she'd had with her boss, about her going back to Alaska. Well, he wasn't going to shut her out now. Uh-uh. Not when she was this close.

She turned onto another street, watching in her rear-view mirror, feeling ridiculous and fearful at the same time. Craig had really managed to spook her. She wouldn't show it, though, not to him.

"I thought I better tell you something," she began, glad she needed to keep her eyes on the road.

"Tell me what?"

"I'm going back to Alaska." Then she braced herself for his reaction.

It came. "Damn it, Marie, aren't you in this deep enough? Are you crazy? You want to go back into the thick of it? Look what's happened already!"

"I'm going on my boss's orders. You have no authority over me."

"Look, Marie..." Craig took a deep breath, obviously trying to control himself. I'll take care of everything up there. You don't need to come."

"I have a ticket. All the way to Valdez this time. I'll be there."

"A pit bull," he muttered to himself.

"I'm just doing my job."

"Let's talk about this. Let's be reasonable," Craig said.

"I want my bonus," she said stubbornly.

"Your bonus."

"You bet. Every last penny of it. As it stands right now, you might get all the credit."

She was aware of his impatient movement.

"You can't stop me," she said, undaunted, "so why bother?"

"What about Tony?" Craig asked.

"Tony's safe now. Joel's dad is a cop. I called and gave them the score."

"What about you, then?"

"I'll take care of myself. I always have." She turned left, glanced in the mirror again. "You're forgetting—I'm no safer here than in Alaska. They already know where I live. It's too late."

She knew Craig was glaring at her. Inadvertently her hands tightened on the wheel. "You see? I may as well be in Alaska, helping." She stopped at a red light and glanced furtively at the car to her left. "The way I figure it, I'm actually better off in Alaska with you than here in San Francisco alone."

"With me."

"That's right."

He didn't say a word the whole time the light was red. He only stared at her. Marie looked straight ahead, tapping her fingers on the steering wheel. She wouldn't give in. Never. She wondered what thoughts were running through his mind, what awful thoughts about her. She told herself she didn't care. She stared at the red brake lights ahead of her until her eyes blurred, feeling his glance crawl over her like thousands of tiny feet. What was he thinking? Did he hate her? But when he finally spoke it wasn't at all what she'd expected.

"Marie," he said, "why did you lie to me?"

"Lie?"

"About your son. About Tony."

"I didn't lie."

"Okay, why didn't you tell me about him?"

"I don't know." Off guard, she revved the engine too much and the car jerked. "Would it have made any difference?"

He was quiet for a minute. "I'm not sure."

"I guess I thought it was none of your business. But I should have told you. I thought about it."

He leaned back, a big man, his presence solid and reassuring and intimidating all at the same time. "I wish you had told me," he said.

"Why? What's the difference?"

"Because your kid's a part of you. For a person to know what you are, he has to know about your kid."

"You really don't want to know me, Craig," she said uneasily, driving on.

He studied her and seemed to come to a decision. "Can you leave tomorrow?" he asked.

"Tomorrow?"

"I'm on a flight tomorrow morning at nine. Can you make it?"

She thought rapidly. "Yes, I can make it." Headlights came at her, hot and white and glaring.

"I'll book a seat for you." He smiled, a thin stretching of his lips. "You win, Marie. This time."

"I'm not your adversary, Craig. Save yourself for him—or them—whoever it is."

"I'll pick you up at your house at seven-thirty."

She nodded, carefully contained, like a vessel of water filled too full, near to overflowing.

"You're going to stick to me like glue from now on. A few days, that's all. I just don't want you wandering around alone. When you drive home tonight make some turns, down alleyways, if you can. Just in case you're being followed."

She nodded again. She didn't dare let herself feel anything—not joy, not fear, not triumph. He'd given in. She was going with him. That was all that mattered.

"Lock up tight at home. If you see anything strange, hear anything, call the police. Then call me, right away. Got it?"

She nodded once more. Her heart sang, and then she wondered how she would be able to bear being close to him, close but so very distant. Well, she'd tackle that when it came. For now she'd wallow in victory. Oh yes.

She pulled up in front of his hotel and just sat there, waiting. She was aware of him getting out, the crunch of the bent door closing. The car rocked a little.

He came around to her side, and she rolled her window down. He leaned over to say something. It was cool out—cool and dark and full of the scent of the sea.

"Drive carefully," he said.

"I'll try," she said, drinking in his face.

"Watch your rearview mirror. Lock up when you get home."

"You said that already."

"I'll see you in the morning."

"I'll be ready."

The drive home was exhilarating. Marie pushed the old Dodge until it whined. The streets were empty. She felt young and alive and oh, so clever. She careened around corners, gunned up hills, drove around in crazy circles.

He cares about me, she thought. *He's worried. He cares. That's really why he gave in.*

Then, nervously, remembering, she looked behind her. There was nobody. No car, no lights—nothing. Silly. No one was following her. And she thought, *He doesn't care. He'd do the same for anyone.*

But she'd be with him. Close to him. Would they stay in the cabin together? Would he be cold and hard, her captain? Did he hate her or love her?

She pulled up in front of the house, doused the lights and turned the car off. Her breath came in short bursts. She gathered her bag and stepped out. A half moon hung above her, smudged by dark clouds that drifted across its face. It was then that she saw the car parked across the street. Its lights were off, but she could clearly see that there was a man sitting in the driver's seat. She had to blink, shaking herself mentally. She stared through the night, uncertain. But the man in the car watched her, following her every move as she climbed the porch steps, unlocked the door and stepped quickly inside.

CHAPTER FOURTEEN

"THERE WAS A MAN watching your house?" Craig repeated, fixing her with a quick glance as the plane banked and lifted through the haze of morning.

"Well, yes, at least I was pretty certain he was."

"He was sitting in his car, the lights off, across from your house? Is that right?" Craig demanded.

"That's about it," she replied, shrugging. "I'm sure it's just scare tactics. I attended a seminar once on this sort of thing."

"Goddamn it, Marie," Craig whispered harshly, "this isn't a game. Will you please grow up and realize what we're dealing with here? Whoever ran that tanker on the rocks has a lot to lose. *A lot.* I told you before, it was nothing short of a miracle that no one was injured or killed in that accident."

He was right, of course, Marie knew, but getting herself all riled up about it wasn't going to accomplish a thing. Tony was living under a roof with a policeman—he couldn't be safer anywhere else on earth—and she was here with Craig, obviously closing in on the guilty party.

"Listen," she said, "the fact that I was being watched tells us that we're closer. Someone is awfully nervous."

"Yeah, me," he muttered, running a hand through his hair. "I can't believe I let you get this involved. I was out of my mind."

"Craig . . ."

"Don't *Craig* me," he said. "I suppose you didn't even pick up the phone last night and try to call me or the police."

Marie flashed him a look. "By the time I picked up the phone, the car wasn't there. It would have been pointless to worry you."

"Pointless."

"Yes. And at the time, I thought of getting a license plate number, but frankly, Craig, I wasn't about to go outside."

"Amazing," he muttered, "you're finally aware that the danger is real, huh?"

"Real or imagined," she said, half to herself. "For all I know, the guy might have been waiting to pick up a date. Paranoia on my part, you know."

"Sure."

She smiled and touched his arm, then reached under the seat and pulled out her briefcase. "Let's look through the trial transcripts again," she suggested. "I know we've missed something."

"You look," he said, impatient, worried, "I'm going to try and figure out where you can go to be safely out of this."

"Well, I'm certainly not going to hide. Haven't you figured out yet that you aren't responsible for me?" Craig didn't answer, and Marie buried herself in the transcripts.

It was all so familiar. Marie had practically memorized whole passages about several of Craig's crew. And every time she reviewed the material she kept coming to the same conclusion: something was missing, something was terribly wrong, it had all been too pat.

"They were eating dinner," she said to herself, tapping a pencil against her teeth, chewing on the eraser.

"But one of them must have left the room. One of them had to have slipped out and gone up to the bridge. How long did it take to run the tanker onto the rocks, anyway?"

"A few minutes," he replied distractedly.

"One of the men must have left the mess and said he was going to the restroom."

"The head."

"Fine, the head. So why didn't anyone notice?"

"You don't notice that sort of thing."

"But someone should have recalled it," Marie said.

"Not necessarily. The accident was a traumatic event. I'm surprised at how much we all did remember."

"Um." She flipped pages. "Tell me more about Bones in New Orleans."

"I've told you everything."

"Only his reaction to your story. What did you talk about before you told him you knew he was the one. Was he composed?"

"Composed?"

"Yes. Was your showing up all of a sudden unsettling to him?"

"God, Marie," Craig replied, "what do you want from me? A psych evaluation of every one of the crew?"

"No. I want impressions. I wish I'd been there with you," she reflected. She flipped a page. "Bones seemed awfully cool during his testimony at the trial," she said. "But it's so hard to tell when I read through it."

"Generally," Craig said, "he's real easygoing."

"Okay then, how was he in New Orleans?"

"Rattled."

"Rattled. Good. Was he upset *before* you told him you wanted money to keep silent?"

"He was surprised....more like shocked, I suppose, when he first saw me at his door."

"Was his lady friend there?"

"Yes. But he made her go to work early."

"Interesting. Obviously he didn't want her to over-hear something."

"You're grabbing at straws, Marie."

"Maybe." She turned another page, and the one be-hind it slipped onto the floor. They both reached down for it simultaneously, and their hands touched. Marie felt a little shock of electricity run up her arm. The spot where they'd made contact felt hot.

She settled herself back in her seat and furrowed her brow. She was trying so hard to concentrate, but it was impossible to remain impervious to Craig's nearness, to the way their thighs were pressed together in the close quarters, to his elbow constantly touching her arm, the muscle working in his tight jaw, his scent. She'd tried so hard to convince herself that it had been for the best when he'd confessed that night at the restaurant, that she'd been as foolish as he to have allowed that...that night to happen.

Oh yes, she'd worked hard on convincing herself, but the miserable fact remained: she still wanted him. Her heart still pumped furiously every time she looked into those cool, impassive blue eyes, knowing that behind them was a lonely man, a man who needed her as much as she needed him. A man she could love with all her being.

"What was that?" she asked, shaking herself. "You said something about Bones talking about Joey Brown?"

He looked at her oddly. "I told you, Bones said the kid used to drink all the time and that he didn't see anything strange in the way Joey died."

"Well, did you point out the fact that you knew Joey personally and that he *didn't* drink at all?"

"No," Craig replied, "I let it drop."

"What did you talk about then?"

"Christ, I don't remember."

"Sure you do. Come on, don't close me out."

Craig shook his head, exasperated. "We talked about John Woods."

"About his skin-diving accident?"

"Yes."

"And?"

"And he said Woody was a thrill junkie, something to that effect."

"So he thought Woody's death was par for the course, too?"

"He seemed to."

"Was Bones nervous talking about the deaths? Did he pace or fidget?"

"Of course he was upset, Marie. Like I said, I showed up at his place out of the clear blue and dug up a damned uncomfortable past."

"You know," she said, tapping a page of Bones's testimony with her pencil, "he seemed too cool at the trial. Way too cool, considering."

"He's like that. I told you."

"Maybe."

"I wish you'd stop trying to read something into every word a person says."

"Um. It's my job. It's the only way I can piece together the scattered facts. I just wish I could get a clear handle on it."

"We may never get one."

"Oh, I will, I will. Eventually it's all going to come together."

"If we don't get killed first," he muttered darkly.

While Marie pored over the pages of the transcript, Craig read the in-flight magazine on Alaska. He seemed to be able to lose himself totally in articles about Inuit art, salmon fishing and the shrinking wilderness to the far north. *Men,* Marie thought, giving him a sidelong glance. And then every time she wanted to talk about a particular item of testimony, he merely shrugged it off, as if she would lose interest and drop the case when he refused to discuss it. Well, she wouldn't, and he should know that by now.

She crossed her legs, shifted in her seat, and felt his thigh pressed against hers. Despite the awkwardness of their situation, Marie was glad to be with him and not running for cover. She was absolutely positive they had someone sweating hard, believing that Craig was going to go to the state attorney general with his so-called new evidence. And that person had shown his hand twice now: first with that call to her son and then by watching her house. But as they pursued each man more persistently, as they pressed harder, the guilty one was going to panic. She knew Craig was right. They were both in danger.

She rested her head on the back of the seat and squeezed her eyes shut. She took a breath. She'd handle the danger. They'd just be extra careful. And because she was in on this with Craig, because she was helping him expose the truth, Pacific was going to have to award her that bonus. They'd hand her one hundred thousand dollars. Wow. And they'd be getting off cheap. You bet.

She half opened her eyes and gave Craig a sidelong look. His calm assurance lent her a feeling of total security. He'd tell her it was false, he'd scoff at her, but it was true—she felt safe with him. More than safe. She felt weak around him, melting inside, all shivery and glowing, miserable and elated at the same time. She yearned fervently for his glance, his touch. She couldn't bear his nearness, but she was terrified of his distance. And she had to cover those feelings up. She had to be brave and intrepid and businesslike around him. On guard every agonizing moment.

She wondered if she would sleep with Craig again, given the chance. She looked down at the papers in her hands, unseeing, and knew she would. Even if he were only using her, she'd let him, because she wanted it, craved it, couldn't sleep because of the memory of that one blissful night.

She lifted her head and studied his profile unashamedly, and asked herself if their relationship had truly been meaningless. After all, she'd lied through her teeth to him that night at the restaurant, trying to save face. And if she'd been lying, perhaps *he* had been lying, too. Perhaps he'd only been trying to protect her.

Sure, Marie. That was what every woman on earth told herself after a one-night stand. Craig didn't give two hoots about her that way. All he really cared about was clearing his name and being reinstated as captain. He was a loner, fourteen years her senior, a hard, unattainable man who belonged at sea. As soon as she helped him clear his name, and his innocence was proven to a skeptical world, he'd sail off into the sunset. *So long, Marie Vicenza, it's been real nice.*

Marie chewed on her lip, turned away from him and stared out the window. Below, she could see the white-capped mountains jutting up out of the cold gray sea— the Alaskan coastline. Myriad islands dotted the icy water, and every so often she could just make out a boat, probably a large fishing vessel. Alaska, wild and free. She wondered idly if she were truly ever going to be free of the congestion and crime of the city. And Tony. She wanted so much more for him, but was it just a pipe dream after all? Was the purity of Alaska only for the very special ones, for men like Craig Saybolt who had the guts to go out and grab life by the tail?

"How's your studying going?" he asked her.

"Oh, fine," she replied lethargically.

"You seem more interested in the scenery." He closed his magazine, put it in the rack in front of him and turned toward her.

"I keep going over the same testimony," she said. "I go over it again and again, and I know I'm missing something, some link."

"You'll drive yourself crazy," he said.

"No, I won't. I'll find it. Eventually." She gave him a weak smile. "But I bet your way works quicker."

"We'll see."

"Craig," she said, taking a cola from the stewardess, "I just noticed this piece of testimony. Let's see... Here it is." She put her finger on a line. "It's Bones talking during a direct examination. He was asked, 'So, you were all eating, all in the same dining room.' Bones corrected him there, saying it was the mess. Anyway, the prosecutor asked, 'And you heard a terrible noise and felt a big shock. Those were your words, Mr. Stratford. So I ask you, if your captain is innocent, as he has asserted, then why is it no one noticed the guilty crew member leave the mess?'"

Marie scanned the page. "Here," she said, "Bones testified that he was positive they were all in there because he recalled an argument over the cook, Joey, only making one serving each of his crab cakes, and Joey swearing there were extras. Bones said...ah, here it is,

'Look, Joey even did a head count and was getting on everyone's backs for eating the extras. I'm sure, sir, that we were all there. I'm positive, sir.'"

Craig sighed and rubbed his jaw. "I remember that testimony. It didn't do me any good."

"No, I wouldn't think it would. But how come Bones was the only one who was so darn sure no one left the mess? I mean," Marie said, "every other man testified that he couldn't recall."

"So?"

"So," Marie said, "either nine of them were lying or...Bones was."

"I think they were all confused. It was a helluva shock to everyone, Marie. Don't put too much stock on any one man's recollections. The jury sure didn't," he said darkly.

"There's something else, Craig," she said, "something we haven't looked at. Suppose they all really were in the mess eating...."

"What are you getting at?"

"I don't want you to scoff. But maybe one of the guys smuggled someone else on board before you sailed. And that person hit you over the head and took the wheel." She folded her arms across her breasts.

Craig was shaking his head. "And just where did this phantom of yours go when the Coast Guard got there?"

"Easy," she said, "he jumped ship right after the accident and was picked up by a small boat waiting for him. There were lots of fishing boats in the area. And what's more," Marie put in smugly, "some of the crew figured it out later. For instance, Joey and Woody did, and that's why they're dead now. It would also explain the others disappearing. They're afraid."

He was silent for a long moment, his cool blue eyes resting on her. Finally he let his breath, and said, "No. I would have seen a strange man come aboard. Impossible."

"But why? *Why* is it impossible? You can't have been watching the gangway every last second you were docked at the terminal."

"Believe me," Craig said, dismissing her, "it was my job to know who was on board."

"Oh, I see," Marie said loftily, "and the great Captain Saybolt couldn't have possibly missed anything."

"You got it. Now, can we drop the subject, please?"

"For now," she muttered.

They landed in Anchorage, and Marie was able to get a standby seat on the short hop over to Valdez. This time, she even had the money, not that she hadn't had to beg Mike for it. She waved the ticket at Craig as they boarded the commuter jet. "A woman of substance," she said and smiled at him, but Craig was looking at her ticket, frowning. "What's wrong?" she asked.

"Nothing."

"Something's the matter. I know that look."

"I was just wondering," he said, helping her into the narrow seat, "what you had to do to get those tickets."

At first she thought she'd heard him wrong. He couldn't be asking if she'd...if she'd slept with her boss. But then, by the look on his face and that clenched jaw, she knew that was exactly what he'd meant.

She shot him a cold glare. "What are you asking?"

"Never mind."

"*What?* Go on, say it."

For a moment he studied her face, his own expression unreadable, then said, "Never mind, I said."

Quickly she put up a hand and shook her head. "Don't you dare insinuate that, Craig Saybolt," she hissed, "*ever*. I mean it. I thought, I *hoped* you knew me better than that."

"Listen," he began, scrubbing a hand through his hair, "I'm sorry, I don't know why I—"

"I do," she interrupted. "You think I'm a tramp." Then she buried her face in a magazine.

It wasn't until they were over the Valdez Arm, on final approach, that it struck Marie like a cold bucket of water: he wouldn't have asked that, he wouldn't have even wondered about it, if he didn't care. Which meant that he *did* care. And suddenly her heart sang.

CRAIG'S CABIN was exactly as they had left it. Tidy, the dishes in a rack, the furniture straightened and dusted, the rugs shaken out. Marie stood in the doorway and marveled at how much she truly liked the cozy little place. A girl could get awfully used to the solitude, the warmth, the man. . . .

"Well," Craig said, clearing his throat, "I guess you're a lot safer here than in a hotel."

"Oh, much," she agreed, trying to sound casual. "Um."

"Should I . . . ah . . . put my bag in the spare room?"

"Sure, sure, that'll be fine."

Clearly he was ill at ease. But not nearly as uncomfortable as she was. She'd only spent one night in his cabin in the woods, and the memory of it caused shivers to crawl along her limbs. She put her bag on the dresser and hung up her slacks and the single skirt she'd brought along. She glanced around the room idly and found it sparsely furnished, sterile. There were no pictures on the wooden walls, no vases or trinkets on the dresser. The rocker needed a cushion. The bed, a double, had a simple white chenille spread on it and a blue comforter folded at the foot. There was a cotton throw rug on the wooden floor, but it was a dull ivory. The room needed color, a woman's touch.

She put her three sweaters in a dresser drawer and was aware of Craig, out in the kitchen, rattling around. He was muttering something, talking to himself, apparently not in a very good humor. She stood on the threshold, folded her arms and watched him, bent over, pulling pots and pans out of a cupboard. Her heart began a slow, cadenced pounding. He was so vital, so cocksure, so rugged-looking, a man's man. She was too used to the city slickers, the yuppies with their razor haircuts, the salesmen with their shiny suits, the blue-collar workers, grimy, tired, their eyes always staring too vacantly. But Craig had an essence to him, an air of manly competence, of self-assurance. It struck her how little he seemed to need anyone, how adapted he'd become to taking care of himself.

"Damn pan, I was sure it was down here." *Clang*.

She sighed and straightened her shoulders. "Need some help?"

"I'm looking for my iron skillet. It was always down under the sink."

Marie smiled. "It's in the dish rack." She pointed. "See?"

He straightened and grumbled something.

"I put it there," she said. "Remember?"

"Oh, yeah, the dinner." His expression altered abruptly, as if he, too, recalled with clarity the events of the last time they'd been there, alone, the perpetual Alaskan sun filtering through his bedroom window, laying a golden stripe across their naked torsos. Marie felt sudden tears burn behind her eyes.

"Dinner," she said, brightly. "I guess I'd better go to the store. I'll call Tony, too."

"No," he said sharply, turning toward her. "*We'll* go to the grocery. I don't want you to even poke your nose outside alone."

Grocery shopping in Valdez was a far cry from shopping in San Francisco. They walked the few aisles on the wood plank floor, and Marie marveled at the poor selection of fresh goods.

"I *was* going to make a salad," she said, determined to be cheerful, turning a head of lettuce over in her hands. "What do you think?"

"Looks fine to me." He shuffled his feet, put his hands in his pockets.

She tried to ignore his discomfort. "I guess we could toss in a cucumber, but the tomatoes..."

"Fine."

"Do you like celery, or mushrooms?"

"Whatever you want."

He wished she weren't there. Her jubilation from the previous night had been worn down to a few obstinate nubs. Mostly she felt a great bubble of misery inside her. It grew bigger and bigger and pressed on her insides and made her want to cry. She fought it, kept trying to squash the bubble down, but it was there, pushing, pushing, compressing her heart and lungs, cramping her stomach and making a lump in her throat.

He couldn't stand her, and he was stuck with her. She'd pushed herself on him, made him take her along, given him no choice. She pushed the cart down an aisle and hated herself.

"Do you like orange juice?" he asked her, appearing beside the cart, holding a carton in his hand,.

She smiled at him, and the bubble inside her diminished momentarily. "I love orange juice," she said gratefully.

While Craig paid for the groceries, Marie used the pay phone in front of the store. She got Joel's mother and asked for Tony.

"Hi, Mom."

"Everything okay?" she asked.

"Sure, fine."

"Good. You remember what we told you about not going home?"

"Yeah." He sounded bored.

"Good." She changed her tack. "And you're letting your hair grow out, Anthony?"

"Yes. Geez, Mom."

"You call Grandma every day."

"Sure, I will."

"I love you, Tony. Be good."

"Geez, Mom."

Craig wasn't bad in the kitchen. While she fixed the salad, he prepared the fish, a white dill sauce and all. Marie had never been too handy at the stove, and she found herself watching him admiringly.

They ate at the small table. "You know, a plant would look great in that corner." She pointed with her fork then wondered if she weren't being too pushy.

"I thought about getting one," he said. "In fact, Tanya, my daughter, suggested it."

"She's been here?"

"Years ago."

"Did she like Alaska?"

He swallowed his mouthful of salad. "Said it was quaint or something like that. She likes city life better."

"Have you, ah, called your kids yet?"

"Yet?"

"Since prison, since you were released."

He shook his head.

She decided to drop it. "The city's fine," she said, "for things like shopping and museums and shows. But I keep promising myself I'm going to get out of there. Live someplace like this," she made a sweeping gesture with her hand, "with Tony. He needs to get away."

"Boys need space," Craig said, "lots of it. Alaska's a great place to raise kids if you've got the time to really show them how to hunt and fish and climb."

"It sounds wonderful...." she said, and her voice trailed away in regret.

It was harder than Marie had imagined, being so near Craig. She was afraid every second that she was going to say something or do something to give herself away. Her feelings were tattered, and she needed time to mend them. But being this close to him only brought home with a miserable constancy just how wounded she was. It had been years and years since she'd let her emotions loose, let herself care about a man this much, and now she knew why she'd kept those tenuous feelings bottled up inside—it hurt too much. She helped with the dishes, took a walk with him in the evening sunlight up into the woods beyond his cabin, even carried in a piece of firewood from out back. His proximity became unbearable. She longed to reach out and touch him, to shamelessly tell him she wanted to share his bed again, no matter how he really felt about her. She wanted to confess her innermost needs and fears, and most of all she was desperate to tell him that she had fallen in love with him.

"Well," she said, putting down the firewood next to the potbelly stove, brushing off her hands like a real woodsman, "I guess I'll hit the sack." She turned around and faced him. He was standing at the back door, his arms folded, one shoulder resting negligently against the frame. He was watching her. "Um," she said, her nerves raw, unable to meet his eye, "I can't believe it's still light out."

"Alaskan summers."

"I like it."

"You wouldn't like the winter here," he observed. "Not many can take it."

"Oh," she said, finally daring to meet his gaze, "don't be so certain."

She tried to sleep. She really tried. She counted sheep, made plans for who they'd see in the morning, mentally rearranged his furniture. She tried thinking pleasant thoughts about Tony and their future together, about a nice place outside the city for her folks to retire to, about a new car, even what color it would be. She tried everything under the perpetual Alaskan sun to drift off into sweet oblivion, but the nerve-racking fact remained: she could hear Craig stirring around in the next room—heard the water in the bathroom sink draining, his bed creaking, his breathing.

In her mind's eye she saw him. Vividly. The strong square line of his jaw, his wide mouth, his broad chest, the texture of his skin, whose memory made her fingers curl futilely. His high forehead where his hair was receding—his only imperfection—and she adored it, loving his flaw the more for being his.

She saw him in her mind's eye and she wanted him and her belly ached as the bubble swelled in her like an unborn child and she curled up into a ball and wept soundlessly.

CHAPTER FIFTEEN

THE AROMA OF COFFEE woke Marie. It took her a second to figure out where she was, and she lay there in the bed a moment, remembering.

She was back in Valdez with Craig, in his cabin. The sun was bursting in around the window curtains in bright bars of light, too bright for early morning.

She rolled over and checked her watch: 7:34. But the sun had been up for five hours.

She could hear Craig moving around in the kitchen, clinking pots, turning on the water, opening a drawer. She wondered if he'd slept well.

She lay in bed in the guest room and recalled the last time she'd been in this cabin. That time she'd been in Craig's bed. She'd watched him while he slept, and then, just before she'd fallen asleep herself, she'd curled up close to him, feeling his bulk against her back, the warmth of his skin and the tickle of his chest hair on her skin. She remembered every touch, every murmur, every exquisite, blazing sensation. She hated to think of why he'd made love to her. He was a man fresh out of prison, he'd said. Had it really been as simple as that?

She had to get up and face him. They had work to do. Craig deserved to have his innocence proven, regardless of how he felt about her. She'd keep her mind focused on that.

She rose finally and pulled on her white slacks and a bright green T-shirt. It was chilly in the cabin, so she shrugged on her white cardigan.

She got her makeup case and opened the door.

"Morning," she said.

Craig was sitting in his armchair sipping from a coffee mug. He nodded.

"The coffee smells good."

"There's plenty."

She raised her makeup case and smiled too quickly. "I better, ah . . . you know, wash up."

He continued staring at her gravely, until she ducked into the bathroom and closed the door behind her, leaning back against it and shutting her eyes, breathing hard.

She had coffee and toast for breakfast. She tried to make conversation, but he answered in monosyllables until she gave up.

"Where are we going first?" she finally asked.

"I thought I'd see if Howie Mayer is coherent. You don't have to come."

"I'm coming."

"Let's not get into this again."

"Why do you think I flew all the way up here? I want to talk to him myself. I've read all kinds of books and been to a dozen seminars on how to know if someone is telling the truth, how to judge people and interview them. That's what I do, Craig."

He studied her, deciding.

"Besides," she added, "it only makes good sense for us to stick together. Safer that way."

A moment extended itself too long. Finally it broke. "All right," he said. "But I want to do the talking."

"Craig, I—"

He held up a hand impatiently. "I know, it's your *job* to question people. You've been to seminars."

"That happens to be the truth."

"I'm sure it is. Still, I do the asking."

She eyed him narrowly. Finally she shrugged. "You won't forget to ask him if he has phoned any of your crew recently? You know, casually try to see if he was the one who alerted whoever called Tony that night."

"I won't forget, Marie."

But it wasn't as easy to get into Mayer's room this time. "Visiting hours aren't till noon," the nurse at the station told them. "And Mr. Mayer hasn't been doing as well as we'd like."

Marie stepped forward. "I'm with the Pacific Group," she said. "Mr. Mayer's insurance company. We've come up from San Francisco to discuss Mr. Mayer's benefits. It's really quite important, and I have a plane out this afternoon." She handed the nurse her business card.

"Well, I guess it's all right then," the woman said. "He's in room 102. Down that hallway. If you'd keep it brief..."

"Thank you," Marie said, smiling graciously.

"You lie well," Craig said when they were out of earshot.

"White lies. Harmless."

"Do you tell those kinds of lies often?"

"No, only if I need to in order to get a job done."

"Anything for good old Pacific."

She looked up at him. "Don't be nasty. I do my job and I do it well. I'm efficient and I get results."

He said nothing.

Howie Mayer was slumped in a chair watching television. He wore a hospital gown and a gray cotton hospital robe and slippers. He was pale and gaunt. His hands shook. Other than the fact that he was sitting up, the nurse was right: he looked dreadful.

"Hello, Howie," Craig said.

The man's creased face quivered, and he opened his mouth. Nothing came out.

"How are you feeling?" Craig asked.

Howie pushed himself up weakly, trying to stand.

"Relax," Craig said. "I'd just like to talk to you for a minute."

Howie tried to say something, swallowed, then tried again. "Captain Saybolt," he croaked.

"I'm not a captain anymore, Howie. They took my papers. I'm plain Craig now." He looked around, found a chair and pulled it up close to Howie. "Yeah," Craig said, seating himself, "it's been rough."

Howie's gaze fell to his lap. Marie wondered if he weren't holding back tears. It was disturbing. If Howie had had nothing to do with the accident, she and Craig would be doing a terrible thing to the man. Maybe they shouldn't . . .

"Yeah," Craig was saying, "it's been about as bad as it can get." He stared at Howie without expression.

Howie mumbled something then looked up. It was the first time he'd actually noticed Marie. "Who's she?" he got out. His eyes were sunken, jaundiced. They leaked moisture. "Haven't I seen you before?"

She nodded, assessing him. So he remembered her. Again, she wondered if he hadn't called someone after their last visit. Someone who had panicked and made that call to Tony.

Craig glanced at Marie. "She's a friend of mine," he told the sick man. "We're going to have a nice little talk, Howie, and we'll all keep it to ourselves."

"Talk?" His voice was barely audible.

"You got in touch with someone from the *Northern Light* crew after my last visit, didn't you?"

Howie shook his head as if confused.

"Sure you did. And that person has been threatening you. It's okay to tell me."

"No," Howie muttered.

"You called that person," Craig said, changing his tactic, "and talked about the oil spill."

"No."

"Let's quit the games, Howie," Craig said levelly. "You see, I have proof you know about that accident, buddy, and it's time you came clean."

Howie was shaking his head vehemently now. His hands trembled uncontrollably. "No," he whispered, his breathing labored. "No, they'll kill me!"

Marie's heart skipped a beat then settled into a steady pounding. Craig pressed him carefully. "Who will kill you, Howie? You can tell us."

"No, no, no!"

It was obvious Howie was terrified, his eyes darting around the room, looking for escape. "Go away!" he cried, then hunched over, trembling, his fists clenching and unclenching.

Marie desperately wanted to push him. She wanted to clutch those fists in her hands and force him to tell them who he was afraid of, who was going to kill him. She was so close to cracking this case she could taste the victory.

"Howie," she said, holding herself in check, "*Howie, No one is going to hurt you. But you've got to tell us who you're afraid of. If we don't know, we can't protect you.*"

Howie emitted a fearful, inhuman wail that must have carried out into the hall, because moments later the door swung open, and the nurse appeared. She was furious. Bustling, she ushered them both out without ceremony then read them the riot act. Marie managed an apology, but Craig kept right on walking toward the exit. She shot the nurse one last glance and then hurried after him.

Outside the sun shone and the air was fresh on a stiff breeze off the bay. She caught up to Craig and tugged at his arm. "Wow," she breathed, "can you believe how *close* we were? He knows! God, Craig, he was terrified."

"So?"

"So, all we have to do now is—"

Suddenly Craig stopped short. "What? Go back in there and shake it out of him?"

"No, but . . ."

And he began walking again, his stride long and angry. She hurried to keep up, puzzled by his behavior. "Craig, I don't understand. What's wrong?"

"I'll tell you what's wrong," he said, still heading down the road, "Mayer was half out of his mind. He might not know a damn thing. He was babbling."

Marie came to a sudden stop. "You're dead wrong," she said, calling after him. "He knows, all right. I'll stake my job on it."

Craig turned to study her. "I hope you're right, Marie," he said, "but even if you are, I don't think there's a chance in hell we're going to get Mayer to say another word."

Marie frowned. "Maybe," she said. "But Mayer's scared of someone. And another thing. Two of your crew have disappeared. I feel safer now eliminating them because of Howie's reaction. I think those two missing ones went underground deliberately. It looks to me," she said, thinking, "that your whole crew might have known who the guilty party was. And they're all scared."

"You always base your investigations on gut feelings?"

"Sometimes. And I'll tell you another thing, Craig, I think it's high time we visit Pete Lund. Of all the testimony I've read, Lund's was the most vicious."

Craig gazed at her for a long moment and then nodded. "Okay, Lund's place next. But *I* do the talking. You got that?"

"Aye, aye, sir." She saluted and followed him along the road with her heart still pounding a little too quickly. *"They'll kill me,"* Howie had said. *"Kill me."*

When they reached Pete Lund's building Craig pushed the doorbell, and Marie heard the muted chimes ring inside. She stood behind Craig, waiting impatiently. She'd stood at this door before.

But this time someone was coming to the door. She could hear him fumbling with the chain and the doorknob. Her heart skipped a beat. Pete Lund was home at last.

"Hello, Pete," Craig said quietly as the door swung open.

"Captain," Pete replied matter-of-factly.

"Not anymore."

"Sorry, force of habit."

Marie studied Pete Lund intently. He was tall and wiry, very blond, with a rough, red complexion. An ordinary sort of man until you looked at his eyes, and then you saw the emptiness inside him, as if the pale blue of the sky showed right through the holes in his head.

"Got a minute, Pete?" Craig said.

"Sure, come in. And your friend, too," he said pointedly.

"Sorry. Pete Lund, this is Marie Vicenza."

"Hello, Mr. Lund," Marie said, holding out her hand.

He took it quickly, giving her a swift, curious glance with those strange colorless eyes of his.

"Looks like you're doing okay, Pete," Craig said, moving around the practically empty living room. Marie had never seen him in this role, belligerent, adversarial. She could have sworn his hair bristled.

"I'm okay, Captain."

"You've been away."

"Yes, on a job in the Lower Forty-eight. I still work for Wesco. But you probably know that."

Neither man seemed interested in sitting down. Awkwardly Marie stood by the front door, watching them, almost holding her breath as they circled each other. She was utterly unprepared for Craig's next statement. He went straight for the jugular.

"You're right," Craig said, "I do know a lot about you, pal. I know you're still with Wesco, and I happen to know I took the fall for you. It was you who ran my ship onto those rocks."

Lund smiled. "You're nuts, Captain. Too many months in solitary, I guess." He held himself stiffly, like a robot, his movements too controlled. The smile stayed frozen on Pete's face.

"I won't turn you in, though," Craig said coldly. "I want money. You got paid off. Now it's my turn."

"I don't know what you're talking about."

"I did twenty months for you. What do you think that's worth, Lund?"

"You're nuts," he repeated. "I told everything I knew on the witness stand. You were there. You heard me. Trying to get revenge on me isn't going to get you anywhere, Captain. All I did was tell the truth."

Craig faced him, a little taller, a lot broader. His fists closed slightly, and a muscle ticked in his jaw. Marie was afraid for a moment, but Craig kept himself reined in tightly.

"Think about it, Pete. Half a million dollars is my going rate to keep quiet. Let me know what you decide. And if you decide not to pay me, I'll go straight to the DA. The same one that prosecuted me. I'm sure you'll do fine in prison."

"Listen, Captain, and I'll give you some advice. Forget about the past. Pick up the pieces of your life and start again. You have kids, don't you?" His empty eyes swung around to rest on Marie, and she felt her skin crawl. "And you have a woman. Threatening me won't get you anywhere."

Marie looked down and flushed.

"Hey," he went on, "I wish you luck. You had a bad time. You made a mistake. Put it behind you."

"Not until it's set right, Lund," Craig said. "I'll be waiting."

Lund shrugged.

"Come on, Marie. My pal here has some thinking to do," Craig said, turning to go.

It was a few minutes before Craig said anything. He strode down the street away from Lund's apartment so fast that Marie had to run to keep up. His face was set, deep lines scoring it from nose to mouth. She knew enough not to say a word.

Finally he swore.

"Lund was lying," she said. "I'm sure of it."

"I don't know."

"Weird guy," she said. "Real cool. Hard to read. But I'm sure he was lying."

"He expected me," Craig said tightly. "He knew I was coming. He was waiting for me."

"Who told him?"

Craig shook his head in irritation. "Who knows? It could have been any of them—Bones, Wild Man, Howie, even Alice Klutznic."

"Do you think Lund did it?"

"Damn it, Marie! Stop asking me. I don't know."

"Sorry."

"Okay, we're going to Klutznic's. The last one we can reach here. Let's get it over with. Then you can go home."

She didn't want to remind him that she could be in danger, that *he* could be in danger. He was too angry right then. Lund had really gotten to him. She could bring up the business about Lund and Klutznic's friendship in Vietnam and the fact that Lund's neighbor had seen Tim visiting Lund. But Craig didn't want to hear it. She guessed he didn't want to hear that he'd never learned very much about his crew. The Iron Man, Captain Ahab, Craig Saybolt.

Tim Klutznic's neat house rested serenely in the late morning sun. A playpen filled with brightly colored toys stood outside the front door. The Ford Bronco gleamed by the curb.

Craig knocked on the door.

"Just a minute!" someone—Alice—called from inside.

Marie and Craig stood silently, side by side, bearers of bad tidings, avenging angels. Marie's face was flushed with the excitement of the chase.

The door finally opened. Alice looked puzzled, then surprised, then nervous, all in a split second.

"Hello, Alice," Craig said, "I'm Craig Saybolt."

"Yes, sure, I remember. We met. You were the captain...." Her voice trailed off.

"Hi, Alice," Marie said.

"Oh, you're . . . the insurance lady. You were here last week."

Marie smiled encouragingly. "That's right. Your husband is a hard man to locate."

"He's still out fishing," Alice said too quickly.

"Do you know when he'll be back?" Craig asked.

She shook her head. Marie thought Alice had paled beneath her freckles, but then just seeing Craig in the flesh would have been unsettling.

"I need to talk to him, Alice. It's important," Craig was saying.

She tried to smile. "Gosh, I'm real sorry. He may be gone for another week or so if the salmon are running well. I never know."

"Where's Tim fishing?" Craig asked in too hard a voice.

Alice took a step back. "I don't know. I'm not sure. Maybe the Columbia Inlet."

And maybe he's not fishing at all, Marie thought.

"And you have no idea when he'll be back?" Craig asked.

"Really, I don't," Alice replied and looked down at her feet. A long moment of silence ensued. Marie saw the woman swallow convulsively. So she had a dry mouth. She was afraid. It was more than just Craig, her husband's ex-captain, showing up. Alice was lying through her teeth.

"I, ah," Alice finally said, clearing her throat, "I have to go now."

Craig studied her an instant longer. "When Tim gets in, you tell him to contact me. He knows where I live."

"I . . . I don't know if Tim . . . I can't make him. . . ." And then Alice's face seemed to crumple under the pressure. "Just leave us alone," she said. "Can't you just leave us be before someone—'' She shut up suddenly and turned white.

"Before someone what?" Marie asked encouragingly.

"Nothing. I didn't mean anything. Before the neighbors notice," Alice babbled. "You're bothering me. Will you just go away and leave me alone?"

"Sure, Alice, we'll go. But if Tim doesn't contact me, I'll be back," Craig said. "Tell Tim that I'll be back."

She shut the door in his face.

"She's afraid," Marie said softly, staring at the blank door. "Just like Howie." She looked at Craig. "What's wrong?" she asked, noticing his grim expression.

"What's wrong? We're hurting people. Innocent people."

Carefully Marie said, "Alice Klutznic didn't seem so innocent to me. You remember her saying, 'before someone finds out'?"

"She didn't say 'finds out,' Marie."

"Ah," Marie said, walking back toward the street, "it's what she *didn't* say, though, that has me thinking."

They stopped at a grocery store and bought some supplies: milk and bread, cans of soup and tuna, a dozen eggs, cheese.

"You need some fresh fruit," Marie said.

"It'll spoil. I'm not home much."

"Here, look at these pears. They look good. Ooh, are they expensive. Your food prices up here are high."

"We have enough, Marie."

"Well, then, some apples. For vitamins and minerals."

"Oh, for God's sake. Get some then," he said impatiently.

She looked up swiftly. She kept trying to be amiable to him, to get along, but he held himself away from her. Whenever she felt that they were getting along, he got angry or sarcastic or defensive.

He carried the bag of groceries back to his cabin and set it down on the kitchen counter. He stood there staring at it, then abruptly turned to Marie.

"I'm going out," he said. "I have some business to take care of."

"You're not going to..." she began.

"No, nothing to do with the case. I have to go to the bank, do a few errands."

"Sure, go on."

"Lock the door after me."

"Will you be gone long?"

He shrugged, turned to go.

"Craig..."

"Yes?" He faced her.

"You seem...angry. Did I do anything?"

"You, Marie? Of course not. You didn't do a damn thing," he said and then he was gone.

She sighed. She locked the door, as he'd told her to. He couldn't stand to be in the same room with her. He'd escaped.

Listlessly Marie put the groceries away. She had to guess where things went. She wondered whether to cook dinner. Would he be home?

The afternoon stretched out before her, sunny and lonely and endless. She wondered over and over if Craig was safe out there walking around Valdez. They'd stirred up a lot of bad feelings that morning. One person, anyway, was a good bit more than nervous. One person was out there somewhere deciding what to do about his ex-captain. Silence him or pay him off. Marie prayed it would be the latter, that Craig would be contacted and an offer would be made. Of course, and she shuddered to think about it, two men were already dead. *Be careful, Craig, be careful.*

To kill time, she took a shower and washed her hair. She tidied up the cabin. There were no photographs—nothing personal at all but some books. She wondered what Polly had looked like—nice, sweet, mild-mannered Polly. No wonder Craig and Marie didn't get along. She was all wrong for him, not his type at all. He needed a calm, perfectly controlled lady, not a hot-tempered, pushy Italian girl. Nor did he need another kid to worry about. His own were grown now. What were their names? Tanya and Craig, "Sonny," Craig had called him.

He didn't have pictures of them, either. But they weren't exactly on the best of terms. It must hurt Craig terribly, although he'd never let on. Still, his children believed him guilty, while a complete stranger was trying to prove his innocence. It had to hurt.

She ran her fingers across the bindings of his few books. Some spy stories and murder mysteries and westerns. Books about Alaska. An interesting one called *Glacier Pilot* about an early flyer named Bob Reeve. She leafed through it idly, studying the photographs. Hardy men like Craig appeared in front of their airplanes in leather helmets and goggles and long coats and high boots. A tough breed.

She made macaroni and cheese and put it in the oven. She even went outside to pick a few wildflowers that grew under the pine trees. The air was sweet and cool, and birds, hidden in the branches, called to one another. A couple of small planes droned overhead.

She sighed, went back inside and locked the door. She put the flowers in a drinking glass, which was all she could find.

She was going to have to go back to San Francisco soon. She couldn't wait for Tim Klutznic to show his face; it might be weeks. She knew she was on the right track, but it might take too long.

What if she couldn't prove Craig's innocence? What if there wasn't time, or nobody bit at Craig's offer? What if she had to go home, alone, without solving Craig's case, without the hope for a promotion or bonus, without the possibility of ever seeing Craig again?

She lay down on her bed and tried to think what she could do next to hurry things along. Nothing. All there was to do was sit and wait. Patience. But Marie didn't feel patient.

She lay there and thought and wondered where Craig was, what he was doing. She wondered, if she'd met him under different circumstances, would he have felt differently toward her? Would he have liked her more if he hadn't been in jail, and if she hadn't been working on his case?

But then, of course, they never would have met at all.

She lay there and thought and remembered how he'd been that night, and she couldn't believe he hadn't felt anything toward her but lust.

He came home after six, opening the door with his key. Marie sat straight up on the bed and ran her fingers through her hair. She got up and went into the living room.

"Hi," she said. "Get your errands done?"

"Uh-huh."

"Hungry?"

He looked at her. "You didn't have to fix dinner."

He smelled as if he'd had a couple of beers. Not that he was drunk or even tipsy. But she knew he'd been sitting in a bar—the Pipeline?—and drinking beer just so he didn't have to come home and face her. She turned away, hurt. "Well, I did, anyway. Do you want some?"

He was staring at the flowers she'd put on the table. He looked a little sad, a little angry. He jerked his gaze back to her. "Anybody come around?"

"No." She got mad then. "Nobody came and broke down the door, if that's what you were worried about."

He assessed her silently.

"Why don't you sit down and eat?" she said. "It's already made."

The atmosphere was strained, too quiet, the tension between them crackling. It was awful.

He ate, his eyes distant, his brow furrowed thoughtfully. Filled with misery, she watched him, appreciating, even through her pain, the character in his face, the strength of him. His strong jaw worked as he chewed, and she wanted to kiss his mouth where she'd kissed him before. She wanted to feel the bristles of his beard scratch her skin and the softness of his lips.

"This is good," he said.

"Thank you."

She remembered the feel of his hands on her, his groans of pleasure, her own cries of fulfillment. How was she going to endure another night so near him?

"I'll do the dishes," he said.

"Don't bother. I'll do them. I am staying here with you for free, after all."

"You don't have to. . . ."

"Why don't you start a fire? It's so cheerful," she suggested.

It was growing cool, even though the sun was still high in the sky. She could see out the kitchen window that fog was curling off the water of the Valdez Arm.

She busied herself cleaning up, grateful she could turn her back on him and not think for a short time. Everything between them was so awkward, so unnerving.

He sat in his armchair, watching the fire in the potbelly stove. She wiped her hands dry and stood in front of the sink for a moment, not sure what to do. Should she tell him she was going for a walk? Should she just go into her bedroom and shut the door?

In the end, she sat on a chair and folded her hands in her lap.

"No television to watch," she said.

"I could get one, I suppose."

"Oh no, I didn't mean..."

"We do have television up here, you know. The same programs the Lower Forty-eight have," he said dryly.

"I'm sure you do. I just meant..." She was running off at the mouth again.

"You don't have to make conversation, Marie. I don't need to be entertained," he said.

Tears stung her eyes. Everything she said was wrong. She blinked back the moisture. "I was only trying to be pleasant."

"You're pleasant enough."

"Somehow that doesn't sound like a compliment."

"I won't play word games with you, Marie."

Something in her gave way abruptly. She found herself talking, the words spilling out of her mouth without conscious thought. "You've looked down on me ever since you found out about Tony. I can tell. You disapprove."

He eyed her with surprise. "What do you mean?"

"You know what I mean, Craig. I was an unwed mother. I got pregnant when I was eighteen years old. I'm dumb, I'm loose, I have a son with no father, not even a stepfather."

"Marie..." He cleared his throat. "I'm no one to judge anybody. What you did was your business."

"But you can't help thinking it. It's the way you are. You and your nice wife and your kids, all born safely after the wedding, I bet," she said heatedly.

"You don't owe me an explanation, Marie. You don't have to—"

"I know. You don't want to hear it. I don't blame you. But I'm going to say it, anyway."

"It's none of my business."

"You've *made* it your business. You find me distasteful, don't you?"

"No."

She got up and held her hands out to the hot stove. She felt the heat burn her cheeks. "You're lying."

"I don't lie, Marie," he said harshly.

She couldn't stop. Her heart aching, she said, "His name was Nick. From my neighborhood. He was a year ahead of me in school, a big senior."

Craig was looking away. He didn't want to hear. But she'd gone too far. She couldn't stop.

"He was smart and ambitious. He wanted to go to college, but his parents couldn't afford it, so he joined the navy. I was devastated. You remember how important love is when you're young? But Nick said he'd come back every leave, and then we'd get married after his four years were up."

"Marie," Craig said, "please don't—"

"He never came home on leave, though." She hesitated, staring down at the black stove. "So that was that.

And I'm over it. I'm a big girl, and I love my son, and I'm glad I have him."

She turned to gauge Craig's reaction. There was an expression on his face that she'd never seen there. All the harsh lines were gone. A softness shone in his eyes. He sat there and struggled with his feelings.

"So now you know," she said, needlessly, into the silence.

He stood up and came to stand in front of her, hesitantly touching her face. "Poor kid," he said with difficulty.

She lifted her chin. "I am not a kid, and I don't want pity."

He shook his head wordlessly, his fingers warm on her cheek, sliding down over the point of her jaw, trailing down her neck.

"I'm making it just fine. This case is my big break, Craig. I've got to solve it."

His hand curled around her shoulder and rested there. She could sense the turmoil within him, the battle for control he was fighting. She was held in suspension, her blood pounding in her head like dark wings.

"Don't hate me, Craig. I was so young," she whispered.

"I don't hate you." He reached around to the back of her head, and his long fingers tangled in her hair as he pulled her close. His mouth covered hers, and her knees went weak, until she was held up by nothing except his hand in her hair, supporting her. His mouth moved over hers, and she closed her eyes and melted with a dazzling sensation. He kissed the corner of her mouth and let his lips trail down to where the pulse beat in her throat. She felt weak, overcome with delight, and leaned back against his hand.

Then he pulled her tight against his chest, and his hands were hard on her back. She clung to him, her face upturned. She heard him groan, and her heart beat out a heavy rhythm: *He loves me, he loves me.*

There was sudden cold then, and emptiness and the staggering withdrawal of his support. He'd pulled away, releasing her, and she almost fell. She stared at him, her mouth still bruised by his, her cheeks hot, her heart pounding a wild tattoo.

"I'm sorry," he said. "It could never work."

"Craig," she whispered, reaching out a hand to him.

"I'm sorry, Marie," he said in a tortured voice, then he turned on his heel and went out the door.

Marie sank into his chair, dazed. After a time she could hear Craig chopping wood in the back. A pause, then a ringing thud and the clatter of the split halves of a log falling to the ground.

She could make no sense of anything. Her heart lied to her, assuring her of this man's love at one moment, then denying it the next.

She sat and watched the sun move slowly across the horizon, never quite setting. She was drained, unable to get up and confront Craig, worn out with bewilderment and battling emotions.

What crazy dreams she'd had. She and Tony up here with Craig. Happy, loving, a family. Tony with his hair grown out and Craig's hand on his shoulder as they held a big fish they'd caught together. This cozy cabin—maybe new curtains at the windows...

It was impossible. He didn't want her. He'd told her in so many ways. And she'd spilled her guts to him. What had she expected: love, respect, commitment? Who was she kidding?

She had problems in her life, sure, but she'd have to solve them herself. She'd thought Craig was a solution. For a few crazy, passionate moments she'd thought Craig would solve everything. She knew better than that. She'd have to do it herself.

If only she could just let go of the awful, driving ambition that ran her life. If only she could be a real mother to Tony, a wife to . . . well, someone.

Maybe she should move to Alaska to try living on her own. Not to be near Craig, no, but because Alaska had captured her imagination, and it was a place for new starts. She could manage on her own. Other women did, lots of them. It would give Tony a chance to get away from the endless, hopeless drone of their lives.

The monotonous thud of Craig's ax came through the walls of the cabin: pause, thud, clatter. Wistfully she wondered why he couldn't love her—the first man she'd loved since she was eighteen years old.

She chewed on a nail, not even realizing it. The fire was dying out, but she felt too tired to put more wood onto it. Maybe she'd just go to bed. Close the door, go to bed and cry herself to sleep, as she'd done for Nick so long ago, as she'd done last night.

Well, it hadn't solved anything then and it wouldn't now.

He didn't want her.

It was a moment before she realized the thud of his ax had stopped. The door opened, and Craig came in, carrying an armful of split logs. He put them in a stack and straightened.

"I think I'll go to bed now," he said, never meeting her eye.

She stared at her hands in her lap.

"I locked the door," he said.

She nodded, still looking down.

"Well . . . good night."

She heard his footsteps, heard the bathroom door close then open, heard him in his bedroom. Still, she sat there, unable to move, trying not to feel the ache in her belly.

Outside the sun still shone, casting relentless shadows, making night into day.

CHAPTER SIXTEEN

MARIE WAS SICK OF IT. Lying there, tossing and turning, longing for a man who didn't want her, a man who lay in the next room, probably snoring and dreaming and sleeping like a baby.

She was angry at herself. She'd decided that Tony and moving into her own place were her priorities, hadn't she? Then why did Craig's reactions matter so much to her?

It was almost two in the morning. She could tell from the light that leaked in around the curtains that the sun was growing marginally brighter already. She was overtired and upset. She should have stayed in a motel, regardless of what Craig would have said.

She rolled over again, too warm under the quilt. What if she really did move to Alaska? Maybe such a move was too outrageous to contemplate. Maybe she was kidding herself, using Tony's welfare as an excuse to be nearer to Craig. Was she that blindly in love?

Well, it didn't matter at the moment. She'd think about it later, when the case was solved, when she and Craig and Tony were safe.

She knew she and Craig had really stirred up the hornet's nest. Soon the guilty man was going to make a move. She hoped he'd offer Craig hush money. Then they'd have him.

But the bonus money wasn't in her hands yet. What if she never got that reward? Could she still make the move? Maybe a bank loan for a while. Pacific had a small office up in Fairbanks, Alaska. Maybe she should consider a transfer there. She knew Tony would go along with her plans. He'd be head-over-heels delighted.

She turned on her other side, kicking at the guilt, closed her eyes and willed herself to relax: the feet, the knees, the thighs, the hips. She worked her way up her body, consciously relaxing her muscles. Her stomach, her—

A branch cracked outside.

Her eyes flew open. A million reasons for the sound filled her mind, crowding one another in a crazy jumble. A man was stalking the cabin, looking for Marie and Craig. She dismissed the idea as unlikely—female hysteria and too little sleep. The branch could have been broken by a natural cause, such as a skunk, a raccoon or a bear. A bear. Weren't there lots of bears in Alaska? The picture she'd seen in that magazine in the hotel lobby came to her—a huge bear on its hind feet, its gigantic teeth bared.

She lay there, holding her breath, her pulse hammering in her ears, listening for another sound, but there was nothing.

Well, darn, she couldn't sleep like this, wondering. She'd have to get up and look. That's all there was to it. She lay there for a moment longer, then swung her legs out of bed and stood on the cold floor, grumbling under her breath. She tiptoed to the window and pulled the curtain aside a fraction of an inch. It was pearly dawn outside. Dawn, at two o'clock in the morning.

Well, this is just fine, she thought. *Almost asleep at last and a stupid little animal has to go and get me all riled up again.*

She was ready to drop the curtain when abruptly a shadow—a movement—caught her attention. Her eyes swiveled. She pulled the curtain aside a bit more. There, a figure moving, hard to see in the faint light, a figure that blended into the dark shadows under the pine trees and vanished.

Marie let out a shaky breath. An upright figure, big enough to be a bear or a man. Maybe she should wake Craig. Oh, for goodness' sakes, it was gone now. Bears probably came around to eat garbage all the time. He'd laugh at the city girl and be really annoyed.

But... what if it came back? Bears were dangerous if confronted. Grizzlies were vicious and unpredictable. Had it been a grizzly? At the very least, it would make a mess of the garbage cans.

She stood poised at the window for a long moment, deciding. Wake Craig or don't wake him. Of course, if she didn't get him up, and the trash was strewn all over the woods in the morning...

Darn it. She yanked the quilt off the bed and draped it around her shoulders. The sensible thing to do was to check the lids on the trash cans. *Then* maybe she could get some sleep. Oh, brother.

Marie tiptoed through the living room, her bare feet icy cold on the wooden floor. He sure could use a throw rug or two, something with color, Indian, maybe. She unlocked the front door, pulled it open slowly. It creaked nevertheless. It was cool outside. Dim light illuminated the clearing in front of the cabin, but the woods were deep in darkness. What if the bear...? But no. She'd hear it right now if it were around. It was okay. She laughed weakly at herself and wished Tony could see her now—his courageous mother.

Pine needles and gravel pricked the soles of her feet as she walked around to the back. A breeze shook branches above her head, rattling softly in the dawn.

She stopped and stood as still as a statue a couple of times, listening, turning her head. There was nothing but the chirp of a sleepy bird and the soughing of the sea breeze in the trees. She moved slowly, watching carefully, around the corner of the house. There were two galvanized metal trash cans, the lids on tightly, and the big propane tank that provided heat for the cabin.

That was it. Normal, silent, untouched. She moved closer, eyes on the ground for animal tracks. A few depressions in the pine needles showed, but they could have been made by Craig when he emptied the garbage. And there on the other side of the fat, silvery propane tank, was a neat stack of firewood. A sawed-off log stood in the clearing, surrounded by wood chips, Craig's big ax still stuck into it at an angle.

No bear, certainly no man—nothing. But there *had* been a shadow moving into the trees. She'd seen it. Or had it been a dream, a product of exhaustion and an overactive imagination?

No. There had been something out there. It had stepped on a dead branch, which had broken, and she'd heard it.

She walked close, looking at the garbage cans, the ax, the propane tank, feeling silly, her heart beating a little too hard. The breeze lifted her hair, and she shrugged the quilt around her more closely.

Her feet were cold. She rubbed one sole against the other ankle to rid it of something sharp. About to turn away she glanced once more at the still life set against the rough cabin wall: wood pile, trash cans, propane tank. Something caught her eye. A protuberance on the side of the propane tank, up near the nozzle. She stepped closer.

How odd. Some gray gooey stuff like putty was stuck to the nozzle. Maybe the tank leaked. Maybe...

She leaned forward in the dusky light. There was duct tape, the putty, something like a battery, wires. A strange apparatus. She followed the path of the wires to where they led down behind the tank. She had to take a step closer and look hard into the shadow created by the tank and the log wall. Her mind was still on bears and breaking branches, and she had to concentrate hard on what she was looking at. She was half wondering what on earth Craig had rigged up back here, when she saw it. A clock.

A clock. How odd. Did Craig have some sort of system hooked up to turn his heater on and off? Putty, duct tape, wires, clock.

For a moment she was held numb by the knowledge seeping into her brain. This was no home-rigged automatic system. It was a—

She gasped, every muscle leaping to action. She never remembered tearing back to the front door, banging it open, screaming Craig's name. And then he was there, tugging on his trousers, and all she could do was pant and point and cry, "A bomb! Out back!"

She guessed he swore. Later she would recall his shoving her outside, commanding her to get as far away as possible, disappearing around the corner of the cabin.

It all happened at once.

Marie, panicked, afraid for him, went rushing around to the back, too, and was just in time to see his arm arc in the dim light and the apparatus go sailing, sailing into the dark woods. She would recall him turning then, poised in flight, seeing her, yelling something—

Then the ground buckled. Marie was aware of Craig grabbing her and throwing her to the earth, lying half on top of her. Simultaneously a terrible noise beat at her eardrums, and moments later debris rained down all around. There was a whoosh and a roar as flames shot into the sky. Black smoke filled the air, choking, stinging.

She lay there trembling, her arms over her head, her cheek pressed hard into pine needles and dirt. It seemed that she lay there for an eternity, but only moments passed before she realized there was quiet. Except for the crackle of flames and the falling of branches it was mercifully quiet.

"Craig?" she whispered.

"Yeah, I'm here. You okay?"

Slowly he moved aside and kneeled next to her. His face was smudged, his trousers torn and black. Blood welled slowly out from a cut on his cheek.

"Oh," she breathed. "My God."

"Are you all right, Marie?" he repeated.

"Yes, yes, I think so."

"It was a bomb. Plastique. It would have looked like the propane tank exploded."

"You're hurt," she said, kneeling opposite him, putting a finger out to touch the cut on his face.

He winced. "I'm fine."

"Do you have a Band-Aid?" she asked.

"Marie." He took her by the arms and shook her.

"I'm okay, really. I just—" Tears began to run out of her eyes, surprising her.

Craig pulled her to him and held her close. "It's all right," he said. "We're going to be fine." His voice was soothing, calming.

Marie clutched at his naked torso and leaned on him for a moment. Then she sniffed and gave a little laugh. "We're kneeling in the dirt, Craig. We better get up."

"We've got to call the fire department," he said, rising. "Are you okay now? I'll have to go down the street...."

"Yes, go ahead."

But a pickup truck barreled up just then and screeched to a stop. A man came running toward them.

"What happened?" the man yelled as they came around the corner of the cabin. "I called the fire department. Holy cow, I could hear that like it was in my own room!"

"It was an explosion," Craig said. "No one was hurt, I don't think."

The sirens began then, wailing above the crackle of the flames. A police car pulled up in front, lights flashing.

People were gathering in the morning light. The flames flickered on their faces, and black smoke smudged the mother-of-pearl sky. Marie shivered and held Craig's hand.

"Saybolt," he was saying to the policeman. "It was an explosion. Plastique, I think. It was on my propane tank."

"A *bomb?*" the policeman asked. "Who in the world...?"

"I have an idea," Craig said. "Look, could I take care of Marie? She's had a bad time."

He steered her inside. "You're sure you're okay?" he asked.

She nodded.

"Sit down. Take it easy. I better go out and answer some questions. This might take a while." He looked at her for a second. "Mind telling me why you were wandering around outside at 2 a.m.?"

"I . . . I heard something."

"Why didn't you wake me, Marie?"

She looked down at her dirt-streaked, black hands. "You would have laughed. I thought it was a . . . never mind."

He came close and stood before her. "Marie . . ." He touched her cheek and rubbed at a spot. "Did you know your face is dirty."

She shook her head.

"You saved our lives, Marie. Do you know that?"

She looked up at him. Something passed between them, some message. Marie didn't know what it was. She only knew it made her insides melt exquisitely. She smiled faintly and put her hand on top of his, pressing it against her cheek. He kept looking at her, though, as if he'd never seen her before. His eyes searched out everything that was inside her, asking, testing, gauging. But that was all right. Craig should know everything about her— everything.

He dropped his hand. "I've got to go now. You're very brave, Marie."

"Oh, I really . . . Craig, I'm still shaking."

"You were brave. Take it easy now. I'll be right outside." He hesitated. "You might want to put something on. Your nightgown is torn."

"Okay." But she sat there, unable to move, smelling smoke, hearing the crack of burning trees, listening to the sirens and people's voices and shouts and orders, feeling the phantom touch of his fingers.

He went into his room and came out with an open shirt hastily thrown on. He held another shirt in his hand, a red plaid flannel shirt that he draped over Marie's shoulders. He tipped her head up with a finger. "Thanks," she said, then he went outside and began answering questions.

It was more than an hour before the pump trucks had the fire under control. It seemed that hundreds of people, an army, had marched by the cabin, shouting at one another. Men came back to the road with blackened faces and holes in their clothes from sparks. They carried hoes and shovels and dragged hoses and swore and yelled orders to other men.

Out front, the radio in the police car squawked and rasped. A mad charade.

Finally Marie stood up and went to the front door. Craig was sitting in the police car, still talking to the policeman.

Automatically she put her hands into the sleeves of Craig's shirt, rolled up the cuffs and made coffee. She felt bruised all over, stiff and sore. She washed her hands to get the grime off, but forgot about her face. She was very tired, slow and fumbling when she made the coffee. Everything seemed surreal.

She went out to the police car. "I made coffee," she told Craig. "Why don't you come in?"

She sat in a chair in the living room, very quiet, sipping from the mug of coffee.

"So this Klutznic and Lund were together in Vietnam. Demolitions experts," the policeman was saying.

"Yes, I believe so."

"Let me get this straight. You were going to expose them, because they'd run your ship onto the rocks three years ago, so they tried to kill you."

"It may have been either or both. It may not have been. I'm just telling you that the explosion this morning certainly points a finger at those men. Lund's in town. Klutznic's supposedly been out fishing." Craig looked grim. "You might check out the deaths of two other crewmen on the same ship. John Woods and Joey Brown."

"You think this pair, Lund and Klutznic, killed those two?"

Craig shrugged.

A smoke-grimed fireman came in. "Fire's under control. It burned Mary Whiteside's tool shed and an acre of forest. I'll make a report."

The policeman shook his head. "You're not gonna believe this one."

"Arson?" asked the fireman.

"Worse than that."

It had started to drizzle. Men went by outside, sodden and black. The cars and trucks gradually moved off.

Marie sat there still, listening to Craig's explanations and the policeman's questions, but she was only half hearing the men. Her brain had finally shifted into gear, and something, something was beginning to nag at her.

In the background she heard Craig saying, "...A threat made to Marie's son in San Francisco." The policeman asked more questions. She racked her mind, pages and pages of testimony filling her thoughts, facts filtering through her consciousness, as if they were trying to fit together like pieces of a puzzle.

What was it? What was she missing? Savant in South Africa, unreachable. Marshall and Bogner, disappeared. Two men dead. Another half dead from alcohol poisoning....

What?

Lund and Klutznic here, both of them, demolitions experts. Petersen in San Francisco, who could have been watching her house. And Bones in New Orleans, nervous when Craig had showed up. Bones had testified at the trial that he was positive no one had left the mess during dinner. The easily believable crab cake story. So Klutznic and Lund...and Bones, the man who should have testified as the rest of them had, who should have said he simply couldn't remember. But Bones must have been scared, must have wanted to brush suspicion away from himself.

It was as if all those pieces of the puzzle slipped into place abruptly, smoothly, leaving no doubt in Marie's mind.

A smile curved the corner of her mouth. *Yes, of course.* She should have seen it all along.

She parted her lips, ready to tell them, then suddenly clamped her mouth shut. She had no proof. How was she going to get proof? It would take months. And then she had it. There was a way. Not even a long shot, really. All it required was the right touch. A woman's touch.

She felt rocky, a little shaky. Her shoulder hurt and her feet were tender. Unnoticed, she went into her bedroom and dressed. Black soot smudges rubbed off onto her white slacks, but she didn't care. She wiped at the dirt on her face and brushed her hair automatically.

She didn't allow herself to think of what would happen next, what exactly she would say or do.

"I'm going out," she said to Craig.

"You okay?" He looked at her with his brows drawn together.

"I'm fine. I need to... I need to make a phone call."

"Stick around, miss," the policeman said. "I'll want to ask you some questions later."

"Oh, I'll be right back, don't worry."

She knew where to go. She'd been there before. She walked quickly, ignoring the twinges her feet gave her.

She should have seen the whole picture months ago. It was so clear once you had all the pieces to the puzzle. No wonder they hadn't been able to figure out who the one guilty party was. No wonder.

It was bright out now. Five o'clock in the morning but bright. The early morning drizzle had receded back into the mountains, into the clouds that hung perpetually over the highest peaks.

What if he was home? Could she face him? Would he do anything to her? He wasn't home, though. She was sure he'd be out with the rest of the volunteers, fighting the last few hot spots of the fire. He'd have to be, to cover himself.

She walked down the now-familiar street, up the walk, up to the door. It never occurred to her how early in the morning it was. Everyone in Valdez was up that morning, anyway.

She raised her hand and knocked on the door. Two quick raps.

It was opened almost immediately.

"Hello, Alice," Marie said. She walked in, past the woman, into the house. She stood in the middle of the room, trying to sense if he were home.

"What do you want?" Alice Klutznic asked. She held the cute, blond-haired baby on one hip. She looked scared, and she looked as if she'd been crying.

"Remember me? I'm Marie Vicenza. From the insurance company."

"I remember." Alice's face was milky-white. Her freckles stood out like stains and her eyes were pink.

"Is Tim home?"

Alice bit her lip and shook her head. A lock of hair fell forward across her forehead, and she reached up to push it back behind her ear.

"Will you talk to me now," Marie asked softly, "before someone else gets killed?"

Alice gave a hiccuping sob and closed her eyes.

"Tell me, Alice, tell me the truth. It was all of them, wasn't it? All ten of them together."

CHAPTER SEVENTEEN

CRAIG HAILED A TAXI at the San Francisco airport and checked his watch. He'd docked in San Diego not more than five hours ago, but only had another thirty-one hours before the *Northern Light* was scheduled to depart from San Diego harbor. He hadn't a minute to waste.

Outwardly he appeared calm and in command of his emotions. Due to his haste in San Diego, he still wore his navy blue captain's uniform—Wesco issue—its brass buttons gleaming in the September sun. The shiny brim of his spotless white cap was pulled low, hiding his clear blue eyes. His shoulders were squared, his stride purposeful. He looked quite impressive, a man with a mission and a vital one at that. A busy man, a captain of a super tanker on a quick business jaunt to northern California, a man of the seas, a commander. Inside, however, he felt like a teenager on a first date, anxious, indecisive. His gut churned.

The incredible truth was that he didn't have any idea why he'd come to San Francisco, why he hadn't telephoned Marie, checked in on her, said hello by long distance. Just exactly what *was* he doing here?

"Mission District," he told the cabby, "and make it quick."

"Yes, sir."

They all called him "sir" now: his respectful new crew on the *Northern Light,* the dockside workers, secretaries, agents, even cabdrivers. Hell, he thought, dogs even got out of his way when he strode past. Respect. That was what he'd missed so much for those three years: his honor, his pride and the respect he'd always been shown as a man who could be counted on to get the job done.

Well, it was over. The nightmare of living on the dark side of respectability was finished. And, he admitted as the cab sped along, vindication tasted pretty darn sweet.

All ten of his crew. Guilty.

It was still hard to fathom. He guessed it always would be. But for money—and they'd been given plenty—he supposed a man would do just about anything.

And Craig knew now that he shared the blame. If he'd been closer to his crewmen, if he'd cared more about them as individuals, they might not have turned on him so readily.

The cab stopped at three red lights in a row. "Never gonna synchronize these damn things," the cabby grumbled.

But Craig wasn't noticing. He was thinking about Marie. He wondered if, without her, he would have eventually found out what had really happened that June day three years ago. He might have. He'd been close. But Klutznic or Lund or one of the others could have gotten to him first, and then it would have been a closed case forever. His kids would have despised his memory all their lives.

But Marie had solved the case. She'd persisted beyond all hope. She'd pushed and insisted and bugged him, and then she'd saved their lives to boot. Such splendid stubbornness.

In two weeks, little Marie Vicenza had accomplished what a fleet of highly paid lawyers and investigators hadn't been able to achieve in over thirty-six months.

Amazing.

The taxi pulled up a long, steep hill, and the rolling jumble of buildings and skyscrapers and green parks of San Francisco lay below, spreading to the glistening bay. An expression came to Craig's mind as he sat musing in the back: he'd been too close to the trees to see the forest. All ten of his crew in on it. No, he wouldn't have guessed in a hundred years.

But Marie had.

And Alice Klutznic had confessed the whole truth—explained the plot to discredit the Alaskan pipeline itself, to make an already suspicious, environmentally sensitive government even more leery of transporting Alaskan crude through one of the last wilderness frontiers. Yes, Alice had spilled the beans and named the men behind the sick plot, but it had been Marie who had gone to her in the first place. "A woman's touch" was all Marie had said to explain why Alice had confessed.

Marie had flown home to San Francisco the very next day after the explosion and had begun to dig into the background of the men responsible for the spill. And it had been Marie, too, who had diligently put the whole picture together on her own, unafraid of those powerful men. She'd uncovered a cartel that three oil men had formed in Texas. She'd gone to Houston—this time with the blessings of her boss—gotten subpoenas of bank records and found that these three men had formed a conglomerate back when OPEC had slashed the price of oil drastically, all but ruining the Texas oil business. The men had bided their time, scheming. Eventually the three oil moguls had made their move. They'd gotten to the crew of the *Northern Light,* through Lund and Klutznic, and caused enough damage to the precious wilderness to shut down the Alaskan pipeline for months while the public demanded safer procedures, double steel hulls on the tankers, new shipping routes, oil spill contingency plans.

Yes, Marie had figured it out. She'd presented bank records to the Alaska attorney general's office that proved the Texas cartel had reopened hundreds of Texas wells, the price of oil had risen, they'd made their fast killing and then backed off. They'd *thought* they were safe. What they hadn't counted on was Marie Vicenza and her unquenchable persistence.

For weeks Marie had called Craig in Alaska at prearranged times at the grocery store phone booth, kept him up to date, boosted his ego. She'd explained that the *Northern Light* had been selected as the tanker to run aground because Craig had been the perfect patsy, known as a maverick due to his Vietnam record, known to have been tough on his crew, so exacting that none of the ten men had really felt much loyalty to him.

The U.S. Marshal in Anchorage was still looking for the two missing crew members, Bogner and Marshall, and Claud Savant was in the process of being extradited from South Africa. Craig was sure that in the upcoming trial in January it would be revealed that Joey and Woody had been murdered by the cartel because they'd threatened to talk. The remaining men—Klutznic, Lund, Petersen and Stratford—were all in jail, their combined bonds set at ten million dollars. Craig guessed that the Alaska attorney general didn't want to see them disappear, too. As for the three oil men, they'd apparently hired the best lawyers money could buy. Craig would

have to ask Marie about their present status—when he
saw her. In a few minutes now...

His stomach clutched.

She'd stopped calling him, hadn't she? She'd given up
back in early August. Maybe she'd been too busy. Maybe
he'd given her no encouragement. He wondered how she
was doing, how Tony was doing. He wondered if she'd
gotten that bonus. If she hadn't, he planned on seeing
that boss of hers himself. He'd go to the very top, if necessary. She'd be rewarded. He'd make damn good and
sure of it.

He stepped out of the cab on Dolores Street and paid
the driver. He recalled the last time he'd been there. The
fog had curled around his legs, and the old house had
been shrouded in mist. He'd met Tony then, and his relationship with Marie had been strained. He'd been confused, his thoughts still too much on himself, on finding
vindication. Yet he was doubly confused now, asking
himself why he'd jumped on a flight to San Francisco the
moment he'd docked. He felt as if he'd been drawn here,
against his will, tugged by powerful, invisible strings.
And he hadn't an inkling what he intended to say to Marie. She might not even be home. He almost prayed that
she wasn't.

He walked past the broken swing on the porch and
raised his hand to knock. Then paused. The closer he got
to facing Marie, the more urgent became his need to flee.
He was aware of how unlike his normal self this behavior was, but he hadn't any way of circumventing it.

He knocked.

Tony answered the door. The first thing Craig noted
was that the youth's hair had grown out. The second
thing he noticed was all the boxes stacked in the hall.
Moving boxes.

"Hey," Tony was saying, "it's you." He eyed Craig's uniform. "You got your ship here...sir?"

"It's docked in San Diego." He saw disappointment flash across the boy's face. And he remembered his promise. "But I haven't forgotten," Craig added quickly, "I owe you the grand tour."

"You mean it? You'll really let me on her?"

"You bet. I keep my word, son."

"All right, dude...sir."

It was then that Craig saw her. She was coming down the old oak staircase carrying a too-large box. "Excuse me," Craig said to Tony and stepped inside past him, climbing the stairs, taking the box—that she couldn't even see over—out of her arms. "Here," he said, "let me."

Craig was aware of her shocked reaction. She stammered, stuttered, teetered on the stairs. He found himself grinning like a kid. What had gotten into him? Why was he even there, for Lord's sake?

"Craig," she breathed as he set the box down in the vestibule. "Craig...it is really—? You're in uniform!" She collected herself and came bounding down the remaining steps and took his hands in hers. He knew he was blushing right down to his kneecaps, but somehow he didn't want the moment to end. Ever.

"...On the *Northern Light?*" she was asking. "Craig, have you got your command back?"

He found his voice. "Yes. About three weeks ago. She's in San Diego harbor, unloading," he managed to say. What an old fool he was becoming, blushing, at a loss for words.

"If your ship is in San Diego," she said, dragging him into the living room, pushing him down into a chair, "how can you be here?"

He dangled his arms over the sides of the chair, tried his damnedest to look relaxed. "She's unloading right now. My first mate is seeing to taking on the supplies." He glanced at his watch. "I've got about thirty hours till—"

"Oh, but that's wonderful!" Marie said beaming, more lovely than he'd remembered. How could he have forgotten those big brown eyes and the spiky black lashes? "We can catch up on everything. Oh, this is wonderful!"

"I'm glad to see you, too," he got out and then noticed Tony standing in the doorway, studying the two of them.

"We're moving, you know," Tony put in, "we're going to—"

"Tony." Marie shook her head at him. "Don't you have packing to do?"

"Yeah, sure, why not," he said, sulking, turning away.

"And Tony," Craig said, "I *won't* forget."

"Thanks." But he didn't sound as if he believed him at all now.

"Won't forget what?" Marie asked as Tony's heavy teenage footfalls receded upstairs.

"Oh," Craig said matter-of-factly, "I promised him a tour of the tanker."

"That was nice."

"And I'll do it. Maybe next trip down he could come to San Diego. I'm sure something can be worked out."

"Um," Marie said, watching him closely, smiling. "Want some coffee?"

"Yeah, sure."

"Black. Come on into the kitchen. We can talk while it brews."

Watching Marie work in her cozy kitchen with its vintage 1930s gas range sent ripples of pleasure along his spine. How well he recalled her in his own kitchen, the way her blouse had pulled against her breasts when she stretched and reached for a can, how cute her rounded bottom looked with the panty line showing, the way her thick curling hair fell in one eye, and she never failed to push it back then nibble on her fingernail. He'd forgotten a lot of those little things about her. What he had not forgotten was that sun-kissed Alaskan night in his bed. Her fragrance, her cries . . .

"It looks like the U.S. Attorney General has enough on the three of them in the cartel for an indictment," she was saying, dragging him back to reality. "Isn't that great? *Plus,* one of them at least will be charged as an accessory to murder. You know, Joey and Woody."

"Sure, yes, that's good."

"And I got my bonus, Craig."

"You did?"

"Yep." She grinned broadly. "What to know how much?"

"It's not really my—"

"One hundred and fifty thousand dollars!"

He whistled through his teeth.

"Well," she said lightly, "I deserved every cent. I saved Pacific a hundred and eighteen million. Think of it."

"Marie," he said, his smile fading, "are you happy? Is that what you wanted, really?" He didn't even know why he'd asked that.

"Of course I'm happy. I'm ecstatic!"

"That's nice."

"Nice?" She put her hands on her hips and faced him. "Tony will have the best education there is. And I'm...I'm moving...."

"I saw."

"And my folks, well, I gave them a third of it. They deserve it all, really, after putting up with me and Tony all these years. But they're selling the restaurant, and with the interest from my money and the sale of the business, they'll be comfortably retired."

"Are they staying here?"

She nodded. "Mama was born here. Right upstairs. They'd never move."

"And you're happy for them," he stated.

"Very."

Marie turned away and poured him his coffee. She was talking all the while, maybe a bit nervously—he wasn't sure. He wasn't sure of anything, actually. Least of all, he wasn't sure why he'd come to see her. He should have just telephoned.

"Klutznic built that bomb," she was saying, "but you knew that. He was a demolitions expert in Vietnam. But Lund, that *creep*, he was the instigator."

"Not surprising. He hated my guts."

"He hated *everyone's* guts, Craig."

"I guess so."

"Anyway, it turned out to be your buddy, Petersen, who called here and threatened Tony. He was the one watching my house, too. Bones, in New Orleans, alerted him."

"It makes sense." He sipped on his coffee.

"My goodness" came a voice at the kitchen door, "it's the captain." Sophia.

Craig felt whatever little wind there was left in his sail vanish. Not many people intimidated him—in fact, he couldn't think of a soul, except Sophia here. "Good afternoon," he said, rising, putting on a brave front, shaking her hand, "Mrs. Vicenza."

"And in uniform. Marie was always a sucker for a uniform. I suppose all women are," she said as if talking aloud to herself.

"*Mama!*"

"Oh, my, what have I said?" Sophia looked sincerely contrite. "Sometimes I just go on, don't I?"

Craig found his voice finally. He even smiled. "I assure you, Mrs. Vicenza—Sophia—my intentions toward your daughter are honorable."

Marie laughed. But Sophia put her hands on her wide hips and scowled. "They better be, young man. She's a good girl. She may be crazy in the head moving to—"

"Don't you have to be at work?" Marie cut in abruptly.

Sophia tossed her head. "Yes, sure, always work." Then she yelled, "Papa! Papa! Are you coming?" and, a hand on the small of her back, she headed through the kitchen door. "Al, I'm waiting!"

Marie sighed and shrugged. "She's such a pain."

"She's protective."

"Yeah, well, I think I'm a little too old for that."

"You're still pretty young."

"Why do you always say that? I'm not. I may *look* young, thank God, but I'm pushing middle age."

"Well . . ." Craig let it go.

They talked about this and that. Actually it was Marie who did most of the talking, he realized. It was as if his mouth had cotton in it and everything he said came out muffled. He drank two cups of coffee and a glass of water.

Marie was sitting across from him at the scarred table with the lace doily in the center. He'd found some spilled grains of salt on the table and had been pushing them around with his index finger for what seemed like hours. A few grains, he noticed inanely, had stuck in a spot of jelly.

"So," Marie said, leaning forward, trying to get his attention, "have you heard from your kids? Have you contacted them?"

He glanced up and nodded. My God, but Marie was a lovely woman, so young, so fresh, so alive. She looked like a Madonna sitting there. So exquisite. She was everything a man could ever ask for. . . .

"Craig?"

"Oh, yes, sorry. Yeah, I called them both in Seattle."

"It must have been hard for you."

"Very."

"And?"

"And, we're going to try to patch things up. Craig, Jr., wants a job on a tanker."

"Not yours, I hope."

He shook his head. "No. I'd be too hard on him, but when he's in port he wants to stay with me. I think it's a good idea."

"So do I. And Tanya?"

"My daughter," he said then smiled, "is coming up this Thanksgiving. She and her husband."

"It won't be easy, will it?"

"No. But I think if we lay all our cards on the table, talk everything out, no matter how hard it is, we'll make it. You know," Craig said, reflecting, "Tanya mentioned something about how difficult it must have been on me when Polly died. She said she hadn't been much of a help then, too hung up in her own pain."

"That's wonderful. I mean, it's wonderful your daughter is communicating. You'll have to keep your chin up and do the same, Craig Saybolt."

And he thought suddenly: if Marie were there, by his side, loving him, he could do it. But he didn't have her. He'd blown it and hurt them both too much to ever expect her to understand. He'd have to settle for her friendship. At least she was not denying him that.

Craig cleared his throat and nodded in the direction of the vestibule. "I take it you found an apartment," he said, his heart feeling like a stone in his chest.

"Yes," she said, "well, I have a line on one, that is."

"You don't have a lease?" He looked up from his folded hands. That wasn't like her, not a bit. Marie always had all the details ironed out. If he knew nothing else about Marie, he knew that much.

But she was shaking her head. "You see, I haven't actually seen the place yet, so I didn't want to sign anything."

"You haven't seen it?"

"Well," she smiled shyly, "it's not quite here in San Francisco."

"Where is it then, Marie?"

"Oh, out of state." Her smile broadened.

He only stared at her curiously.

"I may as well tell you," she said, rather too casually, "it's...ah...in Anchorage."

"Anchorage? *Alaska?*"

"I don't know another Anchorage, do you?"

He couldn't speak. For a long moment, he couldn't even think. Then slowly the knowledge began to sink into his muddled brain. Marie was moving to Alaska. She was going to be only a stone's throw away.

Craig knew then. Suddenly and without a bridging thought he knew why he'd really come to San Francisco. He was astounded by the insight. Astounded and never more certain of anything in his life. He looked up sharply. His shoulders seemed to become more square, and his blue eyes grew bold with determination.

"I want you to come to Valdez," he announced. "I want you and Tony to come and live with me." And then he caught himself. He saw the look of amazement on her face and realized what he'd just said. "My God," Craig whispered, "I didn't know I was going to say that. I honestly had no idea. Marie, I should have *asked* you if you *wanted* to come live with me. My God."

But she was smiling, a knowing look in her eyes.

"When I flew up here today," he went on, still putting his motives together in his own mind, "I didn't know this was why. But I guess I'm ... I know I'm ... I'm asking you to marry me, Marie. I should have a ring, I know, and maybe you don't even want an old codger like—"

"Yes," she said, reaching over to clasp his hands with hers. "Yes."

"What?"

"I'll marry you, Captain Saybolt."

"You will?"

"Don't look so amazed. I love you. I've loved you since that day you darn near made me drive off the road just trying to get you into that awful rental car."

"It was your driving that was awful, Marie," he said and knew he was grinning from ear to ear.

"Well?

"Well what?"

"Do you love me, too?"

Craig lifted a dark brow. What a stupid question. "Of course I love you."

"Lots?" she asked, teasing, her eyes dancing.

"Of course," he stammered.

"And you'll tell me that a dozen times every day?"

"A hundred times," he said, teasing her right back, feeling as young and free as a kid, "now that I have your promise, that is."

"Good. And, well, Tony. He'll need discipline. I can handle it, but if you back me up..."

"What Tony needs," Craig said, "is someone to listen to him. Someone to go out on a fishing boat with him and listen to him. All boys need that at his age."

"And you don't mind?"

"Not a bit. In fact, it'll be a good time for Craig, Jr., to be there, too. We can all three lick our wounds together."

"Oh, Craig."

He could see the moisture glistening in her eyes. "Don't go all soft on me, Marie," he said and squeezed her hands lovingly. Then abruptly he looked up. "Your job with Pacific... did you quit or something?"

She nodded, then shrugged. "Or something, is more like it. I waited until the bonus check was safely in my pocket, and then I confronted Mike."

"And?" He could just imagine.

"Well, I told him what a male chauvinist pig he was."

"And?"

"And he tried to put a hand on my fanny. I hauled off and slapped him."

"You didn't."

"Yes, I did. I wasn't raised in this tough neighborhood for nothing, Craig Saybolt." She laughed. "He fired me!"

And then Craig found himself laughing, too. And they were both laughing, Marie trying to tell him how much she was loving retirement at thirty-one years old.

Finally she sniffed and caught her breath. "You'll have to tell my folks, you know, about our getting married. Ask Al's permission and all that. They're kind of old-fashioned."

"I can handle it. I think I can even handle Sophia. Although," he said, frowning, "I think maybe I'd rather take a full tanker over the Valdez shoals on a rough sea."

Marie smiled and rose, coming around the table, plumping herself in his lap. She took his face in her hands. "I love you, Craig, I love you so much," she whispered.

"Did you know...did you know why I really came here today? Before I asked you to marry me?"

She nodded slowly.

"And you let me go on like that?"

"You were embarrassed."

"Well, damn, Marie, that was a rotten..." But he never finished. Her lips met his and his anger fled like a fleeting squall at sea.

COMING IN 1991 FROM
HARLEQUIN SUPERROMANCE:

THE·BYRNSIDE·INHERITANCE

Three abandoned orphans,
one missing heiress!

Dying millionaire Owen Byrnside receives an
anonymous letter informing him that twenty-six years
ago, his son, Christopher, fathered a daughter. The
infant was abandoned at a foundling home that
subsequently burned to the ground, destroying all
records. Three young women could be Owen's long-
lost granddaughter, and Owen is determined to track
down each of them! Read their stories in

#434 HIGH STAKES (available January 1991)
#438 DARK WATERS (available February 1991)
#442 BRIGHT SECRETS (available March 1991)

Three exciting stories of intrigue and romance by
veteran Superromance author Jane Silverwood.

**This April, don't miss #449, CHANCE OF A
LIFETIME, Barbara Kaye's third and last book in the
Harlequin Superromance miniseries**

Hamilton
H·O·U·S·E

A powerful restaurant conglomerate draws the best and brightest
to its executive ranks. Now almost eighty years old, Vanessa
Hamilton, the founder of Hamilton House, must choose a succes-
sor. Who will it be?

Matt Logan: He's always been the company man, the quintessen-
tial team player. But tragedy in his daughter's life and a
passionate love affair made him make some hard choices....

Paula Steele: Thoroughly accomplished, with a sharp mind, perfect breeding and looks to die for, Paula thrives on challenges
and wants to have it all...but is this right for her?

Grady O'Connor: Working for Hamilton House was his salvation
after Vietnam. The war had messed him up but good and had
killed his storybook marriage. He's been given a second
chance—only he doesn't know what the hell he's supposed to
do with it....

Harlequin Superromance invites you to enjoy Barbara Kaye's
dramatic and emotionally resonant miniseries about mature men
and women making life-changing decisions.

Take 4 bestselling love stories FREE

Plus get a FREE surprise gift!

Special Limited-time Offer

Harlequin Reader Service®

Mail to

In the U.S.
3010 Walden Avenue
P.O. Box 1867
Buffalo, N.Y. 14269-1867

In Canada
P.O. Box 609
Fort Erie, Ontario
L2A 5X3

YES! Please send me 4 free Harlequin Superromance® novels and my free surprise gift. Then send me 4 brand-new novels every month, which I will receive months before they appear in bookstores. Bill me at the low price of $2.74* each—a savings of 21¢ apiece off cover prices. There are no shipping, handling or other hidden costs. I understand that accepting the books and gift places me under no obligation ever to buy any books. I can always return a shipment and cancel at any time. Even if I never buy another book from Harlequin, the 4 free books and the surprise gift are mine to keep forever.

*Offer slightly different in Canada—$2.74 per book plus 49¢ per shipment for delivery.
Sales tax applicable in N.Y Canadian residents add applicable federal and provincial sales tax.

134 BPA KBBA (US)   334 BPA YKMP (CAN)

Name	(PLEASE PRINT)
Address	Apt. No.
City	State/Prov. Zip/Postal Code

This offer is limited to one order per household and not valid to present Harlequin Superromance® subscribers. Terms and prices are subject to change.

SUPER-BPADR   © 1990 Harlequin Enterprises Limited

Coming in March from

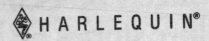

LaVyrle Spencer's unforgettable story of a
love that wouldn't die.

LAVYRLE SPENCER

SWEET MEMORIES

She was as innocent as she was unsure . . . until a very special
man dared to unleash the butterfly wrapped in her cocoon and
open Teresa's eyes and heart to love.

SWEET MEMORIES is a love story to savor that will make you
laugh—and cry—as it brings warmth and magic into your
heart.

"Spencer's characters take on the richness of friends, relatives
and acquaintances."
—Rocky Mountain News

SWEET